MW00440088

THE MISSING BONES

Emily Slate Mystery Thriller
Book 14

ALEX SIGMORE

Dark Woods Press

THE MISSING BONES: EMILY SLATE MYSTERY THRILLER
BOOK 14

Copyright © 2024 by Alex Sigmore

All rights reserved.

This is a work of fiction. Names, characters, places and incidents are products of the author's imagination and are used fictitiously and are not to be construed as real. Any resemblance to actual events, locales, organizations or persons, living or dead, is entirely coincidental.

No part of this book may be reproduced in any form or by any electronic or mechanical means, including information storage and retrieval systems, without written permission from the author, except for the use of brief quotations in a book review.

1st Edition

ebook ISBN 978-1-957536-61-3

Print ISBN 978-1-957536-62-0

Prologue

"HERE, YOU WANT A SMOKE?"

Michelle looked over as Bill reached into his open shirt pocket and produced a packet of Camel lights. She'd snuck a couple of smokes before, behind the school gym with some of the other girls, but those had been just occasional puffs, not an entire cigarette. And every time she did it, she ended up coughing.

This was her first "real" date with William "Bill" MacElroy, star football player and overall stud of Millridge High. Two years ago, when she'd been a freshman, she never would have even appeared on Bill's radar. But she'd blossomed over the past year, which had come with a lot of additional attention from the boys at school. Her mother had complained over and over again they couldn't keep buying her new clothes and that she'd just have to wear hand-me-downs from Rebecca. But her mom didn't know anything about fashion these days, and Michelle couldn't be caught dead in clothes her older sister had worn four years ago. She'd be laughed out of school.

And she *certainly* couldn't wear them on a date with one of the most popular guys in the entire county. Which was what had prompted Michelle to go into her mother's purse and "borrow" a couple of bucks just so she could get some nice things for her date. The summer was just starting, and she was already planning on picking up a job at Ferguson's drug store, so she could pay her mother back then. Hopefully she wouldn't even miss it.

What she definitely wouldn't miss would be if Michelle came home smelling like cigarettes, new clothes or not. The woman had a nose like a blood hound, and Michelle couldn't risk it.

"Thanks, but I'm okay," she said, eyeing the pack.

"Yeah, it ain't for everyone," Bill said, tapping the packet on his arm, which currently held the wheel of his almost-new Camaro. Word around school was that his dad had bought it for him, but he insisted he'd won it in a bet. Michelle didn't care where he got it; she was with the hottest guy in school, in the hottest car out there. She couldn't wait to tell Linda and Patty about this. They hadn't believed her when she said she'd been the one to ask Bill and he'd said yes. Girls didn't ask guys on dates, at least that's how it had been. But Michelle had seen the way Bill eyed her in the halls. And she'd decided to take a chance.

One that had paid off in spades.

Bill pulled one of the cigarettes from the packet with his teeth and pressed the lighter in the console that sat between them. "You don't mind, do you?"

Michelle cranked the window down a bit, allowing the warm summer air in just enough so it didn't destroy the hair she'd spent an hour fussing over. "No, not at all."

"Thanks," he said. "Sometimes I just gotta relax, you know?"

"Why?" she teased. "Are you nervous?"

The lighter in the console popped and Bill pulled it out to

press his cigarette against the coil, igniting it. He then turned to Michelle, taking his eyes off the road. "Should I be?"

She gave him a sly grin. God, he was so *handsome*. This was really going to happen. Tonight would be the night, she just knew it. Even though it was their first date, she didn't care. And she didn't think he did, either.

"Where are we going again?"

Bill turned his attention back to the road, pulling a long drag on the cigarette. "My buddy told me about it. You know Chris Hendricks?"

Of course she knew the star of the football team. Chris was one of Bill's best friends and teammates. He *also* happened to have been eyeing Michelle more and more in the halls lately. She couldn't help but feel that part of the reason Bill had said yes was so he could "claim" her before anyone else could. Then again, he didn't have the best track record with girls at school. The rumors were that he'd take you on a few dates, then end up dumping you for someone else and continue the cycle. But that wasn't going to happen to Michelle. She would make sure of it. "Yeah, I've seen him around."

"He was out on his dirt bike and happened to find it. Brought me and a couple of guys up here fishing a few times. It's a great little spot. Super quiet and secluded."

"Oh yeah? What are you thinking about doing up there? I thought we were going to see a movie or something."

"Oh, I've got something much better than a movie in mind," he replied, shooting her a wink. "You're gonna love it." He reached over and caressed her bare thigh.

Heat immediately rose in her cheeks—and other places— when he touched her like that. She didn't care what they were doing, she was just thrilled to be here. She wished she could go back to that nerdy little girl who had just started ninth grade and tell her that in just a few years, she would be on a date with one of the most popular boys in school and *he* would be the one coming on to *her*. Her ninth-grade mind wouldn't have been able to comprehend such a thing. But here she was. All of her decisions had led her to this place, and she was feeling courageous.

She opened her legs just a little bit more, and his hand began to explore. The rush of adrenaline was like nothing she'd ever felt before, and it felt like her heart might explode from her chest.

Michelle leaned her head back and closed her eyes, focusing on Bill's fingers moving over her skin, feeling the rumble of the car underneath her, the sensations combining and pushing her closer and closer to the edge already. She let out a small gasp as Bill's hand found its way to her crotch.

And then it was gone.

She opened her eyes to see Bill had both hands on the wheel as he turned off the main road onto what looked like a dirt driveway. Disappointed, but not wanting to let it show, she tried to regain her composure. "Where is this?"

"Some old, abandoned place I think," he replied. "But just wait, it gets better." The driveway seemed to be less of a driveway and more of an overgrown path. If not for the lights illuminating the grass ahead of them, Michelle wouldn't even be able to tell it *was* a path. All of a sudden, she didn't feel so good about this. Where was he taking her?

"Bill, I—"

"Hold on, almost there," he said. A moment later, the trees opened up and disappeared behind them, revealing a large body of water. It wasn't big enough to be a lake, but it was certainly bigger than a pond. And it was a clear night, so clear that Michelle could see the crescent moon and even the stars reflecting off the glassy surface of the water.

Bill pulled up and cut the engine. As soon as the lights when out, it was like the entire sky lit up all at once. A million different stars all staring down at them; a blanket of dots, covering the entire sky.

"It's...beautiful," she whispered.

"Told you," he said, snubbing his cigarette in the car's ash tray. "Come on, that's not the best part."

He got out and rushed around to the other side of the car, trying and failing to get Michelle's door open before she could, but still attempting to guide her out of the car. Immediately, her gaze was drawn up at the endless sky, but some part of her brain registered that he was at least attempting to be gentlemanly. "Here, come look at this," he said.

Michelle looked back down at the water, noticing for the first time a dock that led out into the water. It was large enough that both of them could walk side-by-side down the wooden planks, and there even looked to be small slips where boats could be docked.

"This connects to Rappahannock River, over there," Bill said, pointing to the far end of the pond. "But I guess it's off the beaten path, so no one else knows about it. At least, I've never seen anyone else out here."

"It's amazing," Michelle replied.

"Wait until you see the water." Bill grinned, taking her hand, sending another shockwave of adrenaline through her and bringing Michelle back to Earth a bit. She looked around, finding an old house sitting a few hundred feet from the edge of the water. And a small outbuilding that looked like it held boats attached to the dock.

"Does...does someone live here?" she asked.

"Nah, at least, I've never seen anyone." Bill dropped his cigarette and put it out underneath his shoe.

He was right, the house was dark and looked abandoned as far as she could tell. The place was completely secluded, no other houses were even in sight. And they had been driving for a while, which was probably why they could see so many stars out here. No light pollution to obscure them. She'd always heard you could see more stars out in the country but had never really come out to do it.

"I guess you bring all your dates here," she tried teasing as he led her down the dock, her new heels click-clicking against the wooden planks.

"Nope, never brought anyone here but you," he said. "I mean, I didn't find out about it until the end of the school year either, but still. I could have brought Stacey McKinnon out here, but things weren't going so well between us by then. You're the first person to see it."

"Yeah?" she said. She didn't want to hear about Stacey McKinnon. But she also recalled her mother telling her to be careful whenever she went out with boys. She'd never gone into details; she'd just told Michelle that she always needed to be aware of her surroundings when she was out on a date. Michelle looked around again. It was becoming more and more apparent that they were completely alone out here. But she didn't want to think about that.

She wanted to think about Bill's hand on her thigh again.

When they reached the end of the dock, Bill took a seat on the edge, his legs dangling down. Michelle followed suit, but removed her new shoes so she wouldn't accidentally drop them in the water. Her mother would definitely notice if she came home barefoot.

"Amazing, isn't it?" Bill asked, leaning back and staring up at the sky.

"Yeah, it's beautiful," she affirmed, turning so she was facing him and not so subtly giving him a better view of the open buttons on her blouse.

He must have sensed her inquisitiveness, because he gave his eyebrows a little wiggle and smirked before standing back up.

"What are you doing?" she asked as he began to pull off his shirt.

"What does it look like?" he tossed his shirt aside and began to unbutton his jeans. "Whadaya say?"

Michelle glanced at the water. It was perfectly still, not even a ripple from a mosquito broke the glass-like surface. She wasn't a strong swimmer, but she'd been able to hold her own when she was younger. But getting into that water would ruin her hair. And there was no telling what was down there in that muck.

Bill tossed his shirt and pants aside, before unabashedly removing his underwear, completely revealing himself. She wanted to look away, but all she could do was stare open-mouthed at him as he grinned as wide as he possibly could before jumping off the dock, cannonballing himself into the water.

Michelle reflexively held up her hands to try and stave off some of the water, screaming as she did, but it was no good. He had soaked her in one jump.

"Might as well get in now," he called out. "Give your clothes time to dry!"

The adrenaline that had previously abandoned her came roaring back. Could she really do this? What would her friends say? But he was right, she had to get out of her wet clothes now and try to dry them before going back home. Because there was no question what her mother would say if she came back sopping wet.

Screw it, she thought and stood, pulling off her top and jean shorts.

"Damn," she heard Bill whisper to himself as she undressed, which only bolstered her resolve. Before long, she was completely naked, but instead of giving him a full show, she pinched her nose and jumped in, feet first. She completely submerged herself with the jump, but found her feet didn't touch the mucky bottom, thankfully. She hated not being able to see to the bottom. But tonight was all about taking chances, and Michelle had never taken a chance like this in her life. Tomorrow, she would be a completely different person.

"Wow," Bill said when she came up for air. "I wasn't sure you'd actually do it."

"Yeah, why not?" she asked.

"Well, don't you have a reputation of being kind of a—"

"—a nerd?" Michelle finished for him.

"Well, yeah," he replied.

She swam a little closer so they were mere inches from each other. All her other senses were obscured, and all she could focus on was the boy—the man in front of her. She wrapped her bare arms around his neck while continuing to tread water. "Not anymore," she said, and before she could chicken out, she pressed her lips to his, rewarded with the immediate warmth of his breath on her tongue. He was eager, but not unexperienced as he explored her mouth. Their bodies pressed up against each other and she felt his firmness practically poking her in anticipation.

After a few minutes, she pulled away. "Let's take this up to the bank. Might be a little easier," she whispered.

"Yeah," he said, breathless. "Good idea." The dock was too high to climb back up and if there had ever been a ladder, it had long ago disintegrated. Bill started swimming to the shore first and Michelle worked to keep up. With a little persistence and sense of urgency, she managed it. When Michelle finally felt the first bits of dirt and sand under her feet, she found she could just walk up to the bank where Bill, his skin slick with water, had taken a seat and was watching her with hungry eyes.

She couldn't help but feel his desire, which continued to embolden her. She'd never felt anything like this before and didn't want it to stop. But just as she was halfway out of the water, her foot struck and lodged into something hard and stiff beneath her. She tried shaking it away only for it to grab tighter, and she screamed out.

Bill was up and running to her in a second as Michelle tried to scramble her way out of the water. Whatever was on her foot had taken hold, and all she could think about was getting out and getting away. Bill grabbed her arm, helping her out of the water and on to the bank. But when Michelle looked down, all the blood seemed to drain from her and she felt the world going dark.

Wrapped around her foot was the white bone of a human skull.

Chapter One

I JUST KILLED MY MOTHER.

It's all that goes through my head as I slam on the brakes, my car screeching to a halt and the seatbelt biting into me as the inertia tries and fails to send me sailing through the windshield. I *saw* her, there was no mistaking it.

One second I was driving along, thinking about my recent promotion, looking forward to moving into my new home with my boyfriend, and the next, there she was on the side of the road, her eyes as large as saucers and as wild as a hyena's. There was nothing I could do...she just...stepped out in front of the car, and before I could even swerve out of the way, she was gone.

My heart is almost in my throat as I throw my seatbelt off, jerk my door open, and jump out of the car, practically tripping over my own legs as I stumble out and try to get back to the unmoving figure lying on the side of the road. It's like the entire world stopped—the street dark and empty as I run to confront what I've done. My mind is a jumble of thoughts and images, and none of them make sense, so I just decide to ignore them all. All I know is I have to help the woman I may have just killed.

When I reach her, she's lying on her side, facing away from me. As I reach out with my shaking hand, I stop.

Can this be real? Did I really see my mother's face?

Despite the horror I might find upon turning her over, I must know. There's no going back. Her long, black overcoat is slick with water from the wet pavement—or perhaps it's blood, I can't tell. But I reach out and take her shoulder, gently pulling her towards me. She rolls lifelessly to the side and I gasp, falling back and hitting the pavement.

Her eyes are closed, and her hair is much grayer than it was the last time I saw her. But it is undoubtedly the face of my mother. The soft chin, the high cheekbones, the smooth skin. She has a few more wrinkles, but it is the face I grew up knowing and loving. Burning tears begin falling down my cheeks.

Still, I know I can't just sit here. I have to *do* something.

I scramble up place my fingers against her neck. Her skin is warm, and I can feel a pulse. I don't see any obvious damage from where my car struck her, but that doesn't mean it doesn't exist. She's alive, which means she needs medical attention, *now*.

"This is Agent Slate," I say into my phone, my voice shaky and stern at the same time. "I've got an injured pedestrian, vehicular accident, I need immediate assistance, emergency services. Send an ambulance."

"Agent Slate, what is your location," the 911 operator says on the other end of the phone.

I give her the nearest cross section.

"Don't move the victim," the woman on the other end reminds me. "I have someone in route. They'll be there in less than five minutes."

Five minutes is an eternity, I think.

"I need you to stay on the phone with me," the operator says. "Is the person breathing?"

I pull back the overcoat and can see the soft rise of her chest. "Yes, and she has a pulse."

"Is she in any immediate danger?"

I look around again, still no vehicles on the road and no other pedestrians either. "No, I don't think so."

"Okay, just stay there and describe everything you can to me about what happened," she says. I try going through it, but I keep getting distracted by the woman in front of me. I didn't want to believe it; I didn't want to believe she could still be alive. And some part of me still knows it's impossible, but I'm here, looking at her. She looks so like my aunt, but it can't be her—the woman Liam and I discovered when we were searching through Millridge's records. She's too old. And my mother's little sister wouldn't look *exactly* like her.

I don't know what to think anymore. All I know is I need for this woman to be okay. I need to talk to her, to hear her voice again. I need…I need answers.

The operator is still asking me questions, but I've stopped answering. All I can do is sit and watch as the woman continues her shallow breaths. She could have internal bleeding, or a concussion. And if I touch her again, it could be deadly.

Finally, I hear the sirens of the ambulance as it approaches. Part of me tries to get up off the ground, to flag down the vehicle, but all I end up doing is sitting there, waiting for them to come along. I catch a flurry of activity out of my periphery as two men run over and begin asking me questions. It's like I'm hearing them through a fog as they assess my mother (*not my mother?*), getting vitals and attempting to find out where and how she's injured.

I answer the questions as best I can without taking my eyes off her. Even when they finally move her to the stretcher and get her loaded into the ambulance, I never break my gaze. Stupidly, I realize I'm still holding the phone up to my ear and the operator is trying to get my attention.

"*Agent Slate!*"

"Yes, I'm here," I say.

"The paramedics will take it from here," she says. "Do you need me to inform your Agent in Charge?"

"Um, yes," I say. "Please notify Deputy Director Janice Simmons with the FBI." She agrees before hanging up, and I find one of the paramedics is telling me where they're taking her. It's like the world is moving in slow motion as they close the doors to the ambulance and one of the paramedics sits in the back with my mother, preparing an IV.

I feel a hand on my shoulder before I finally snap out of it.

"I said we're taking her to Walter Reed," he says. "Can you meet us there?"

"I...I don't think so," I tell him, because I know my car is part of a potential crime scene. I should stay and wait for the investigation, but I can't do that. "Never mind. I'll follow you there."

He nods and I'm back in my car, pulling my seatbelt back on. We're already at the hospital and I'm watching them remove her from the back of the ambulance. Now I'm in the ER, where doctors are assessing her condition. I have no sense of the passage of time, its as if it's coming in waves.

The doctor is asking me questions. I answer them to the best of my ability. One of the machines starts screaming, and people rush to my mother's side. I want to go to her but feel a hand on my arm, holding me back. I look over to find Janice. When did she arrive?

The machines beep again, and blue lights flash all over the ER. They're losing her and all I can do is stand here, watching. I feel another hand on my shoulder and see Liam. He pulls me into a hug, but I've gone numb. He tries to guide me away from the activity, but I can't move. Janice is saying something, but the sound of the doctors yelling is all that fills my ears...

~

"Em?"

I blink a few times, and find my head is pounding. I sit up, pressing my hand to my forehead. It does nothing to alleviate the migraine that seems to have infiltrated my brain. "Liam?"

He's squatting beside me, his hair slightly messed up and his suit wrinkled. I'm on a couch in some unfamiliar room, but it's very white and clinical. There are a couple of generic art pieces on the walls. Then I remember: the hospital.

I try to shoot up out of my seat, but Liam's hands keep me rooted to the spot. "Whoa there," he says. "Take it easy."

"What's going on? What happened to her?" I ask, the memories coming flooding back. I glance up to see Janice is standing in the corner, leaning against the doorway, her gaze locked on mine.

"They are still working on her," Liam says. "She had a lot of internal bleeding. She's in the operating room."

"Is she going to make it?" I ask, tears prickling my eyes again. I know it's completely irrational, but I can't help it. She's my *mother*, as much as my logical brain doesn't want to accept it.

"They don't know," Janice says. "We'll have to wait and see."

"Em," Liam says softly. "You need to take it easy. You had a panic attack and passed out in the ER. Do you remember?"

"No," I say, rubbing my head again. "I don't remember much of anything after leaving the accident. Just snippets."

"I'm getting a doctor," Janice says and disappears from the doorway.

I turn to Liam. "What's going on?"

"I don't know," he says. "I only got here about an hour ago. Do you remember talking to me at all? Or to the doctors?"

"Not really," I say. "I remember one minute you weren't there, and then the next you were. Same with Janice."

"Zara is on her way too," he says. "Janice called us once she got the message from emergency services."

"Liam, there was nothing I could do," I say, wiping the tears away. "She just...stepped out in front of the car. I didn't have time—"

"Don't worry about that right now," he says. "We just need to make sure you're all right." He runs his hand over my forehead, pausing as if to take my temperature with it. He then cups his hand around the back of my head and presses my forehead to his, briefly. "*I* need to make sure you're all right."

"Here," Janice says from behind us. She's all business bringing the man in the white coat in behind her. Liam steps back as the doctor gets down on one knee and shines a light into my eye. "Look up, please," he says. "Down. Left. Now right." He takes my pulse, as well as has me turn my head and performs a couple other cursory tests before standing back up.

"Agent Slate, I believe you had an acute panic attack due to stress. But the symptoms don't seem to be lingering and all your responses are normal."

"That's a relief," Liam says.

"Em!" Zara appears at the doorway and deftly maneuvers around Janice, who tries to stop her, before side-checking the doctor and barreling into me, wrapping her arms around me and nearly knocking me back.

"Jesus, Foley, get a hold of yourself," Janice says.

"Are you okay?" Zara asks in my hair.

"I'm okay," I say. "Apparently it was just a panic attack."

She pulls back and looks me directly in the eyes, holding me by the shoulders. "You sure?"

I nod a couple of times. "I think so."

Zara turns to the doctor who is rubbing his shoulder from where she knocked into him. "If you're going to prescribe drugs, give her the good ones. Not those watered-down placebos you guys pass around."

"I don't believe Agent Slate *needs* any drugs," he replies. "Her vitals have already returned to normal and she's not showing any lingering symptoms."

"Thank you, Doctor," Janice says, approaching. "Now if you'll excuse us, we have some classified business to discuss."

"If you need anything else, reach out to Dr. Ramirez. I'm going off-shift," he says, shooting Zara another annoyed look before heading out. She doesn't even flinch. Instead, her attention focuses back on me.

"What happened out there?" she asks.

"I think that's something we'd all like to know," Janice replies.

I take a deep breath, then do my best to relate everything I could remember from leaving the office after a meeting with Janice on my "new" position in the Bureau.

"Em, I don't want to alarm you," Liam says, "but I can confidently say that is the same woman I saw outside the house that burned down in Ohio."

"We can also probably assume she was the person driving the car that kept trying to drive us off the road," Zara says, referring the multiple occasions when an old Ford erratically followed us.

"I assume this is also the person who has been sending you these letters?" Janice asks.

"But...she can't be..." I'm stammering, unable to wrap my head around it. "My mother is *dead*."

"What about your aunt?" Liam asks. "We found that information about her in the library up in Ohio."

I shake my head. "She's too old. Emily would have been younger, by about five or six years at least."

"It's the only explanation," Liam says. "Regardless of who she looks like, she has to be your namesake."

I'm still reeling from finding out my mother may have

named me after her sister, a sister who was never revealed to me when my mother was alive.

"We have another issue to address," Janice says. "The accident itself. Because you drove away from the scene, you may have potentially destroyed evidence. I have Caruthers at the location now, trying to find anything he can. But DC Police is going to want to open an investigation."

I let out a long breath. "I couldn't stay there and wait. Not without knowing what was going to happen to her. I need to make sure she'll be okay."

There's a knock at the door and we all turn to see a tall woman in scrubs. Her dark hair has begun to escape the net she wears around her head, and a mask hangs loose around her neck. "I'm Dr. Longwood. Are you the agent who came in with the older woman?"

I stand. "Yes, I'm Agent Slate. How is she?"

She glances at all of us. "We need to find a way to notify the next of kin," she replies.

My heart goes into my throat. "Why? What's happened?"

"It's just a precaution," she says. "But I don't want to say more without informing the family first."

"Well, *she's* family," Liam says, indicating me. "She's the woman's niece."

"Oh," Dr. Longwood says. "Then may I have a word in private?"

"No, it's fine," I say, trying to maintain my composure. "You can speak freely, everyone here is a federal agent."

"Very well," she says. "Unfortunately, we found some bleeding in the brain and had to induce a coma. Right now she is stable, but I don't know how long she will remain that way. The next twenty-four to forty-eight hours will be critical."

"What's the prognosis?" I ask.

She pinches her features. "I'd say at this point, fifty-fifty she comes out if it without brain damage. If you wouldn't mind, I need you to fill out some forms."

I nod. "I can do that."

"And if you have any other family, you may want to contact them to let them know. I've seen cases like this go both ways. And usually it's best to err on the side of caution."

"I understand." Though it feels like everything around me is falling apart. The full shock of it hasn't hit me yet and I'm running on autopilot, I know it. I need to fill out the forms, that's the first thing to take care of. As long as I have something else I can focus on, I can function.

"Coll, go with her," Janice says. "Foley and I will deal with DC when they get here, which I'm sure they inevitably will."

"Yes, ma'am," Liam says. We follow Dr. Longwood out into the hallway. But somehow, I can't help but feel I'm about to sign a death certificate.

Chapter Two

THE REST of the evening was filled with mind-numbing busywork, but at least it gave me something to focus on other than the woman in the ICU. Eventually, Liam convinced me we needed to get back home and get some rest, but I demanded we go see the woman before we left. I could only see her from a distance, and she didn't even look like the same person with all that stuff hooked up to her, but a desperate hope tugged at me, even as I watched the machines beep in their regular intervals.

Everything I need to know about my family, about my history, is contained in that woman's brain, which may or may not ever work properly again. And I just don't know how to function until I get the answers I need.

Thankfully, Liam is there to coax me back home, where I'm greeted by a sleepy Timber. I manage to fall into a dreamless sleep, which is over much too soon before it's time to get back up and start the day over. When I pick up my phone, there's a message from Janice telling me not to come in today, that I need a day to recover.

While that seems like a relief at first, as we fix breakfast and go through the motions, I realize that if I end up sitting around the house all day, I'll just go crazy. And alternatively sitting in my mother's hospital room would drive me even crazier. I need something to do, I *need* to work. If for no other reason than a distraction.

"Um, what are you doing?" Liam asks as I come in the bathroom while he's tying his tie. Our new *shared* bathroom, which I've barely spent any time in considering we still haven't unpacked our lives into this new place we've purchased together. It's a lot more spacious than the bathrooms at either of our former apartments.

"I'm getting ready for work," I tell him, turning on the shower.

"No, you're not," he says. "After everything that happened last night? You need—"

"Don't say I need time," I tell him, tossing off my robe and stepping into the shower, which is already hot thanks to this house's tankless hot water heater. "I need to focus on my job. Have I ever done well when I've had 'time off'?" I make air quotes before closing the glass door.

Liam finishes tying and straightening his tie. "Okay, fair point. But you also don't do well when you push yourself too hard. If it were any other normal day, maybe. But you're supposed to be starting your new role at work, are you going to be able to do that after everything that happened last night?"

"I have to," I say. "I don't have a choice. Plus, the challenge will keep my mind from wandering."

Though, odds are Janice is going to see me in the office and order me right back home. And there is no way on Earth Dr. Frost would ever authorize this. Maybe if I convince Janice that I'll go speak with Frost today, she might give me some leeway. Plus, the department is a mess right now. With Wallace's exit and the new reorganization of the hierarchy, everyone and everything is up in the air.

Twenty minutes later, having just rinsed off and done the

bare minimum to get myself ready, I come out to find Liam tossing Timber bites of leftover scrambled egg in the kitchen. All the furniture is still wrapped up, and the stool Liam is sitting on still has the plastic around it, but he hasn't let that stop him. In fact, the only thing that looks like it *has* been unpacked is the box of Timber's toys, which are strewn all over the house.

"I called Tess to let her know we'd need her today," he says. "She'll be here in a few hours."

"Thanks," I say, reaching over and giving him a hug. "And thank you for not arguing with me about going in. It's important that I do this."

"I know," he says. "Plus, I know a losing battle when I see one. Better to raise the white flag now and save myself the trouble."

I elbow him as I search the kitchen for a to-go container for my pre-work coffee.

"They're in one of the boxes," he says, reading my mind. "We'll have to do with the office swill for a while."

"Fair enough," I say before leaning down and giving Timber a kiss on the top of his head. "Be good today. Have fun in your new house. We'll be back later."

He whines, but his tail still wags. It kills me every time he does this because he acts like we're leaving him forever. I toss him a biscuit from a nearby box, and he dutifully takes it to his bed as Liam and I head out. This house has a garage, but it's so packed full of our crap there's no room to pull in yet, so we head out the front door to Liam's car. In the daylight, I check the front of mine to see if I spot any damage, but there's nothing to see. It's strange, I would have thought there would be at least a dent or something. I figure it's probably best I don't drive the car any more than I need to until the investigation is over, which I'm sure to get a call about today.

I'm lost in thought the entire way over to the office, mulling over the events of last night, trying to figure out if I could have done anything differently, or if I missed something. I'm so zoned out that I don't even realize when we've gone through security and pulled into the underground garage.

"Get your game face on," Liam says, cutting the engine. "If you're gonna face Janice…"

"Right," I say, resetting myself. I need to convince her I'm okay to work, that I can handle the pressure of a new job. In fact, I'm actually looking forward to the distraction. It'll be a challenge for sure.

We head through another layer of security after leaving the underground deck and entering the building, and I can't help the butterflies in my stomach as the elevator rises floor by floor. As soon as the doors open, I catch sight of Caruthers, whose eyes go wide upon seeing us. He gives us a curt nod, and Liam and I head down to the department, pushing through the double doors.

"Son of a bitch, I knew something was up when you didn't answer my texts," I hear Zara mutter from somewhere off to my left.

I turn to find her looking over the shoulder of another agent I don't know as they're reviewing some information on the agent's computer. She excuses herself and comes around, wrapping me in a hug before I can stop her. "You are too damn stubborn, you know that?" She lets go and glares at Liam. "And *you.*"

He holds up his hands in defense. "Hey, I tried to stop her."

"About as hard as a puppy tries not to pee on the rug when it's excited, no doubt," she replies. "Janice is going to be pissed."

"I know," I say. "I'm going to speak to her now. Do you really think sitting around the house all day would have been a good idea?"

She huffs. "You don't have to just sit around the house,

you know. You can actually go out and do things, go to a park with Timber, or a museum, or take a drive somewhere—"

"—car's evidence—" I remind her.

"—*whatever*, I'm sure you could have thought of something."

I nod my head. "Maybe. But without something to occupy my mind…"

Finally, she relents. "Ugh. You are just impossible sometimes." She grabs Liam by the arm. "C'mon, she's gonna need us if she's going to get through this in one piece." We head over to what used to be Fletcher Wallace's office before he was summarily dismissed for conduct unfitting an FBI Agent, namely conduct he'd taken towards me. Janice is in there, ordering the workers accompanying her what to do with all of the files and equipment. She looks up in surprise as Zara, Liam, and I appear in the doorway.

My old boss's eyes flash a moment before she pinches the bridge of her nose. "Not off to a good start, Slate." She pulls her vape pen from her pocket and takes a few pulls before replacing it.

"I have a job to do here, you said it yourself," I tell her. "My personal life shouldn't interfere with that." She remains unconvinced, staring at me like I have two heads. "This department needs all hands on deck. Especially after the exit of SAC Wallace."

Still, no movement on her part. I know she's sizing me up, trying to determine how serious I am. "It's one day, Agent Slate. I told you to take *one day*."

"That's one more day I'm not doing the job you gave me. A day longer that a family may have to wait for answers on their loved ones, a day where a fugitive can get further away. A day can make a big difference." I don't show any softness; Janice responds best when people are stoic, emotionless. I do my best to emulate that.

Finally, her gaze shifts to Zara and Liam. "You two aren't helping your cases either."

"This isn't on them," I say. "I made this decision, and they both tried to stop me. But they know me better than that. And I think you do too."

She lets out a long breath. "Fine. If this is the way you want it. Come with me." She breaks into a stride, leaving the room and brushing past all three of us. It's so abrupt I'm almost not ready for it, but I quickly catch up while Liam and Zara follow closely behind. Janice walks with imminent purpose, not slowing down for anyone. She leads us through the department until we're on the other side, close to one of the bullpens. Behind it are a row of offices, all with windows that look out on Pennsylvania Ave. We cross the empty bullpen to a corner office, and I happen to see my name emblazoned on the door.

"Wait a second," I say. "This is *my* office?"

Janice steps aside so I can get a good look. The room is big, with windows on two sides, flooding the office with light. There is a large desk in the middle, and I happen to see that all of my stuff from my other desk has already been brought in here and placed haphazardly on top. There are also shelves and cabinets along one of the walls without windows and a large rug covers most of the room, its plushness apparent even with my shoes on. There's also a couch on the fourth wall, though it looks somewhat older in style.

"Surprise?" Zara says, weakly. "We had hoped to finish setting it up by the end of the day so it would be ready for you tomorrow."

I turn to find her beaming at me. Liam as well. "Did *you* know about this?"

He gives me a sheepish grin. "I knew *of* it, but I hadn't seen it yet."

"Welcome to your new office, SSA Slate," Janice says. "As the head of your own division, the Bureau has relinquished this office, which you are to use as you see fit in the pursuit of your cases." She points to the couch. "Get used to sleeping on that, because as of now, your responsibilities here have doubled."

I can't quite believe it. When Janice told me I was getting a promotion, I'd expected maybe they would give me a cubicle with two more walls, not an entire office with views of some of the most iconic parts of Washington, DC. Other than the couch, everything in the office seems brand new, like it has just been renovated. I take a minute to soak it all in. Is this really where I'm going to be working from now on?

"So, what do you think?" Zara asks, her voice betraying hope.

"It's amazing," I say, awestruck. "I'm...speechless."

"Here," Janice says, handing me a set of keys. "Your back-ups. The door has a fingerprint lock, which you'll need to set immediately. In addition, I have some paperwork you'll need to fill out. I hope you didn't think you'd come bursting in here and get started on cases today."

"Well, I kind of—"

"Speaking of which," Janice adds without stopping. "You have broad authority to choose the cases you feel are the most important and to use your team's resources to work those cases. But don't think this is a free ride. The whole reason any of this is possible is because of your track record. That is a record you will need to maintain and improve if you want this to remain a permanent situation. You're being given these resources because you are the best at closing the tough cases. We expect that to continue."

"We?" I ask.

"Me, and the director," she says. "As I mentioned before, you are free to choose your team—" she shoots a glance at Liam and Zara, "—but keep in mind each of your team members will always have their own cases as well. A lot of this job is resource management and allocation."

"I understand," I say.

I catch Zara nudge Liam. "Kinda seems like Em's the only one getting paid for all this 'extra' work, doesn't it?"

"Hey, I'll cut you in if you want to take on the paperwork," I tell her.

She chuckles. "Staying here after hours to write up reports? No, thank you. That's prime gaming time."

Janice clears her throat. "I need to impress upon you how important it is you succeed in this, Slate. I've put my neck out for you here, and I've convinced the director this program can succeed with the right person in the job. *You're* that person. You've told me you can handle this. Now I expect you to deliver."

Her words are like being splashed with cold water, and I straighten my posture. "Yes, ma'am. I won't let you down."

"Good. Get settled and familiar with the space, then come and see me in Wallace's former office and we'll go over that paperwork." Her gaze lingers on me for a moment before she excuses herself.

I walk over to the desk and place my hand on the back of the leather chair. It's firm yet forgiving.

"Okay, now that that's over," Zara says, "I'm calling the couch!" While it's not particularly long, it fits Zara well enough. "We'll designate this whole area Zara's realm."

Liam smiles as he stands on the other side of the desk, watching me.

"What?" I ask.

"Are you happy?"

"I'm…I don't know what I am," I say. "It's a lot of pressure."

"You've handled worse," he says.

He's right. I have. But this is a big step. Just a year and a half ago, I was on the verge of losing this job, of maybe even facing federal charges. And now here I am, a Supervisory

Special Agent in charge of a brand-new team. I can hardly believe it. "I don't know how to feel."

"C'mon Em," Zara says, extricating herself from the couch and joining us. "You deserve this."

"I wasn't the one who infiltrated and took down a terrorist cell," I remind her, "or who was almost blown up in a house fire." I glance at Liam.

"No," he says. "You're the one who has tracked down and closed more cases than just about any agent in this office, despite all the obstacles thrown at you. Don't you understand? That's why Janice gave you this opportunity. Because no matter what is thrown at you, you find a way through. Your resilience is not a skill many of us have."

Zara produces a nervous laugh. "Just look at me. Do you think I'm ever going undercover again?"

I can't help but smile. "Thank you. Both of you. I don't know what I would do without you."

"Keep doing what you're doing," Liam replies. "And you'll be just fine."

"Yeah," Zara adds. "And now there's a bonus, you get to boss us around."

That actually produces a laugh. "Only if I decide to add you to the team."

Her entire face drops. "You wouldn't!"

I shrug my shoulders. "I dunno. Maybe some requirements are in order."

She rounds the desk looking like a pissed off fairy and I back off, "Okay, okay, you're on the team!"

"That's better," she says, smug. She turns to Liam. "That's how you do it. Can't let the power go to her head."

"I'll be happy to submit to any requirements you may have," he says.

"Ugh," Zara replies. "I'll go get the door sock. Just let me know when you two are done."

"I'm sorry, the *door sock*?"

"Yeah," she says, throwing a wink over her shoulder. "You know, for all the bow-chicka-wow-wow you'll be doing in here."

"That is *not* what this office is for," I insist.

"Um, that is *exactly* what this office is for," she laughs, side-eyeing at Liam. "*AmIrite?*"

His mouth is open but nothing comes out, and I can see his cheeks beginning to redden.

"Okay, both of you need to get out of here," I tell them. "I'm never going to get anything done with all these distractions."

"Yes, boss," Zara says, shooting me a little salute. "But seriously, Em. Congrats."

Liam seems to have regained some of his composure. He reaches over and gives my hand a squeeze. "She's right. We'll celebrate when we get home."

I smile. "Thank you. *Both* of you."

As they leave, Zara continues to rib Liam about the door sock, and I find myself alone with my thoughts again. It's still overwhelming, and as much as I want to revel in this moment, I find myself being drawn back to the hospital again and again. And the events of last night. While I'd hoped today would be a good distraction, it appears getting my mind off hitting my own mother with my car won't be as easy as I'd hoped.

Chapter Three

"HELLO?" I ask, knocking on the open door.

Dr. Kurt Frost glances up from writing something on a notepad, surprise on his face. "Agent Slate?"

"Yeah," I say sheepishly, sliding all the way into the door frame.

He stands, removing his glasses. "I wasn't sure I would see you again after SAC Wallace was terminated."

"Neither was I," I admit. "But I spoke to Deputy Director Simmons. She thought it was a good idea I continue these sessions for as long as I need them."

"I see," he says. "Well, come in. I have some free time now, or if you'd like we can set up an appointment for later in the week—"

"Actually, there is something I need to discuss," I say. When I first started seeing Dr. Frost, I was convinced it was just Wallace's ploy to spy on me, or at the very least to discredit me. But it turns out Frost is the genuine article, and these sessions have proved to be helpful. If nothing else, it's helped me get outside of my head some.

Frost indicates I take a seat on the couch as he closes the

door. "I understand congratulations are in order. I heard about your promotion through the grapevine."

"Oh, yeah. Thank you," I say.

"You don't seem that excited." He takes a seat behind his desk again, pulling out his signature yellow pad.

"No, I am," I say. "It's just...there's a lot going on right now." I give him a CliffsNotes version of everything that's happened in the past week. The strange car, the woman stepping out in front of me, the accident, all of it. He sits and listens without interrupting.

When I'm done, I sit back and take a deep breath.

"Emily, tell me. What was your relationship like with your mother?" he asks.

I furrow my brow. "Um, good, I guess? I was an only child, so I was her primary focus, but I never felt like she was smothering me. She was kind in a way I've never known anyone else to be. She had this sense about her, like you knew that everything would be okay simply because she was there. That she could take care of anything. That's what I remember most about her."

"Did you ever witness your mother doing anything...well, anything you might have objected to?"

I'm not sure I understand what he's asking. "Like what?"

"For instance, did she ever raise her voice or get angry? Did she ever do anything you found questionable?"

I search my memories, sure I can think of something. But the longer I think about it, the more I realize that I don't think she ever did. I'm not sure I ever heard her raise her voice once. Even when I did something wrong, it was usually Dad who got more upset. "I remember one time when I almost accidentally lit the carpet on fire. Dad was livid, but Mom... Mom just wanted me to know that sometimes people made mistakes and that didn't mean they were bad people. But sometimes they just didn't know better."

"Didn't know better?" Frost asks.

"Yeah, I remember her saying that a lot. Anytime I would do something wrong, she would turn it into a lesson instead of a punishment. One time, I was five or six I think, I thought it would be fun to hide after she put me to bed. When she came in to check on me and couldn't find me, she got really upset. But when I finally came out, she said she was just relieved that I was all right. She told me that she had been afraid something had happened to me, and that all she wanted was to make sure I was okay."

"Would you say, then, your mother had a lot of empathy?" he asks.

I nod. "She did. Even when I was older, she said people always did what they did for a reason, and while sometimes those reasons could be bad, usually it was because people were hurt or suffering themselves. For instance, someone broke into the corner store down the street from our house. She said it wasn't because they *wanted* to break in, but probably because they didn't have enough money, and were desperate for food."

"I see that's a lesson that's stayed with you," he says.

"I guess in a way, it kind of informed who I am as an agent," I reply. "I always look for the underlying reasons people do things. And more often than not, it's not because they are monsters. I mean, some of them are, sure. But usually, it's because they are hurt in some way and don't know how to deal with it."

Frost nods before standing again and coming around the desk to sit in the chair across from the couch. "Would you agree you hold your mother in very high regard?"

"Doesn't everyone?" I ask.

"No, they don't. Not everyone is as lucky as you. Mothers can be abusive," he says. "Or absent. But yours was neither."

"I guess…I was lucky," I say.

He takes a deep breath before crossing one leg over the other. "So how does it make you feel then, to see her again?"

I go still. "I…uh…you're not suggesting that the woman in the hospital is actually my mother."

He makes a noncommittal gesture. "You tell me."

"I mean, my brain *knows* it's not her," I say. "I watched them bury her. I was there for the funeral."

"But…?"

I let out a long breath, unable to believe I'm about to admit this. "But…it was a closed casket. I never actually saw her body." He's about to speak again but I interrupt. "I mean, I did, but only from a distance, before my dad ordered that they close the casket for the ceremony." I ball my hands into fists and release them again, over and over. "I…um…I wasn't doing very well at the funeral. It took me a long time to get over losing her so young."

"Maybe it's something you never did get over," he suggests.

"Maybe."

"So, tell me about this woman in the hospital. Who do you think she is?"

"I mean, I *thought* she was my mother's sister. The one I discovered in her hometown's records. But that girl was six years younger than my mother. This woman looks exactly like my mom would look today."

"Are you sure?" he asks.

"What?"

"You said yourself, it's been almost what, eighteen years since she died? How would you know exactly what she would look like now?"

I pause. "Well…I…" I trail off, not sure how to respond.

"Either way, I see two possibilities here. The first is that your mother faked her death and has been hiding from you this entire time. Her only daughter, the one she adored. *Or* this is a relative of yours, your mother's sister, who may not have even known you existed until recently. Whichever is more likely, both involve your mother keeping secrets. You said your mother never spoke of her family."

"Except to say that there weren't any of them left," I say.

"Which was a lie." I look up to see his gaze boring right into mine. "Can you think of any other time, that you know of, when she would have lied to you?"

"No, I don't think I can."

"But it's possible."

I straighten back up, suddenly feeling uncomfortable. "What are you getting at?"

"I want you to consider something," he says. "You have this idealized picture of your mother in your head. Of course you do, it's only natural. You lost her at a young age, and she was your primary parent. All of which is understandable. But in the years since, you have put this woman up on a pedestal, when in fact, she was just as human as you and I. She made mistakes, she was not perfect. And I want you to keep that in mind as you investigate this case.

"We already know your mother lied to you at least once. I don't want your bias towards her to strip away your skills as an investigator. Because whatever this is, you are going to need those skills to get to the bottom of it."

"Are you saying my mother was involved with something illegal?" I ask.

He purses his lips. "I want you to keep an open mind. What I am saying is this case is very personal to you, which means all this extra 'stuff' that's out here will cloud your view of what is really going on. You just told me how much all of this is weighing on your mind. I know how you operate, and you always throw your whole self into anything you work on. But in this case, you are too close to see things with the same clarity."

I get what he's saying, but I don't like the implication that I can't handle getting to the bottom of this because I'm too close to it. I was too close to Matt's case as well, and eventually

I uncovered the conspiracy behind it. Not that I think there is a conspiracy behind this woman, or if there is, it's not on the same scale.

"Tell me, what would you do if this were one of your regular cases?"

I laugh. "I don't think I have regular cases," I tell him.

"Fair enough. But humor me."

"I'd follow the evidence," I say. "But this isn't my case. It isn't *anything* yet. We just have a woman in the hospital."

"One you suspect of sending you cryptic letters and attempting to run you off the road," he replies. "It sounds like the making of a case to me."

He's right. And given I now have broader authority to pick and choose which cases I want to go after, I could spend my considerable resources looking into Emily even further. But at the same time, Liam and I have been doing just that for the past three months and have barely gotten anywhere. I don't think it would look very good for my first outing as SSA to be something I'm personally connected to, especially if there's nothing to find.

"As much as I'd like to, I can't put my personal needs over those of the FBI. I have a responsibility to choose cases that will have the most impact. I'm a public servant. Which means putting the needs of others before my own."

"In true Emily Slate fashion," he says. "But I want you to be mindful of how much of yourself you're giving away when you're working. With you, it's often results 'at all costs.' And sometimes those costs include your mental health. I think this new chapter in your life is a good opportunity to start curbing that behavior. You won't be effective very long if you burn out."

I nod, having heard this song and dance before. And part of me agrees with it. But at the same time, if I'm closing in on a suspect, I'm not going to take a mental health day. I just won't do it. Some things are worth sacrificing; I knew that when I took this job.

"All I'm saying is, give yourself some grace and try not to push yourself too hard."

I stand abruptly. "I won't. Thanks for seeing me on such short notice."

He sighs like he knows his words have rung hollow. "This is a new chapter for you, I just want to make sure you're with us here for a long time."

"I know," I say. "And I appreciate it. I'll keep it in mind, really."

"Very well. Feel free to schedule some more time whenever you're ready."

"Thanks," I tell him and head out before he can hit me with any more platitudes. Why is it that half the time I leave his office I feel more frustrated than when I went in? I know Dr. Frost means well, but maybe this wasn't the best idea.

If he really thinks I'm not going to do everything I can to get to the bottom of whoever this woman is, he doesn't know me as well as he claims to.

Chapter Four

BY THE TIME I finally get through all the paperwork Janice prescribed, as well as upgrade my security clearance and familiarize myself with the new areas of our databases I now have access to, it's past six. I told Liam to go home and I'd catch an Uber as soon as I was finished, but it's taken me longer than I thought. Not to mention over here on this side of the office, I'm separated from the usual group of agents and I don't see as many people as I'm used to. It's almost like my own little world over here so I don't get to see when people arrive and leave.

As I shut everything off and close my door, I pause to reflect on my name emblazoned across the front. Maybe it's just a series of fancy decals, but it's what those decals represent that means so much. I can't believe I have my own corner office, and starting tomorrow, I'll be running my own team. I already took a cursory glance at all the files in the database. There were so many more than I had expected. This is not going to be easy by any means, but I'm excited to start. And other than my meeting with Dr. Frost today, I've been able to keep my thoughts off the woman in the hospital for the most part.

But as I'm making my way down to the main lobby to meet the Uber I've called, I can't help but drift back in that direction again. I'm not sure if the hospital would inform me of any change in the woman's condition or not as there's no concrete proof I'm her next of kin. At least not until all the tests come back.

As I get down to the lobby, I cancel the Uber and call for another one—this one going to the hospital instead of back to the house. I just want to pop in for a few minutes to see if there's been any improvement or if they've found anything yet. I shoot a text to Liam letting him know I'll be a little later than I expected and to go ahead and eat. I don't want to hold him up, and I know Timber's patience can only be stretched so thin. That dog is more accurate than an Omega Speedmaster.

When we reach the hospital, I can't help my heart from thumping in my throat again as I show my ID to the nurses guarding the ICU. They demand I put on a mask before entering, which I do as I follow the lead nurse in. She directs me over to where the woman is still lying, her condition unchanged since yesterday.

"No improvements at all?" I ask.

"Not as far as we can tell. Brain activity is still minimal."

"Any word back on her ID?" I ask.

"We turned all that over to DC Police this morning," she says. "You'll have to direct any questions about that to them. We're just trying to keep her alive."

Staring at this woman hooked up to all these machines is so strange. I'm pulled back to those final moments with Mom in the hospital, seeing her hooked up to all manner of devices as she slowly wasted away. At first, I didn't understand exactly what was happening, but as the days dragged on, it became clear that my mother was never leaving the hospital. And in fact, she died only a few days later. I was in school when it happened, and Dad told me I wouldn't want to see her like that, as previous evening she had been fine. Well, fine enough that I could pretend like everything was kinda normal. Even though I insisted, he wouldn't hear of it. He said it was nothing a twelve-year-old needed to see.

And now, here I am, in the exact same position again eighteen years later.

"Is there anything else you need, Agent Slate?" the nurse asks.

"No, thank you," I reply, my voice soft and even, but I'm barely even listening. Instead, I'm back in those days after Mom's death. Frost is right, there is no way my mother would have faked her own death and left me and Dad on our own. That wasn't her nature. Which means this *has* to be the other Emily. The one in my grandmother's belly in that picture. The aunt I never knew about, and who has apparently been trying to goad me into believing she is my mother.

And yet, I can't get this nagging feeling out of my gut that I'm missing something. There are too many unanswered questions, too many unknowns. I need to treat this like I would any other case, which means the first thing I should do is confirm this woman's identity. I need to know for sure this is the woman who wrote the letters, who almost killed Liam in that house, and who tried to run me and Zara off the road. I'll leave everything else up to the DC police, but at the very least, I need that. Once all doubt has been eliminated, only then can we move forward. But I doubt DC Police is going to share their findings, at least not for a while. And I don't feel like getting into a pissing contest with whoever has been assigned the case. Not to mention I'm probably a suspect considering my car is the reason she's in this predicament.

I glance behind me to see that the nurse has retreated to the station near the door. I wave her back over.

"Yes?"

"I need a blood sample from the victim," I tell her. "The

FBI has opened a case in the matter, and we need to assess her identity. Is there an extra sample I can use?"

The nurse gives me a grimace before turning to the refrigerator that sits below the counter in the ICU. "We have additional samples on hand for processing. Tell me what you need, and I can get it for you."

"Sorry, but this has to be an internal FBI matter," I tell her. That and I don't want DC Police getting word of anything we might find. This needs to be for my eyes only, at least right now. "We have teams for this kind of thing."

The nurse sighs before reaching into the cold unit and pulling out a sample in a glass vial. "You'll need to get it back under forty degrees within thirty minutes," she says. "Otherwise it loses its viability."

"Thanks," I say as she hands it over. I place it in a small evidence bag I pull out of my jacket pocket. Had I asked as a relative, I doubt she would have complied. But as an FBI agent, I have the authority to request samples when they're needed. Though I don't miss the nurse's stink eye as she returns to her duties. She was here last night too, when I was claiming the woman in the bed was my aunt.

But I don't have time to worry about the nurse. I need to get this back to the office before it goes bad. I head down the corridor and pull out my phone, dialing quickly.

"This is Caruthers," the voice says on the other end.

"Caruthers, it's Slate," I say, striding down the hallway with purpose. "I need your assistance."

"What's the case number?" he asks.

"There isn't one. Yet. I need you to open up a new file, for my eyes only. I'm sure you heard about the woman I ran over."

"I'd caught wind of it." Good ol' Caruthers, the man was practically unflappable. Which was precisely why I called him. I don't want to pull Zara and Liam into this, they've both already risked so much for me. Now to see if my shiny new SSA title can pull any weight.

"I'm dropping by a blood sample; I need you to run it and see if it matches the one I have on file. I also want to pull her fingerprints, see if we can't get a hit in the system somewhere." I'll fill him in on the rest when I see him in person, for some reason I don't want to talk about it over the phone.

"I can do that," he says.

"Thank you," I reply, relieved. I wasn't sure that was going to work. Some part of me worried my authority had already been curtailed by the accident, or only applied to people I authorized for certain cases. But it seems Janice has trusted me with a lot more. "Let me know as soon as you find something. Day or night."

"I'll get right on it," he says. "Oh, and Agent Slate?"

"Yes?"

"Congratulations on your promotion."

Chapter Five

BY THE TIME I get home, it's well past nine and my stomach is rumbling. That took longer than I expected, but at the same time, I think the risk will be worth it. If for no other reason than my own piece of mind.

Finally, the Uber drops me off and I barely have the door open before Timber practically runs into me. All the lights are still on, but I don't see Liam anywhere. And then my heart drops when I catch sight of the kitchen counter. He's fished a pair of candlesticks from some box, though neither have been lit. But it's clear from the silverware that's been carefully arranged—and the glasses full of what I'm sure is room-temperature water by now—that there either was or was supposed to be a romantic meal set up here.

"Oh, hey," he says. I see him yawning as he walks down the hall leading to the bedroom.

"What's all this?" I ask.

"Your celebration, remember? New job and all?"

"Oh," I say, feeling like such a shit. "Right. Liam, I'm sorry, don't tell me you didn't eat anything."

"I wanted to wait on you," he says, stifling another yawn.

"But don't worry, Timber got his dinner right on time. And his post dinner snack."

I rub Timber's head a few times as I toss my jacket over the end of the one of stools Liam has unwrapped for the occasion. Dammit, what was I thinking? Oh yeah, I was being selfish again, only thinking of what *I* needed. Here he's gone to all this trouble being all perfect like he always is to celebrate me, and what did I do? I went back to the office to drop off the sample so Caruthers would have everything he needed first thing in the morning.

"Had to work later than you thought, huh? New jobs are like that, sometimes," he says.

"No," I say, my face stern. "That wasn't what I was doing."

His eyebrows form into a *V*. "What?"

I take a seat on one of the stools. "I already know what you're going to say, just trust me when I say I had to do it. For me."

"Do what?"

"I opened an investigation into the woman in the hospital. A quiet investigation."

"Em, I could have helped you—"

"That's just the point," I tell him. "I'm keeping this quiet on purpose. The only reason I'm telling you is because I'm not about to start off our new lives together in this house by lying. And I know DC is already working on their own investigation. But I think I have some rights here. If this really is the woman who has been sending these letters, I deserve to know who she really is." I glance over at the makeshift place settings again. "I'm sorry about dinner. I will make it up to you."

He pulls his lips into a line, and I'm sure he's about to lay into me for keeping him in the dark, even if it was only for a few hours. But instead, he pulls me close and holds me in a hug for a moment. Timber whines and Liam reaches down, pulling him close too. I feel his little butt wiggle against my leg, just happy to be part of the group.

Finally, Liam lets go. "How about some dinner?"

"You're not mad?" I ask.

"Why would I be mad? You're right, you *do* have a right to know who she is. I also know you're not going to be able to think straight until you get some answers." He rounds the kitchen island and heads to the refrigerator, pulling out a bottle of champagne.

"That's great, make me feel even worse," I say. "At least yell at me or something."

He stifles a chuckle. "Em, it's *okay*. Trust me, I get it. I want answers too. I mean, she almost killed me." I reach out, taking his hand and giving it a squeeze.

"Do you think we should notify Detective Michaels?" Despite my reluctance, he *is* the detective in charge of the investigation into the arson up in Ohio. But because I spent the better part of two days being grilled by the man, I'm not thrilled about the idea of looping him in on this. Especially since he still considers Liam a suspect.

"It might not be a bad idea," Liam says. "He might want to coordinate with DC police down here. If she does wake up, he should probably be there."

"Yeah," I say, reluctant. "I suppose. Still, I don't like the idea of just handing her over to him before we figure out just what her game has been."

"We could always wait and see if she wakes up first, *then* contact him," he suggests. "Did the nurses note any changes in her condition?"

I shake my head. "Not as far as I could tell. Still minimal brain activity. But I managed to procure a blood sample."

"Procure?" he asks, arching an eyebrow.

"For Caruthers," I say, though I know how flimsy that sounds. "In my defense, I didn't go there planning to do it."

"But you'd been thinking about her all day and couldn't focus until you got an update," he says, giving me a grin.

"You know what? It's scary how much you already know about me. We've only been going out for what, six months?"

"Aren't we trained to observe people?" He holds out the bottle of champagne. "Want to do the honors? By the way, this is just a preview. We'll have a real party once we get the house in order."

I take the bottle, unwrapping the foil from the top before going to work on the metal screw around the cork. "Thank you. For understanding."

"I'm always here for you, you know that, right? And not to judge you or berate you. I'm here to support you, in any way I can."

I smile. "Ditto." I pop the bottle and the cork goes flying. Timber turns to attention at the noise, looking around before chasing after it. I pour some in each of the two empty glasses Liam has placed before me. "You know, I wouldn't be able to do this without you here."

He takes his glass, clinking it against mine. "Just imagine. If I'd never met you, I'd still be stuck in Stillwater, maybe even still working under Burke." He mimics a shudder. "Scary."

"Here's to finally finding answers," I say.

He nods, holding up his glass. "To answers."

"Okay," he says, clapping his hands together. "Now that I'm awake and have a slight buzz, it's time for your celebratory dinner."

"Liam, you really didn't have to—"

"Shh, shh, shh," he says, placing a playful finger against my lips. "It'll be worth it, trust me."

We banter while he pulls out all the stops, removing dishes from the refrigerator he obviously fixed some time before. *When did he have time to do all of this? Was I really gone that long?* As the food warms in the oven, we share a charcuterie board full of thin meats and exotic cheeses before he presents me with a decadent plate.

It's a perfectly cooked piece of white fish, presented on a bed of mushroom risotto and surrounded by spinach and vegetables. Liam grins as my eyes practically bug out of my head. The smells coming off this thing are immaculate.

It's all so mouthwatering, I forget we don't even have a table to eat at yet. We sit side by side at the kitchen bar, with Timber practically drooling at my feet as the smell of the lemon and spices fill my senses and ignite some part of my brain that I know is mistaking this for crack cocaine. Each bite is delectable, and by the time I've cleaned my plate, its nearing midnight. Timber, having consumed more than two full bread rolls, blinks sleepy-eyed as I insist on cleaning up. If Liam's going to cook like this every night, I'm going to need to start putting in some serious gym time. Because there's no way I'm giving up this food. It's just too damn good.

"Where did you learn to cook?" I ask. "It's like you're a professional chef."

He chuckles, wiping down the countertop. "You just haven't ever had a proper meal before," he says. "You can't subsist on take-away food all the time. Well, you *can*, but you miss the aroma of life."

"Is that what we're calling it?"

"That's what my dad calls it," he says. "But it was Mom. She taught me everything she knew. Gerald...well, he never really got into cooking. But it was something she and I bonded over."

I nod. Liam's family life is almost as complicated as mine. But thankfully a lot of that has calmed down in the past few months, after our visit up there. "Well, tell her thank you from me. She taught you well."

"And now, for part two," he says.

I glance at the clock. "Shouldn't we be getting to bed?"

"Trust me. You'll sleep better. Stay right here." He heads

down the hallway to the bathroom, and I can hear running water. My curiosity getting the better of me, I follow him after a few minutes. The bathroom is full of steam and a lavender aroma.

"What is this?"

"Hot bath," he says. "It will help you sleep better."

"Liam, this is too much," I protest.

"Oh no," he says, standing. "This is all purely selfish. Because when you toss and turn all night, I don't get any sleep. And I've got this new slave driver of a boss I need to make sure I impress at work tomorrow. Which means I need a good seven hours, at least."

I approach him, looking up into those gorgeous hazel eyes of his. "Slave driver huh?"

"Oh yeah. She's a real ball buster." He smiles.

"Then I guess you better get a good night's rest." I reach up and press my lips to his, feeling the heat of his body against mine.

I never do make it into the tub.

Chapter Six

Liam and I head back into work again, and I can already see a new pattern forming. Before, when we were coming from our separate apartments, we wouldn't see each other most days until we made it to the office. As our relationship developed and we began staying over more and more at each other's places, we'd always take separate cars into work in the event we needed to go back to our own homes.

But now that we're both living in the same house, there's no sense in taking two cars, even if one wasn't about to be part of a police investigation. We both get up, get ready together, have our coffee—if we can find it in all the packed boxes—and share a ride to work together. In some ways it's frustrating; I'm not used to steering around another person before spitting out my toothpaste. But in other ways, it's really nice because unlike before, there is always someone around. Even though I've had Timber, I haven't needed to adjust my life to another person since Matt died. I'd forgotten what that was like, and since he and I never worked together, I never felt the same closeness I do with Liam.

I don't know why, but part of me thought maybe we'd run out of things to talk about. But with him, it's easy to keep the conversation flowing, even during the half hour commute. When we reach the office, I feel a different sense of confidence that wasn't there before. I've never been one to shy away from my job, or feel like I don't belong, but I think the promotion has given me a certain sense of validation that I wasn't aware was missing.

Liam peels off to his desk, leaving me with a few additional words of encouragement before I head over to Zara's desk, which now sits up against my old, empty desk. She's already hard at work as I approach but smiles when she glances up.

"Hey boss, can't wait to see what you come up with."

"Don't start that," I say.

"Start what?"

"Don't call me boss. It's weird."

"Yeah, but it's also factual," she replies. "How about chief? Big man? Head honcho?"

I glare at her.

"Big kahuna."

"Zara," I say.

She giggles. "Yeah, okay. I'll stick to *appropriate co-worker term of full equality but also not really because now you're getting paid the big bucks.*"

"I'm really not," I tell her. "It's only a one-level increase."

"Oh," she says, her face falling. "That doesn't really seem worth it then."

I scoff. "Thanks."

"Always here to help," she chirps.

"Speaking of which, I could use your assistance on something."

Her eyes go wide. "Really? Are we working a case already?"

"Well, not exactly." Her face pulls into a frown. "C'mon, I'll explain in my office."

"Don't need to tell me twice." She grabs her coffee from

her desk and follows me to the other end of the department. My door remains locked from last night, so I assume housekeeping doesn't have access to any of the offices on this level. It's probably something I'll have to schedule; I think I remember that in Janice's paperwork somewhere yesterday. But I did manage to set up the biometric lock, so when I grab the handle, the door automatically clicks open.

"That's so cool," Zara says. "I wanna get one of those for my place."

Once we're inside, I close the door behind us. "Okay, don't freak out, but I have to tell you something."

"That's never a good start," she says, setting her coffee down on my desk.

I give her a rundown of what happened at the hospital last night and what I've got Caruthers working on. I watch her face the whole time, but she remains impassive. When I finish, I wait for her to say something, but she just stares at me like I'm a comic bombing up on stage.

"What?" she finally says.

"Aren't you going to jump on my back about not involving you?" I ask.

"No," she says before taking a sip of her coffee. "Should I?"

"It's just, in the past—"

"Em, you don't have to consult me on every decision you make," she says. "Especially not now. You have operational authority. *And* this involves you. I think you did the right thing. I mean maybe I wouldn't have gone in there and swiped a blood sample—"

"I didn't swipe it," I correct. "I opened a case."

"Okay, whatever. You have a right to know what's going on. Have DC police contacted you yet?"

"Not yet," I say. "And I'm not sure what they're waiting on. I would call down there, but I don't want to seem too eager."

"That's probably a good idea," she says. "Caruthers is reliable. He'll get the job done. What did Liam say?"

I purse my lips. "He was strangely understanding, even though he'd gone to the trouble to make us a nice dinner to celebrate and I totally blew it. In fact, both of you have been way more tolerant than I thought you would be."

"That's because you got used to having your ass handed to you by Wallace all the time," she says. "Those days are over. You're in charge now. And I know you won't cut us out. I mean look at right now. You brought me in and told me what's up first thing this morning. That's a lot better than running off to Louisiana by yourself to try and protect me." She comes around the desk and wraps an arm around me, pulling me close to her side. "This is different."

"Okay," I say. "But there's something else."

"What?" she asks, her voice flat.

"I need help going through all these cases. Look at this." I log into my computer and show her the database showing all the open cases that I now have access to. They number in the hundreds.

"Whoa," she says, then looks at me with bright, wide eyes like a kid who has just seen a pile of presents under the tree. "Can I?"

"Be my guest," I say.

She lets out a high-pitched squeal before sitting down and scanning through all the cases. Zara has this ability to navigate a computer faster than I can follow. She's almost like a machine herself in that she's so quick to absorb and disseminate information. I watch in amazement as she flies through each of the files, scanning for relevant information, reading the summaries, cross-referencing them against each other, and diving deep into the details, never slowing down.

"Em, this is crazy," she says after a few minutes, though the windows are still opening and closing with rapid speed. "I had no idea any of these existed."

"Neither did I," I admit. "I guess this is what all the SACs see. I guess Janice gave me access so I can figure out where to divert our resources."

"They're listed by date," she says. "Not order of severity. This is going to take some time."

"Which is why I need your help," I reiterate. "They expect me to go through all of this on my own and figure out what's best for the team. But this will take me a year."

"No," she grins, spinning around in her chair. "We can do it. But first, who is on the team?"

"Well, you and Liam, obviously," I say. "And I think bringing in Nadia and Elliott wouldn't be a bad idea."

"Finally warmed up to them, huh?" she shoots me a wink.

"Considering Wallace is completely out of here and they both have helped save cases for us in the past? Yeah, I'm ready to trust them with some more."

"Great," she says, grinning. "Anyone else?"

"I think that's enough for now, don't you? But I guess I should formally request that you join, considering it's optional. Remember, Janice said you'd still have your own casework."

"My casework I can handle," she says. "I'm a master at time management. So yes, I accept."

I mock wiping my brow. "What a relief."

She turns back to the computer. "So now all we have to do is figure out where to begin."

WE SPEND THE BETTER PART OF THE MORNING GOING THROUGH everything in the database, eventually coming up with a list of cases that we deem "high priority" given the number of victims currently involved or the potential for future victims. I'm determined to make the biggest difference I can right out of the gate because I want to make sure this program succeeds. Though, it's strange, not being handed a case by a superior. That's all I've been used to for the past five years. And now that it's up to me, I find there's a lot more pressure. What if I choose the wrong kinds of cases, or someone bites it because we're working on a "cold" case instead of something more recent? And what if we can't make any headway on the cases we do choose? Janice is expecting results, and while I've never really focused about that before, now the pressure is very apparent. I'm starting to understand why higher-ups in our organization are so stressed all the time.

"Okay," Zara says. "I think we have a good selection here. Most of these are recent cases that have been trouble for one reason or another, and there are a few that are even local. Though, I guess now that you're the boss we don't have to worry about your flight restrictions, do we?" She cackles while I stare at her, nonplussed.

"Very funny."

"In fact, you could authorize private transportation for any case now," she suggests. "I mean, talk about a party bus."

"I think someone in accounting would still notice," I say. "I'm not running this place."

"Not yet," she points at me with the end of a pen.

"Not ever. You know what being the director is like. You have to talk to politicians all day, or speak in front of Congress, or hold press conferences. None of which I want to do."

"Right," she says, nodding. "No bullshit."

"No bullshit," I affirm. "What's your call out of the list we've collated?"

She scans over the fifteen or so cases we've pulled together. "I dunno, I kind of like this one in Atlanta. Possible drug movement across states. Never know how big that could be. Might lead to something massive."

"Not my style," I say. "I'm thinking something a little more urgent."

She leans back in her chair. "Such as?"

"This one," I say, pointing to the screen. "Two dead girls who are suspected to be part of a prostitution ring. Maryland Police, DC Police, and the Customs and Border Protection have all been working on this one for months, but haven't made much headway."

"It's always the dead people with you," she says, coming to look over my shoulder. "Em, this isn't a big case. I have a dozen others that are higher priority."

"I know," I say. "But that's the point. No one is paying any attention to this one. Why would they? It's two dead sex workers. Not exactly lighting up the switchboards." I turn to look at her. "But those are two human beings whose murders have barely been investigated. People with families, loved ones out there wondering what happened to them. They deserve as much attention as any of the other cases on the docket."

"If you're sure," she says. "But if you're looking to make a splash with your first case, I'm not sure this is it."

"I know," I admit. "But what I really want is to help those who've been overlooked. Like these two have."

She lets out a long breath. "Okay. Do we have anything on them yet?"

"Crime scene photos," I say, showing her images of both victims as they were found in the apartment. "Anything strange stand out about these?"

"Their clothing, for one," she says. "Expensive."

I grin. "I knew you'd pick that up. What else?"

She furrows her brow. "They're both fully clothed in the photos."

"Exactly," I say. "And sex worker victims are usually killed either in the act itself or just after. I don't know about you, but it doesn't even look like these two ever got undressed."

"The John killed them before they even had sex?"

"That's what it looks like. Which means there's more to this than just two dead women. It puts all sex workers at risk. These might not be the only two victims."

"Now that I think about it," Zara says. "Why are they there together? Were they killed at the same time? Or did one walk in one something she shouldn't have seen?"

"That's what we need to find out," I say glancing over the crime scene photos again. Both women look to be of Asian descent, which may explain why CBP was involved.

"I have to admit, I think you've got something here. Of course, it doesn't hurt that it's local," Zara suggests, giving me a look.

"What?" I ask.

"Nothing. You wouldn't happen to take a local case so you could stay close to a certain hospital, would you?"

"Why can't I do both?" I ask.

"Oh, you absolutely can," she says with a smile. "Just thought I'd point it out."

"Here," I tell her, giving her the case number. "Get started and see if you can at least track down which site they came from. In the meantime, I'll try to pull everything together to present for the team."

"Don't you have to first let everyone else know they're *on* the team?" she asks.

"Riiiight," I say, reining in my zeal. Just because Zara was enthusiastic about accepting the position, doesn't mean everyone else will. I'm pretty sure I can count on Liam. It's the other two I'll have to convince.

She chuckles as she heads for the door. "Best get on that. I'll start working on this right away, bo—, I mean, uh, big momma."

She quickly closes the door behind her before I can throw something at it.

Chapter Seven

"First off, I want to thank you all for agreeing to be here. I know this is extra work on your parts, so just know how much I appreciate it."

I'm standing at the head of one of the two bullpens we have in our department, looking out on Liam, Zara, Agent Nadia Kane, and Agent Elliott Sandel seated in the first couple of rows. Each of the bullpens only has about a dozen or so chairs facing the speaker's podium, but even with the four of them it still looks empty. Like I'm talking to a room full of ghosts.

Thankfully, it didn't take as much convincing to get Nadia and Elliott to join as I had originally thought. Nadia was enthusiastic, but Elliott seemed to enjoy drawing out our conversation. I don't know if it was because of our history or if that's just how he is, but eventually he relented, saying it would be an "interesting experiment," whatever the hell that means.

To say I'm nervous is an understatement, despite the fact I know and have worked with all these people intimately in the past. But there's just something about having the attention on you that changes how you see a situation. And it's not that I've ever been one to shy away from public speaking, but I don't like the spotlight. I never have. Whenever I've been encouraged to appear publicly about a case, I tend to find any excuse I can to get out of it. Even back when James Hunter was discovered and arrested, it was all Janice could do to get me to stand on the stage behind her as she spoke to the press about everything we'd found. Thankfully, she isn't here to watch, which I think would completely throw me off my game.

Before walking up here, I tried to remember that Wallace did this dozens, if not hundreds of times. And if he could do it, then so can I. I also tried to remember this is not about me, no one cares if I'm nervous or not. We're here to help people, and those people are trusting me to get my shit together and solve some crimes. Which also means I can't allow myself to be distracted, wondering if Caruthers has made any headway yet or not. I have to put that completely out of my mind and focus on the job at hand.

"Here's what we've got. Two victims, both in their late teens or early twenties. Both found still fully clothed, strangled by the neck. Neither woman had any ID on her, though the suspicion is they were local sex workers." I catch Liam's supportive smile, which helps me relax a bit. Though, I do feel a little strange about giving him orders. The same way I feel strange when Zara tries calling me "boss." While I've always wanted to move up the ranks in the Bureau, I never really thought about what that would entail. And now that I'm here, I feel more disconnected from my friends than I have in a while. Which is ridiculous, we're all still working in the same office; it's not like I've moved up to the eighth floor and I'm rubbing shoulders with the deputy directors. But still, I feel something of a separation that wasn't there before. A separation I hadn't expected.

"Suspicion from who?" Nadia asks.

"This case came from Maryland PD and Customs and Border Protection," I say. "They've been working on it for a few weeks without making much headway." Though, what Zara and I managed to find in the few hours since makes me think they weren't looking very hard. Just another one that had fallen through the cracks.

I turn my attention to the screen behind me. It took me the better part of an hour to pull together a simple presentation to show the group. I hope this is something I can get better at as time goes on, because wrangling together computer presentations is not my forte. Now that I'm up here, it feels like a fourth grader could have put together a better summary. I press the button on the little remote, and the screen behind me fills with the pictures of both women from the crime scene, splayed out on the floor of what looks like an upscale apartment. We have the address on file—it's in one of the nicer parts of town. To the untrained eye, they probably wouldn't raise any sex-working flags, but there are small tells.

"The initial investigation couldn't find the murder weapon or weapons," I say. "But the autopsy concluded it to be an electrical cord of some kind. No witnesses and no one heard anything. CBP has come up blank trying to identify the two individuals."

"Which means what, exactly?" Nadia asks.

"Runaways, domestic abuse victims who got themselves into worse situations, who knows?" I say. "But that's not our primary focus at the moment. We need to find the person responsible and make sure they are held to account. Then, in doing so, we might be able to also address that larger issue."

"Who found them?" Liam asks.

"Maintenance man for the apartment complex. Neighbors began complaining of the smell, and he went in to investigate. That was three weeks ago."

"Who owns the apartment?" Elliott asks, having not spoken until now.

"We're still working on that. You all have the case notes there in front of you. And Zara has already done some pre-work on this." I motion to her to take over, though she stays in her seat.

"It took more digging than I wanted to do," she says, "but I found something interesting that might point us in the right direction." I toss her the remote and she clicks to the next image, which is of a website called "Red Sunset Photography." The image on the front of the webpage is just as it says, a beautiful photo of a red sunset against the water.

"Looks like a place you'd get bad photography done," Elliott says.

"Close." Zara clicks to another page, which shows the "about" section. "They describe themselves as a bespoke, yet discreet model agency, where women are available on an hourly basis for nude 'photography' needs." She uses air quotes. "Basically, it's a place to hire prostitutes, but they're just covering their asses here."

"And this is the site the two dead girls were advertised on?" Liam asks.

"Zara?"

She types for a moment and the page changes, this time showing a "menu" of sorts, each with a different woman in various states of undress. Zara scrolls through the site until it lands on the image of a woman calling herself *Lucy Lieu*. "Here's one of them. I haven't found the other yet."

"They're still on the site?" Liam asks.

"No, this is a previous iteration I was able to find using some internet sleuthing. It's been updated now, and Lucy isn't there anymore. But she's advertised as costing four hundred 'roses' for one hour, eight hundred for two, twelve hundred for three and so on and so forth. The interesting thing about this site is this information isn't publicly available without a member code. Or, in my case, a serious desire to break into places I'm not supposed to be."

"Why go to the trouble?" Nadia adds. "There are plenty

of escort service sites out there easily found with a Google search. Why put everything behind a membership wall?"

"False exclusivity," I say. "Combined with the fact they're charging such high prices makes me think they have some high-paying clients. The men and possibly women who frequent this site aren't going to be your run-of-the-mill Johns looking for an hour or two. These people are looking for an experience."

"Not to mention, if the women are undocumented, they don't want any information to be publicly accessible," Zara adds.

"Which could also come back on the agency," Liam says. "They wouldn't want the investigation. No wonder they tried scrubbing them from the site."

"Exactly," I say. "In fact, depending on the client, the agency might have even helped cover for them."

"So we go after the agency," Nadia suggests.

"It's a start," I reply. "Zara has managed to find an address, so we can at least speak with someone who represents the…company."

"That's not going to make things easy," Elliott says. "If they did help cover it up, they won't be looking to speak with the FBI."

"Which is why Maryland PD and CBP haven't been able to make headway," I say. "But we're going to. We need to know who is running this service, how many people are involved, and where their models are coming from. But more than that, we need to find their client list, which is going to be a bitch and a half. But that's why we're here. To do what no one else has been able to manage so far."

I switch off the monitor behind me. "We're going to break this into teams. Liam and Elliott, I want you two looking into the victims. Find out as much as you can, no detail is too small, especially anything that might point to an ID. I doubt

Lucy Lieu was her real name. Even if you have to start looking overseas."

Liam exchanges a glance with Elliott. "No problem."

"Zara, you and Nadia keep working on Red Sunset. Find someone from the company we can speak with in person. I want to know who owns the company, where they live, where they work and how to get to them. And see if you can't find out who owns or leases that apartment. I did a quick search before coming in here, but the local records are frustratingly nebulous. Talk to the neighbors or anyone else that lives around there, especially the people who reported the smell and the maintenance guy. We need to start fresh, make sure we're not missing a beat."

"You got it," Zara says, nodding. "What are you going to do?"

I smile, gathering up my materials. "Lucky me. I have a budget meeting."

Chapter Eight

AFTER FORTY-FIVE MINUTES of mind-numbing information, I have decided I am definitely not a numbers girl. Not only are budgets extremely boring, but I'm not sure I like knowing how the agency operates behind the scenes. The only time I ever needed to worry about a budget in the past was when I accidentally booked a private plane for a flight and was "grounded" for spending too much of the Bureau's money. But upon seeing the budget they're working with; I can say without a doubt that my little "snafu" was nothing more than a blip on the overall plan.

The way Wallace made it sound, the Bureau was on the brink of financial collapse, and I was the primary cause. Of course, I should have realized that was nothing more than him being an insufferable blowhard, trying to blame me for his own shortcomings. It may have taken a few months, but the Bureau getting rid of him was one of the smartest things its ever done.

As I'm making my way back to my office, I can't help but reflect on my first official meeting as SSA with my team. Despite a few small hiccups, I think it went extremely well. And the more time I have to think about it, the more I feel like we're working on the right case. Maybe it's not the biggest or flashiest case out there, but it's important nonetheless. Though, I am worried it might not meet the burden of proof to keep our team around. Janice said she was counting on me to make the right decision. I only hope I don't disappoint her.

When I reach my office, I have an itch to catch up with Zara and Nadia to see how they're doing, even though it's barely been an hour. It's strange not being in the middle of the action, and I'm not sure I like it. There's no rule about me not getting directly involved, other than the fact I need to manage the team, but I don't know if I can be both leader and member at the same time. It's a balancing act for sure. I log in and search for any updates from anyone, but nothing has come through. I'm about to call Zara when my phone rings anyway. I smile; it seems we're both on the same wavelength after all.

"This is Slate," I say.

"Agent Slate," an unfamiliar male voice says. "I'm glad I caught you. This is Detective Striker with DC Police."

Right, the accident. I'd gotten so caught up in the case I hadn't thought about it for a couple of hours. I'm not sure if that's a good thing or not, but it's promising, at least. It seems I've managed to curb the typical obsession, at least a little. Is that what they call growth?

"What can I do for you, Detective?" I ask.

"I wanted to call to introduce myself," he says. "I'm heading up the investigation into the accident on Monday night. Do you have a few minutes to answer some questions?" His tone is open, friendly. He's making it sound like this is something he *has* to do, even though both of us know it's not necessary. I can't tell if that's on purpose or not. False friendliness is a tactic I am well familiar with.

"Sure, I suppose," I say.

"Great, I'm down at the sixth precinct building. Just tell the duty officer you're here to see me when you arrive. He'll buzz you right through." He hangs up before I can protest, causing me to grit my teeth. I walked straight into that one.

Whatever. I should just go down there and get this over with. It will give my team some more time to make headway on the case. I head down to the garage and sign out one of the company cars, seeing as mine is still at home, but I can't help but curse under my breath the whole way.

Thankfully, the morning traffic is light and it's still before lunchtime. There are a few protest groups out, but that's nothing unusual for DC with the weather finally starting to warm up. Spring has never been my favorite time of year by far, but even I can't help but admire all the beautiful trees and flowers in bloom.

The sixth precinct is on the west side of the city and is a tall, four-story building shoved in between a series of other commercial buildings. There's a parking area around back where I pull up, showing the officer on duty outside my badge. He waves me through, allowing me to park in the sparse lot. Otherwise, I would have needed to find a parking garage somewhere.

As I walk up to the back of the building, I can't help but notice the weathered yet intricate designs carved from marble to make up the façade. The building stands as a testament to the city's rich history and is probably at least a hundred years old or more.

As soon as I enter, I'm greeted by tall portraits along the walls in ornate frames, with the patina of age, their regal faces softened by time. The floorboards, polished and shiny, creak with every step, and I wonder just how many people have come and gone before me. I catch the scent of leather and old paper in the air, almost emanating from the walls themselves. A large wooden desk sits in front of me, looking like it was carved from a single, massive tree. Officers and detectives mingle near the desk, their voices a low murmur punctuated by the occasional cracks of a nearby radio. I also catch the scent of freshly made coffee, my mouth watering without my permission.

One of the officers at the desk looks up as I approach.

"I'm Agent Emily Slate. Here to see Detective Striker."

"Sure," he says, pointing to a door off to my right. "Through there and up one flight. Striker's office will be on your left at the top of the stairs. Here, I'll buzz you through and let him know you're coming."

"Thanks," I say, heading for the door set into the marble wall. Above me, the label on the ten-foot-tall portrait identifies it as William B. Webb. They just don't build police stations like this anymore.

Through the door, the station is a little less glamorous, and I find the metal staircase encased in a cinder-block stairwell with rows of windows along every other landing. The morning sun shines through, illuminating the space in bright, white light, and when I reach the second floor, it takes my eyes a second to adjust to the change.

As the desk officer said, Striker's office is on my left and the door is open. I knock once before entering. The office is about half the size of mine at the bureau, but looks far more lived-in. Behind the well-worn desk sits a man in a dark blue suit, though his tie and jacket are off, and his black suspenders contrast the light gray button up with its sleeves rolled up. I can already tell Striker is a career man, someone who has been in this business a long time. I put his age around forty, maybe forty-five, though his face is clean-shaven and his dark hair has only barely begun to gray. But it's the lines in his skin that give him away. Lines that have probably seen their fair share of brutality and injustice in this world.

"Detective Striker?" I ask.

"Ah, Agent Slate," he says, standing. He'd been holding a set of photos, examining them as I came in, which look to be photos of the road where I ran over my aunt. He extends his hand as I approach and I take it, giving it a firm shake. "Sorry to bring you all the way down here like this, I know you probably have more important things to worry about."

"It's no trouble," I say, matching his energy and tone. If we're going to play this game, then so be it. He isn't sorry for bringing me down here any more than he's upset about hanging up on me. In his eyes, I'm a suspect, through and through. This is Detective Michaels all over again, except instead of combative and accusatory, Striker is friendly and disarming.

"Have a seat," he says, indicating one of the two old leather chairs that sit across from his desk. "Can I get you a coffee? Or a water?"

"Coffee sounds great," I say. "I caught a whiff of it downstairs."

"Oh," he laughs as he heads to the door. "That's Jameson. Brings in his own blend every day. He's spoiled every one of us. We just about revolt each time he goes on vacation. Hang tight, I'll be right back." He heads out, leaving everything on his desk in plain sight. I don't know if he's trying to bait me into looking at what he's working on or if he really is just that nonchalant about it, but I stay rooted to my chair. I have no idea if he's got a camera in here and he's watching me from another room or not, but I don't need to give him any reason to suspect me. I already know how this looks. And if I weren't an Agent in the FBI, I probably would have been brought in much sooner.

Striker returns a few minutes later with a warm cup, steam escaping out the small hole in the lid. "Tell me this isn't the best thing you've ever tasted."

"Thank you," I say taking the cup. "Impressive credentials." I nod to the series of plaques and commendations that adorn one of the walls of his office.

"Oh, thanks," he says. "My wife insists I keep those up. But really, I forget they're there half the time." I take a sip and an explosion of flavor hits my lips. Either I've been drinking the wrong brand or the coffee at the bureau really is just *that* bad, because this is on a different level. "Good, right?" he asks.

"It's great," I say, relishing the taste.

"His family is from Columbia. Apparently, they know something about coffee down there," Striker says, taking a seat across from me. "Okay, I'll try to make this quick and painless." He levels his gaze at me. "We're both officers of the law here, so you already know what I'm going to ask you. But for the sake of the record, I have to do it anyway."

I nod. "Understandable. I'd be doing the same thing in your position."

"Why don't you tell me what happened, from your perspective."

I lay it all out for him. What I had been doing that night, driving back from the office after my meeting with Janice. And how she just stepped out in front of me before I could even do anything. And how I stayed with her until the ambulance arrived, then followed it to the hospital.

"And you didn't see her until she was in the street?" Striker asks.

"She must have been purposefully staying in a shadow," I reply. "One second there was no one there, and the next, boom."

Striker sits back in his chair, looking at the photographs on his desk. He picks them up and hands them to me. They are shots of the street from different angles, all taken in the daytime. "There aren't any surveillance cameras in that area," he says. "So we don't have any footage of the event."

"I'm sure that's by design," I say.

"How do you mean?"

I considered not giving him this information, but if he doesn't already know, it will come out sooner or later, so it's better I be upfront with him. "I believe this woman has been stalking me for the past few months. Starting with a series of letters I began receiving back in January."

"Letters?" he asks, arching an eyebrow.

"Cryptic ones," I say. "Written in handwriting very similar to my mother's. However, my mother died when I was twelve." This time both eyebrows go up. "I've been investigating this on and off ever since, but information has been hard to come by. A fellow agent of mine went up to Ohio, to my mother's childhood home, and was almost killed in a fire that burned the house down. And just last week, a reckless driver tried to run me and another agent off the road multiple times."

He blinks a few times. Clearly this was not what he was expecting. "And you believe this woman in the hospital has something to do with it?"

"I think she's my aunt," I tell him. "One I didn't know about before. But my—Agent Coll who works in my department, he found a photo of my mother's family in that house, showing my grandmother pregnant with another child. As far as I knew up until then, my mother was an only child."

He furrows his brow then takes a sip of his own coffee. "That's…quite the story. So, if this woman was stalking you, why would she step out in front of your car?"

"That's the million-dollar question," I reply.

"Had you seen her before the accident?" he asks.

"I know what you're thinking. No. I didn't go looking for her. I didn't even know what she looked like until—"

"Then how do you know this woman is the one who has been stalking you?" he asks, his anxiousness getting the better of him.

"Because she looks exactly like my mother," I reply.

He leans forward and folds his hands together, glancing to his left and right like he's trying to make a decision. "I have to admit, Agent Slate, this was not what I expected to hear when I asked you to come in today."

I scoff. "But you did want to know if I had a personal connection to the victim. And it turns out that I do."

He nods. "I did. However, this complicates things."

"Have you been able to positively identify her yet?" I ask.

He hesitates. "What is your aunt's name?"

"Emily," I say. "Emily Katherine Brooks. According to the information I found in Ohio."

His eyes go wide again, and I almost laugh. It's all so absurd, but I have to admit I get a certain amount of joy out of trying to describe it to someone else. It's I've pushed him into the twilight zone, and he doesn't know where to go.

"Are all your interactions so…complex?" he asks, writing down the name.

"You'd be surprised," I tell him. "There's something else."

By now I think I've thoroughly given him an aneurism because he makes a wide motion for me to continue. "Please, by all means."

"The Millridge PD is looking into the arson that destroyed the house. The agent who was almost killed in the fire managed to see someone else there, and positively identified the woman in the hospital as the same woman he saw at the fire. If you call Millridge and ask for Detective Michaels, he can give you more information about his case."

"That's…very helpful," he says, writing down Michaels's name.

"Look, I know how this seems—if I weren't a decorated agent with the FBI, I would probably be talking to the public defender right now. But I want answers as much as you do, and I hope like hell she wakes up, because she is the only one who can explain to me why my mother decided to lie about having a sibling. If I could have stopped in time, I would have."

He taps his pen against the desk a few times as he assesses me. I know he's looking for any tells, or any indications I might not be telling the whole truth, but I decided before I even walked into this building I was going to be a hundred percent honest with Striker. He's my best chance at figuring out this woman's motives in the event she doesn't wake up.

"I just have one final question," he says. "Where is your vehicle?"

"It's in the driveway at my house," I tell him. "I looked for any dents or fluids, but I didn't see anything."

"Those could have come off while you were driving to the hospital," he says.

I nod. "I know. I purposefully haven't driven it since that night. You're free to take a look at it, if you wish."

"That's all right," he says. "I trust you." He stands and extends his hand. "Thank you again for coming down and taking the time to speak with me."

I shake his hand again. "I know it's a lot. Will you at least keep me updated once you confirm her identity?"

"I'm sorry, Agent Slate, but until the investigation is closed—"

"Of course," I add. "I shouldn't have asked."

"But I may have more questions."

I nod. "I'm right down the street. Thanks for the coffee." I raise the cup and he nods appreciatively. As I leave his office, I'm left with the sense Striker doesn't fully trust me, despite what he says. Having been in his position before, I know how it all sounds. It will take him some time to disseminate everything I've just told him. And in the meantime, I'm going to keep running my own investigation.

Because no matter what, I doubt he's ever going to tell me the whole truth.

Chapter Nine

BY THE TIME I get back to my office, it's past lunch and no one on my team is anywhere to be found. I head down to the cafeteria to grab something quick and catch sight of some of the people who used to be in my department but were transferred after the big shakeup with Hunter. It's nice to see them again, but I only offer a quick hello before sequestering myself in one corner and keeping myself occupied with my phone, reviewing the glut of information that seems to continue to fill up my inbox. In the past two days I've received over three hundred emails. Trying to read and parse them all is impossible, so I've taken to glancing at them, determining their relevance and deleting them if I can. Most are updates on other cases, or CCs on matters that have nothing to do with me. But because I'm part of the leadership team now, it means I'm looped in on a lot of matters outside of my direct purview.

"Ugh, this effing budget meeting," I mutter, deleting what looks like notes from the meeting for all department heads.

"Agent Slate?"

I look up to find Caruthers standing at my table, a mostly empty tray in his hands. All that's on it is a singular apple.

He's always been tall, though that disparity is exaggerated when he's standing in front of me.

"Agent Caruthers," I say. "Everything all right?"

"Mind if I join you?" he asks.

"Please," I say, putting my phone away. He sits across from me, his back perfectly straight. Zara used to work closely with Caruthers, which was how I knew I could trust him. He and I have crossed paths on more than a few occasions, but we've rarely been assigned to the same case.

"I thought you might like an update on your case," he says. "And given your...previous instruction, I thought it might be better to discuss it here, rather than in your office."

If Wallace were still my boss, I would have said he was exactly right. This is the kind of thing I wouldn't have wanted him knowing about. But now that I have my own office, with my own closed door, I don't think this kind of subterfuge is necessary. But at the same time, I'm anxious to learn what he's found.

"You found something?" I ask.

"I ran the fingerprints from the Jane Doe in the hospital, along with the blood sample," he says. "She's B positive, if you're curious. As I'm sure you know, as part of your hiring process, the Bureau collects information on all your direct family members, living or dead. Which means your mother's fingerprints are in the system. I had Amelia do a direct comparison. They were not a match. The woman is definitely not your mother."

I let out a breath of relief. I was pretty decided that was the case, but knowing for sure feels like a question answered. "Thank you. Was she able to find any match?"

"Nothing in the system, but I'm not giving up," Caruthers says. "I'm also running a DNA test on the blood sample you gave me."

I nod. "Good. Maybe we'll get lucky. But I'm confident in

saying now this is most likely my aunt. I think the blood test will prove that."

"There's something else," Caruthers says. "DC Police knows we are investigating the woman as well."

"Striker?" I ask.

He nods. "He called me directly to obtain a copy of the fingerprints. But I don't understand how he knew. My tech didn't see anyone else at the hospital when he went to fingerprint her."

"When did he call?" I ask.

"First thing this morning," Caruthers says. "I would have notified you earlier, but you were in meetings and then out of the office."

"I just had a meeting with Striker," I say. Just as I suspected. Despite his friendly demeanor, he was already aware we were looking into the woman ourselves when he met with me. That man has a hell of a poker face. "Does he know about the blood sample?"

"Not as far as I'm aware," Caruthers says.

"Let's try to keep it that way. I don't want to show our hand any more than necessary."

"Understood," he says. "If I find anything else, I will let you know immediately." He moves to get up.

"One other thing," I tell him. "You may want to try contacting a man named Amos at the Millridge town records building. He helped Liam and me when we were there, looking for information on Emily. He might be able to assist."

"I will get right on it," he says.

"Thanks. This really means a lot."

He gives me a curt nod before heading off again. I look down at the sandwich on my tray, feeling both vindicated but also frustrated. I still don't know the reason behind everything Emily's been doing for the past four months. At the same time, I'm a little unnerved Striker already knew we were taking fingerprints of our own. It makes me wonder how he could have obtained that information. But he can't say I wasn't honest with him, which was part of my strategy.

It's something I can't seem to get out of my head for the rest of the day.

~

FOR ONCE, I ACTUALLY MANAGE TO BEAT LIAM HOME. WHEN I arrive, there's a note from our dog sitter detailing Timber's activities for the day. But he's still wired as soon as I arrive, running zoomies all over the house before I can even set my stuff down. "Whoa," I tell him. "Is this how you are every evening? I thought Tessa ran you at the park for a good hour?" He's probably just stressed because he's in a new place, *again*. When I moved to the apartment after leaving the home I had with Matt, Timber took some time to acclimate. But something about this seems more…intense. I take him to the backyard and let him run around some while I throw the frisbee, and it seems he's more than happy to burn off the energy.

It's funny, I've barely spent any time back here since we decided to buy the house. I just haven't had the time. But it's a large, fenced yard with plenty of room for him. In fact, we'd have enough room for another dog if we wanted one. It's something we've discussed, and I think Timber could really use the company during the day when Liam and I are at work. It's something I'll bring up again when he gets home.

Timber is in the middle of a run after the frisbee when he abruptly changes direction and zooms past me, headed for the back door. I open it just in time to see Liam step in the front door and Timber just about barrels into him.

"Hey," he says, setting his stuff down on the kitchen counter. "You made it back early."

"I couldn't read one more expense report, otherwise I think I would have shot someone," I admit. I know Janice warned me that this job came with a lot more paperwork, but I didn't realize how tedious it would all be. I thought I'd at least be able to read interesting case files.

I plant a kiss on Liam's lips. "How was your day? Did you and Elliott make any progress?"

His face drops. "Not much. We took another look at the victims, but there's very little to go on. We're waiting to hear back from a couple of sources. Maybe I'll have something for you in the morning. Did Zara and Nadia make any progress?"

"I haven't heard from them," I admit. "And Zara would let me know as soon as they had something. I hope I didn't make a mistake in choosing this case."

"It wouldn't have been there if it wasn't a tough one, right?" he asks. "Plus, it hasn't even been a day."

"I know," I say. "I'm just impatient." I pause long enough for him to look up.

"What?"

"I spoke with Caruthers today. The fingerprints aren't a match to my mother. It has to be Emily."

He comes over and offers a hug, which I accept. "Em, that's great. See? You were right."

"So why don't I feel any better?" I ask, pressing my face against his chest.

"I don't think you're going to feel better until you get to speak with her, face to face. Until then, you'll always be wondering."

"I suppose," I say. As we're fixing dinner, I fill him in on Detective Striker and his investigation.

"What did he say about Michaels?" Liam asks.

"He said he'd reach out. Whether he will or not, I don't know. Are you thinking about the fire?" He nods. "Michaels needs to know, one way or another," I say. "If for no other reason than to take both of us off his suspect list."

Liam glances up from chopping some peppers. "Do you want to call him?"

"Not particularly. The last thing I want to do is insert myself any further into Striker's investigation. I can already tell he doesn't trust me." While I don't exactly feel threatened by the man, I also can't get this nagging feeling off my shoulder that I need to be very careful going forward.

"Maybe it's best to just let it play out," he suggests. I hate to admit it, but he could be right. I have a bad habit of trying to make things move faster than they're supposed to. I tried it with Michaels and it backfired on me. Who's to say the same thing wouldn't happen with Striker? I should just let his investigation play out and focus on my own work. It's not like whatever he does will make Emily wake up any faster, which is all I really want.

"Maybe."

Timber nudges me with his head, looking for a snack from the prep area. "Oh, right. That's the other thing. What are your feelings on a bigger bed?"

"A bigger bed?" he asks, smiling.

"Yeah. For a second dog."

Chapter Ten

"Good morning," I say, trying to push down the feeling of being on display again. I'm back up at the podium in front of the bullpen, with the other four agents all sitting there, staring at me. A warm cup of coffee sits on the small table to my side, courtesy of Liam. "Liam, Elliott, let's start with you."

Elliott clears his throat. "We managed to take a look at both bodies, which are still in the city morgue. No one has come to claim them, which leads us to believe they aren't local."

"It also looks like they fought back, given some of the bruising patterns on the autopsy reports," Liam adds. "Not to mention there was some material under their fingernails, but it wasn't enough to get a clean sample, so nothing was done. And we have no identification on either of them. No missing persons reports in a four-state radius match their descriptions."

"Clearly we can't leave things up to the boy's team because they don't know how to get it done," Zara says, shooting Liam a grin.

"Did you manage to make any progress?" I ask.

"We split the work," Nadia says. "Zara worked on the

company while I tried to find out as much as I could about the apartment. The crime scene has been cleaned up, but the apartment has not been used since the murders."

"Did you find out who was renting it?" I ask.

Nadia gives me a wide smile. "It was listed as rented by a company called Productive Holdings on a month-to-month basis. They didn't renew for this month. However, that's just a shell company for Red Sunset Photography, or more accurately, their parent company, XRC Productions, LLC."

"Wait," I say. "The internet escort agency rented the apartment?"

Nadia nods. "And that's not all. They have four other active apartments throughout the city. We believe they rent these spaces so they can control the entire escort transaction."

"Which supports the theory that the agency helped cover for whoever killed those women," Zara adds. "And that's not all. Tell 'em what else you found."

Nadia cheeks redden slightly, but she continues. "I made a thorough inspection of the property and found evidence that there may have been video recording equipment set up at one point in time. Though, I can't confirm if it was there when the murders took place."

"Someone has video of what happened," I say, pondering.

"*Potentially* has video," Nadia says. "I don't have enough information to confirm that yet."

"Still, it's a good find. Great work, you two."

"Oh, and we're not done yet, folks," Zara says. "I'm still working on finding out who runs Red Sunset and XRC, but I believe we have the next best thing: a client."

"Wait, how did you find one of their clients?" Liam asks.

"There's a camera on the lobby of the apartment building," Zara says. "I had the building manager pull it for me, and I logged everyone who went into the apartment complex. I managed to weed out the residents, so then I was left with the people who were just coming in for some hanky panky. On three different occasions, I found the same face. A repeat customer. And you'll never believe this." She gets up, and turns on the monitor behind me, messing with her phone until she's sharing her screen with the group.

"Can anyone tell me who this is?" She shows us a grainy picture of a man from a bit of a distance. He's walking towards the camera and disappears under it. He looks vaguely familiar, but I can't exactly place him.

"Is this the lobby?" I ask.

"Sure is." She turns to the group. "Anyone know who he is?"

"Kenji Okusaka," Elliott says.

Zara's face falls. "How'd you know?"

"I pass his billboard every day when I'm going home," Elliott says.

"Who is Kenji Okusaka?" I ask.

"C'mon Em, don't you ever pay attention to the billboards around town?" She adopts an overly happy tone. *"Need a new Bentley? Call Kenji!"* When I still don't respond, she throws up her hands. "You're hopeless."

"He's a car dealer?" I ask.

"He's *the* luxury car dealer for the larger Washington-Baltimore area," Elliott says. "He has at least half a dozen dealerships between here and the coast."

"And his face is on every single one of his billboards," Zara says. She pulls up another picture from her phone, this time of a man with a too-large smile standing beside a very expensive looking car. "Tell me that's not him."

"The resemblance is uncanny," I say. "Nice find."

"Thank you," she says, and returns to her seat.

"When was the last time he visited the apartment?"

"We have him going in on February twentieth and coming back out on the twenty-first," Nadia says.

"Wait," I say. "If there was a camera on the lobby, then it

should have picked up whoever came in the night the two women were killed."

"That's the odd thing," Zara says. "The report from the coroner puts their date of death on March fifteenth. However, I took a look at all the footage. There's no one going in or coming out of that apartment after March twelfth. And the coroner wouldn't have been off by three full days."

I look back through the information I pulled from the case. "The maintenance man found them on the seventeenth."

"Him I have video of," Zara says.

I turn to Nadia. "Were the two girls living there? Permanently?"

"Hard to say. The whole place was cleaned out. But it's possible. Then again, it could have been nothing more than a meetup location. There were no personal effects that I could find. None that were left behind, anyway."

"Shit," I say. "What about another way in or out of the apartment?"

"Sure, there were plenty of windows. And the fire escape."

"Then that must be how they got in." I turn back to Zara. "Do you have any footage of the girls coming or going from the apartment?"

She shakes her head. "None. Just the residents and the occasional John."

I cross my arms, pacing in front of them. "So, did they live there together? Or did someone not want them showing up on the camera? XTC or whoever they are—"

"XRC," Elliott says under his breath.

"—must have known there was a camera in the lobby."

"You're thinking they weren't allowed to leave," Liam says.

I nod. "It's looking that way. Which means it's much more likely we're dealing with a trafficking situation here. We need to find out who is running this company."

"We could check the other four apartments Nadia found,"

Elliott suggests. "If the women are living there, we could at the very least extricate them."

"But without knowing who is behind this, they would just disappear and start again somewhere else," I say. "Though I like the idea of setting up surveillance. It won't hurt to gather as much information as possible on those other locations. In the meantime, I think it's worth speaking with Mr. Okusaka. I want to know how he got involved with this company, and who he knows."

"How are we going to get him to talk?" Zara asks. "All we have is him entering the lobby of an apartment building. It's not like we can show him explicit photographs."

"We don't have to," I say. "All we have to do is make him believe." I check the time on my phone. It's a quarter till ten. "What are the odds Mr. Okusaka is in the office today?"

"Office? He's probably out playing tennis or something," Zara says.

I point to Liam and Elliot. "Liam, keep working on finding out who these girls are. Coordinate with CBP if you have to." He nods. "Elliott, I want you and Nadia to start setting up surveillance on the other four locations. Let's see if we can't find any more repeat customers. And in the meantime, Zara and I will go speak with Mr. Okusaka personally."

"Wait, don't you have an assessment meeting today with Janice?" Zara asks.

"I'm sure we'll be back in plenty of time," I say, grabbing my files. "Okay team, let's get moving."

∼

"I LIKE HOW YOU MANAGED TO INSERT YOURSELF INTO THE investigation," Zara teases as we're headed to the Four Links Golf Course. Her intuition had been right, if a little off, and a quick check of Mr. Okusaka's social media informed us he was out on the course today, taking advantage of the nice weather.

"I'd like to see you sit through one of those budget meetings and not be bored out of your mind," I say. "I never really understood the concept of meetings that could be emails, but if there was ever a shining example…"

"That bad, huh?"

"Gordon just went on and on about allocations," I say. "I swear I think it was a test of endurance. Or he was trying out some new kind of torture technique that should absolutely be banned across the globe."

"Em," Zara says. "Have you maybe considered that all this extra work isn't what you really want to be doing?"

"What do you mean?" I ask. "I've always wanted to move up in the organization."

"Right, I know. But did you know how much of a pain in the ass it was *before* you got the promotion?"

"What are you saying? That I should have stayed a regular field agent? Been assigned another boss like Wallace? Or someone worse?"

"No, but I know how good of a field agent you are. So does everyone else. And on some level, you know it too. Which is why you're in this car with me instead of Liam or one of the others." She gives me a pointed look.

"I don't know," I admit. "It wasn't like I was expecting the promotion in the first place. It…just kind of came out of nowhere. And it seemed silly not to accept it. Especially coming off this Wallace nonsense. I figured the best way to make sure I'd never have to deal with any of that again was if I was my own boss. Not to mention the added bonus of being able to choose my own cases."

"Which you kind of already do," she says, holding up three fingers. "Fairview, Millridge, and Stillwater."

I chuckle. "Okay, maybe I've been more rebellious lately.

But that's just because of Wallace's pig-headedness. If he hadn't been so—"

She places a reassuring hand on my arm. "It's okay, I know. But the bad man can't hurt you anymore, okay?"

I jerk my arm away as she chuckles. "Yeah, yeah. Maybe this isn't the job for me. But I'm only two days in. I think I need to give it some more time, don't you?"

"I dunno. You have a pretty strong gut. And it's usually correct. If something doesn't feel right to you, I don't think you need a solid month to think about how not right it feels."

I let out a long exhale. "Maybe. We'll see."

"At any rate, I'm *loving* this," she says. "You weren't the only one who thought Wallace was nothing more than a blowhard. I just wish Janice had pressed formal charges against him."

"You and me both," I say as I spot the sign for the Four Links Golf Course. It sits among a tasteful set of shrubs and blooming flowers. Subtle, but also screams money. As I pull in, we pass rows of shiny, expensive cars, half of which I've never even seen before. Looks like everyone is taking advantage of the weather.

"You going for the valet?" Zara asks.

"Don't you remember? I'm in charge of the budget now." I give her a quick smile before pulling up to the valet station. Call it a bonus for sitting through all these meetings. "Okay. Showtime."

Chapter Eleven

ZARA WHISTLES as we walk into the lobby. "Money, money, money," she sings under her voice to the tune of some old seventies' song. She says she's been trying to branch out and listen to decades other than the nineties, but it's slow going.

I have to agree with her sentiment, though. I knew golfing was an expensive sport, but if the lobby is any indication, I now know it's way out of my reach. The floor is an intricate pattern of cream and emerald marble bright and shiny, like it has just been polished. In fact, I wouldn't be surprised if a man with a mop follows everyone around just to wipe up any smudges. The walls are decorated with ornate paintings in dark-trim frames of different golf courses—none of which are this location given the oceans and seas in every picture. Above us, arched ceilings house tasteful but elaborate chandeliers, glittering in the sunshine and throwing pinpricks of light all over the space.

The whole place has an air of superiority about it, as if to say, *you don't belong here, go home*, which, I have to admit, already raises my hackles. The lobby itself is mostly empty, but that's because it's hardly a welcoming area, and there are only few seats to be found. A man in a pressed black suit stands near the doors to another section of the club, glaring at us.

"Target acquired," Zara whispers. I nod and we make a beeline for the man scrutinizing us. As soon as we make our approach, his face goes completely neutral.

"Good morning," he says. "How can I help you?"

I hold out my badge, and Zara does the same. His eyes flash upon seeing we're FBI. "I'm Agent Slate, this is Agent Foley. We're here to speak with one of your members. Mr. Okusaka."

"What's this regarding?" he asks.

"That's not your concern," I reply. "But this matter is of some urgency."

"I believe Mr. Okusaka is out on the green. He probably won't be back for a few hours," the man replies without missing a beat.

"Then we'll just have to go to him," I say.

"I'm afraid only members are allowed on our greens," he protests. "The delicate nature of the environment—"

"Stop right there," I say. "We don't have time for this. If you want to impede a federal investigation, be my guest. But you are bringing a lot more trouble on your own head than you would be by just pointing us in the direction of your little golf carts and telling us how to find him."

The man raises his chin as if he's been slapped, before swallowing. "If you will proceed through here, down the corridor, you will reach stairs that will take you to the lower level. Cart rental is down there. They can probably tell you which hole Mr. Okusaka is on."

"Thank you," I say, taking a step back before shooting a look at Zara. She just rolls her eyes as the man opens the door to the corridor for us.

It's more opulent down here, but I've seen more than enough and pay no attention to it. The corridor opens up to an expansive sitting room that looks out on the green with two-story glass windows. Large, plush seats take up most of the area, some with tables. There's also a wide fireplace at one end of the room surrounded by high backs. The corridor hallway splits a long bar in two, which takes up the entire back wall. There are about a dozen or so people in here, some near the bar, but most lounge in the chairs and carry hushed discussions. What strikes me as most odd is that only some people are in golf attire. Others are wearing full business suits.

"Where the deals are made," Zara says.

"Yep. What would we do without powerful people getting together in their little cabals?" I look around for the stairs and find them near the large glass windows. People glance at us as we walk by, and I swear I recognize more than a few of them as powerful people on the Hill. It also doesn't escape my notice that their conversations pause as we pass. I can't even imagine the deals happening in this room.

We make our way down the stairs to another area with a young woman behind a long counter. She smiles at us as we approach. "Looking to rent a cart?" she asks. "Have your caddies arrived?"

"We don't have caddies," I say. "We just need the cart." I show her my badge. "And we'd like to know where Mr. Okusaka is on the course."

"Oh," she says, surprised. "Of course." She slides a set of small keys across the counter. "His group started about an hour ago, so they should be around hole ten or eleven by now. They like to take their time."

"What's the quickest way over there?" Zara asks.

She pulls out a paper map and unfolds it for us. It shows the entire green, along with all the driving trails. "You'll have to go this way," she says, using her finger to follow from the main building along the trail to holes one and two. "Keep going until you reach here, hole six, then there's a trail where you can cut over to ten. Shouldn't take you more than five or ten minutes."

"Thanks," I say taking the map and the keys.

"Take cart number seventeen," she says. "It has a full charge."

We push through the double doors and head around the side of the building to where the carts are parked. A couple of mechanics are there, working on two of the carts. They don't bother looking up as we find the one with the subtle seventeen on the side.

"Drive or navigate?" I ask Zara.

"Drive." She grabs the keys enthusiastically and jumps into the cart, sliding all the way over.

"Okay, out from here and take a left." The cart jerks forward, and I have to hold on to the side as Zara presses the pedal to the floor. As she turns the cart, I swear I feel the two wheels on the left side leave the ground. "Jeez! Cool it, this isn't a sports car."

"No, it's better. It's like a go-cart," she says. "Trust me, I can handle it." Her foot never leaves the gas as we navigate bumps, hills, curves, and everything in between. As we pass other golfers, half of them gawk at Zara's speed while a few try yelling something at us, but I don't catch it. I'm busy holding on to dear life and the map simultaneously.

When we reach hole six, Zara takes a hard right turn into what looks like woods, though there is a worn path just barely big enough for the cart. "Hang on!" she yells. This path isn't paved like the others, and there are tree branches and other obstacles in the way. And while I think they might slow her down, they do nothing of the sort and my ass leaves the seat more than once as we bounce over the roots and rocks.

"Z!" I yell.

"Isn't this great?" she yells back.

"No!"

She just cackles with laughter as we break through the bushes and back onto a paved road in front of us. Zara swings the cart to the left before slamming on the brakes, jerking us to an immediate stop so abrupt I almost take out the flimsy plastic window on the front. To our right are two other golf carts parked about twenty feet away, near a group of men decked out in polo shirts and khakis, staring at us.

Zara draws in a deep breath through her nose before checking her phone. "Four minutes, eighteen seconds. I bet it's a new record."

"What the hell was that?" I demand, still trying to catch my breath.

"That, was how you make the rest of us feel when you're in a real car," she says, glaring at me.

"What are you even taking about?"

"I dunno, Ms. Speed Demon, you tell me."

Okay, so sometimes I drive fast. Probably faster than I should. But that's just one of the perks of being in law enforcement. Plus, it's not like I'm an *unsafe* driver. I'm just… enthusiastic. "You mean all that was just your way of telling me to slow down?"

"Well, that and it was a lot of fun," she replies. "I can see why you like it so much."

I scoff. "You're insane."

"That's why you love me," she grins, getting out. I follow suit. All six of the men are now openly gawking at us.

"If nothing else, that was a hell of an entrance," I say as we make our way to the group.

"Maybe we threaten him with a ride back if he doesn't cooperate," she teases.

"That'd do it." I hold up my badge to the men, all of whom are wearing sunglasses. But even from here, I can pick out Kenji Okusaka easily. He looks exactly like the picture on the billboard. And like the surveillance video. "Good morning, gentlemen. I'm Special Agent Slate with the FBI. This is Special Agent Foley. We'd like to have a few words with Mr. Okusaka."

"What for?" Okusaka says, his driver club at his side. He looks like he was just about to take his swing.

"It will only take a minute," I say. "Would you mind us speaking in private?"

"I'm in the middle of a game here, Agent," he says, his voice rising. "You'll need to make an appointment with my office." He turns back to the green. The other men in his group, one of whom I am sure is a state senator, continue watching us.

"It has to do with Red Sunset," I say. "But if you'd like, I can ask you the questions here."

He freezes before turning to us and giving us a placating smile. He hands his club to the caddy that's standing only a few feet away. "Mark, you go ahead," he says to the man closest to him. "This will only take a few minutes." He marches toward me like he's on a mission before passing both me and Zara on the way back to the golf carts. The other men watch as we follow him until we're out of earshot. I glance over to see that Mark hasn't taken his swing. None of them have.

"Let's make this quick," he says, shooting furtive glances at the rest of his group.

"In a hurry?" I ask.

"Just tell me what you want to know," he replies.

"So then you *are* familiar with Red Sunset Photography," I say.

He crosses his arms but drops his head, shuffling his feet. I exchange a knowing glance with Zara. "Wow. I figured we'd have to pry it out of you."

"What do you want me to say? That I'm proud of myself? Just tell me what you want and let's get on with it. I'll cooperate as long as you don't mention it to my colleagues."

"Are any of them members, like yourself?" I ask.

"No," he replies. "It's an exclusive group."

"So we gathered," Zara says. "How did you become a member?"

"Personal referral," he says quickly.

"From whom?" He looks up, alarmed. But it's more than that, there's some fear there too. I glare at him, silently willing him to tell us, but he just keeps looking back over at the group who have huddled closer and seem to be talking amongst themselves.

"Who is it?" Zara asks. "The longer you stall, the longer this takes."

"I can't," he says.

"You can't what? Tell us?"

He shakes his head. "They'd kick me out. They'd know. No one reveals their sponsor."

"Is that how it works? Every member needs a sponsor?" I ask. He nods. "Mr. Okusaka, I think we both know this is more than just an escort service." He winces as I say it, considering his group of posh golfers again. He is *very* worried about his reputation. And I think that's something we can leverage. "These women, they aren't here legally, are they?"

He grits his teeth.

"And because they're not here legally, they can't make complaints to law enforcement, and you can do *whatever you want* with them, isn't that right?"

"Look, I've never hurt anyone," he says. "You can ask them. That isn't my thing."

"Then why not go with a premium escort service?" I ask. "One where you know the woman has autonomy?"

"Don't you get it?" he hisses. "That's part of the fun. Knowing they are under your complete control. That they couldn't say no, even if they wanted to."

"Yeah, that's not messed up at all," Zara says. "Not to mention illegal."

"Don't talk to me about legal and illegal," he replies.

"Didn't your own FBI just find a mole inside your own organization? Or did I misread the news?"

"This isn't about the FBI, Mr. Okusaka," I say. "This is about an exclusive prostitution ring which involves human trafficking and two dead women."

His eyes go wide. "Two dead women? Who?"

"We're looking into that," I say. "We doubt the names they were using on the website you frequent were real."

"You don't think I had anything to do with that, do you? I already told you, I never hurt anyone."

"You *did* have something to do with it," I say. "By supporting this organization with your patronage. You helped fund it, and thus you had a hand in everything that came after."

He scoffs. "Please. That's like saying I'm responsible for global warming because I own a car."

"You do own a series of dealerships," Zara points out. "So yeah, you are more responsible than most."

"This is ridiculous," he hisses again, looking back at his group. "I had *nothing* to do with the death of two women." He's holding himself even tighter, and I can tell we have him on the ropes. Just a little more and he'll give.

"We don't know that for sure. But we do know you frequent a certain apartment a few times every month. Do you always use the same girl? Or do you like to shop around?"

He grimaces. "The same girl," he says.

"What's her name?"

"She goes by Amee Sapphire." I don't think that's going to be one of the girls in the morgue, but we'll double check on the website to make sure.

"How many other members in the organization?"

"How the hell should I know?" he asks. "I don't run the place."

"Who does?" My questions are coming quick and hard, as

I'm trying to keep him as truthful as possible. But he's doing a good job of deflecting.

"You think they would tell *us that*?"

"Listen, Mr. Okusaka, you're going to need to give us something," I say. "Because right now I've got you on video going in and out of the apartment where we found two dead girls, and unless I can find another suspect, you're going to stay at the top of my list."

He runs a shaky hand through this black hair, his eyes going wild. "I told you; I can't give up my sponsor."

"Why, because they'll kick you out? Big deal," Zara says. "I'm sure you can get your rocks off somewhere else."

"No, you don't get it," he says. "I'm under contract. If I reveal the company, they'll come after my business. These people don't mess around."

"You mean they're blackmailing you," I say.

"More like…making sure I don't get out of line."

I turn away from him, pacing back and forth. We could force him to tell us, but what would that get us? If they found out, they'd just close up shop. I think we're going to have to go about this another way. I come back to find him trying his hardest not to look back at his group.

"Okay Mr. Okusaka. I'm willing to overlook your part in a human trafficking organization *for now*. And in exchange, you are going to become a sponsor yourself."

"What?" he asks.

"You said the only way someone gets into this little club of yours is by personal introduction. You're going to do that for one of my people. And let me be very clear, if you don't cooperate fully, the *FBI* will be the ones you have to worry about ruining your little empire, not Red Sunset. Understand?"

"You want me to help you get a mole inside?" he asks. "And then you'll leave me alone?"

"You won't go to jail," I say. "How's that?"

He nods. "Okay. But they do an extensive background check on every member. If they find out you're FBI—"

"Let us worry about that," Zara says.

"No, it will come back on me," he says.

"It's either this, or I cuff you right here," I say.

"Fine, fine, yes," he stammers. "When?"

I turn to Zara. She's the one who will have to coordinate a fake persona for someone on the team. I'm thinking Liam is probably our best bet. "I'd say no more than a day or two," she estimates.

"Okay," he says. "I'll be in my Crystal City office tomorrow. Do *not* come by my house."

"Worried your wife will find out?" I ask, and his eyes turn into full saucers. "Yeah, we know. We do background checks ourselves."

He grumbles something under his breath that I don't catch, but I don't need to. His meaning is plain. "We'll see you tomorrow, Mr. Okusaka."

He turns and heads back to his golf buddies, throwing on a fake smile. Zara and I head back to our cart. This time, however, *I* take the driver's seat. "I think that went rather well, don't you?"

"Sure," she says grinning. "I just can't wait to see Liam's face when you tell him about his new assignment."

Chapter Twelve

"YOU'VE GOT TO BE KIDDING," Liam says. We're sitting in my office back at the Bureau. He's been working with Customs and Border Protection all morning trying to identify which country the dead women came from. Right now, his working theory is China, but he's still deep in it.

"Priceless," Zara says from behind us. She's back on the couch, working hard on her laptop. "I knew that look would be worth it."

We both ignore her. "I think this could work," I tell him. "We just need to get you in there. It's the only way we're going to find out who is running this thing."

"And how does setting me up with an escort help us?" he asks, incredulous.

"You're not going in there for sex," I say. "You're going as an investor. But you'll have to communicate through the girl, since they don't have a link on their website for 'investment opportunities,' unless I missed something." I lean around him to look at Zara.

"Nope."

"That's what I thought. You'll claim to be an investor

looking to expand and try to get in contact with someone in charge."

"I'm not sure about this," he says. "I don't exactly look like the type."

"Sure you do," Zara says. "We just need to get you a suit that fits."

"What's wrong with my suits?" he asks.

"Too *Men in Black*," she says. "Think more…Pitbull. How fast can you grow a goatee?" He glares at her. "Okay, forget the goatee. Em, does he have chest hair? I think we could go with an open collar."

I have to stifle a laugh. "He does, but it's kind of thin."

"Um, I'm right here," he says.

"Scraggly chest hair," Zara mutters. "Okay, we'll go for the classy look."

"What is she doing?" Liam demands.

"She's working on your cover," I say. "According to Okusaka, these guys do a thorough background check."

"Which means I need to build Leo Burnett a history no one can tell is fake. Which takes a lot of work these days, trust me."

"Who is Leo Burnett?" Liam asks.

"You, dingy," I say. "That'll be your undercover name."

"And you're from New York, so get rid of that Appalachian accent," Zara says.

He turns back to me. "Em, this is crazy. I can't go in there with only a day's prep."

"I know. It's short notice. I'm just trying to prevent us from finding any more dead women in empty apartments."

"Okay," Zara says, standing. "I think I have everything I need. I'm going to meet up with Jacobson and Ronaldo. We'll get working on this new persona." She heads out, leaving me and Liam to ourselves.

He sits back, sighing. "I don't guess I could convince you to give this assignment to Elliott?"

I make a face and he laughs. "I'm not sure Elliott would be the best person for this job. He's a little too…clinical. I need someone who can put the girl at ease. And honestly, I'm pretty sure they're going to be recording you anyway, so you need to act the part all the way through."

He scoffs. "Won't it look a little weird when I don't actually end up having sex with her?"

"Just claim she's not your type," I say. "Don't worry, once you start talking money, it won't matter."

"If you say so," he says. He taps his fingers on my desk a few times before smiling at me.

"What?"

"You. You seem much more like yourself now. The past couple of days, I feel like you've been trying to toe this line and have been worried you might make a misstep."

I raise my eyebrows, sitting back in my own chair. "Yeah, Zara said something similar. She thinks maybe this job isn't for me."

"I'm not saying that," he replies. "But maybe there's room for balance. I don't think you need to completely delegate *everything* as SSA. You're obviously good in the field. Integrate yourself into the process. Don't just sit back and let us do all the fun stuff."

I arch an eyebrow at him. "Even if it keeps me here late at night catching up?"

"It's about what makes you happy. And I think working the field is where you shine. Don't worry, the only one who'll be upset about a later dinner is Timber, and I can make sure he's fed on time."

I sigh. "I dunno. Maybe Zara is right. I never gave a lot of thought to being SSA. But between me and the four others in this department, there's a lot of stuff that goes on behind the scenes that I'm not sure I want to deal with. I haven't even told you about the meeting to discuss the *feasibility of improving goal targets for the next two years*. I'm going to have to take about ten caffeine pills to stay awake in that one."

He chuckles. "When's your meeting this afternoon?"

I check the time on my computer. "In about fifteen minutes."

"Do you have time to discuss something non-case related?"

"For you? Try and stop me," I say.

He gets up and closes the door to my office, causing my smile to drop. Whatever this is, it must be serious. "I've been thinking, after what you told me about Detective Striker."

I sit up a little straighter.

"Given that he already knew what Caruthers was doing before he called you in to talk to him, I think maybe I was wrong before. Maybe we *should* bring Detective Michaels in on this."

"You? Want to contact Michaels?" I ask, incredulous.

"Only because I'm not sure Striker is going to give you a fair shake at this. I can positively ID her as the woman at the fire. If Michaels thinks we're trying to withhold that information—"

"He might try coming after you again," I say, completing the thought. Michaels is old school, meaning he doesn't look much past the facts and the figures of a case. He's been working this arson ever since February, and as far as we know, Liam is still his primary suspect.

"It doesn't need to be anything more than a courtesy call," he says. "That way you stay out of Striker's way, and at least he's up to date."

"How do you think he'll react?" I ask.

"The same way he does about everything. With all the enthusiasm and drive of a sloth."

I chuckle. My initial thought was to contact Michaels immediately, but at the same time, I don't want him coming down here and claiming jurisdiction only to get into a custody battle with Striker. That doesn't get me any closer to finding out just what this woman wants from me.

But if we want to clear Liam off Michaels's plate, maybe it's the right call. I grab my phone. "You're going to do it now?" he asks.

"Might as well," I say, pulling up his number on my contact list. "I'll be in a meeting for the rest of the afternoon. And I'd rather it come from me than you."

"Guess I can't argue with that," he says as the line rings.

"Michaels," he answers on the other end, his voice gruff.

"This is Supervisory Special Agent Emily Slate," I say. "I have some updated information about your case."

He pauses for a moment on the other end. "You received a promotion."

"That's not important," I tell him. "We think we have your arsonist in custody down here in DC."

"Is that so?" he asks, emotionless as always.

I proceed to give him a quick rundown of the events of the past few days, along with the make, model, and license plate of the car that tried running me and Zara off the road.

"And why do you think this is my arsonist?" he asks.

"Because Special Agent Coll has positively identified her as the woman he saw outside the Brooks' home the day it burned down," I say. "If you'll recall, he told you there was someone else there."

"I see," he says. "But this woman is in a coma?"

"That's right," I say.

"So she can't defend herself or confess to the crime."

I grit my teeth. "No, not at the present."

"Huh." He says it aloofly, as if he were sitting on a dock somewhere, watching the birds fly by. "What's her prognosis?"

"We're hoping for a full recovery," I tell him. "But it's still up in the air. As you can imagine, we have quite a few questions for her ourselves."

"I bet," he replies. "As it is, Agent Slate, this isn't very helpful. Now if you had called with a signed confession, I might have had reason to come down there. But as far as I can tell, all you have is an unconscious woman in a hospital bed—"

"And an officer of the law placing her at the scene of the crime," I say.

"A crime of which he himself has been accused," Michaels finishes. I want to punch the man right through the phone. "I appreciate the call, Agent Slate, but unless there is some concrete proof connecting this woman to the fire, I believe I will continue with my own investigation."

"C'mon Michaels, we both know Liam didn't do it. And if you had anything on him, you would have charged him while we were still up there. Do your job, for once. You're not going to accuse a federal agent of arson without an ass load of evidence and it's clear you don't have any."

He's silent on the other end.

"The detective down here in charge of the investigation is named Striker. He's looking into the accident."

"Do you have her vehicle?" he asks.

"We don't, I'm not sure about Striker. I know they're looking for it."

"Very well," he says. "Thanks for the tip, Agent Slate. I'll keep my ears open." He hangs up before I can say anything else.

Liam gives me an amused grin. "Well, that went about as I suspected."

"He's frustrated because he doesn't have any suspects," I say. "And he's trying to pressure both of us because he's got nowhere else to turn. Hopefully now he can focus all of that energy somewhere else."

"Do you think he'll contact Striker?"

"I hope so. But what we really need is for her to wake up. Because he's right, without a confession or some evidence tying her to the scene of the crime, your testimony will only go so far."

"Let's hope for a miracle," he says, standing. "Thanks anyway, for calling Michaels. Even though he's an ass, I think it was the right thing to do."

I nod. "Of course."

"See you tonight?"

"I'll get back home as soon as I can," I tell him. "You know, as much as I like carpooling, I think I might have to start bringing my car again. This is costing me a fortune in Uber fees."

He laughs. "I could always get Timber, bring him back here to pick you up."

I smile. "You've never tried to wrangle Timber in a car for more than thirty minutes. It does *not* go well," I tell him. "He is not the kind of dog who can go on long trips."

He gives me a knowing nod. "Well, at least you'll have a warm meal waiting for you when you get home." Giving me a quick wave, he heads out.

I have to admit, I wasn't sure if I would be able to do the domesticated life again. And I know we're only a few days in, but it's a nice contrast to how things have been for the past year. Usually, I would go home to Timber and an empty house, eat something out of a can for dinner, and go to bed to start it all over again the next day. But just having a human there to go home to is…well it gives me a reason to get away from this place, which is something I haven't had in a long time.

As I gather up my things, preparing to head to my next meeting, I can't help but wonder if it's something I'll ever get sick of.

And if I do, what happens then?

Chapter Thirteen

"NOT BAD, if I do say so myself," Zara says, standing back and looking at her handiwork. She put herself in charge of Liam's wardrobe for his undercover mission and has gone all out to make him look like someone who might invest in a company such as XRC, Productions, LLC.

He's decked out in a fitted dark blue suit with a patterned button up shirt and no tie. And his light brown shoes are a nice contrast. Even I have to admit she's done a fantastic job bringing his style up to date.

"It's too tight," he says, looking in the mirror.

"That's just the style these days," she replies. "This isn't the 2000s when everyone wore suits two times bigger than themselves. Plus, it does a great job of accentuating your ass."

"Zara!" I say.

"What?" she exclaims. "Just look at it! He's working it and doesn't even know it."

"Just ignore her," I tell him. "It looks great."

Liam looks over his shoulder, checking the mirror one more time. "If you're sure."

"Here," Zara says, handing him a pair of sunglasses. "And finally, you'll need this in case you need to pull out your wallet for any reason." She plops a leather wallet in his hand. It looks worn and well-used. I take it from him and open the inside. Liam's face stares back at me from a fake driver's license showing his cover ID, as well as a bunch of other erroneous information. As I dig through the wallet, I find insurance cards, credit cards, and a couple of business cards as well as some cash.

"You really went all out," I say, folding it all back together and handing it to him.

"We needed to be thorough," Zara says. "There's no telling how deep they'll look."

We spent the better part of the morning meeting with Okusaka again as he showed us how to access the member portal on the website using his credentials. From there, he was able to make the recommendation to add Liam to the "club." And about ten minutes after that recommendation, Liam received an email with a link to an online form he had to fill out. Zara helped him fill in all the information "accurately" to match the cover she and Nadia set up for him. The two of them had been here later than I was last night making sure Leo Burnett was ironclad.

Okusaka said there would be some final approval Liam will have to go through before they'll admit him and give him full access, so we're using the additional time to cross any errant t's and dot all our i's.

"Don't forget, you need to keep your chest up, walk confidently," Zara says, puffing her own chest out.

"I thought I already did that," Liam says.

I just grin as I check my phone, looking for any update from Caruthers. It's been two days since I've heard from him, which is making me nervous. And while most of my focus is on this case, I still can't help my thoughts being drawn to the woman still lying in the hospital.

Zara's phone vibrates, and she pulls it out then replaces it after a quick look. That's not quite like her. Usually, she responds to notifications immediately. I catch her shooting furtive glances around the room, and when she notices me looking, she turns all her attention back to Liam. "Yep, I think this will do nicely."

Liam straightens his collar. "So do I get to keep these once the job is over?"

"That's up to Captain Budget over there," Zara replies.

"No, they belong to the Bureau," I say, standing. "Though, I might be able to pull a few strings." He *does* look good, but I have other matters to attend to. "As much as I love haunting the locker rooms, I need to get back to it. Let me know if you hear anything else from Okusaka."

"Yeah, I should head back up too," Zara says. "I've been neglecting my other work because *someone* needed me for a special mission."

"Should I leave the suit on?" Liam asks.

"No," we both say at the same time.

"Okay, just a question," he says under his breath and begins taking the jacket off. Zara throws me a look that seems to say *"Men, right?"* and we head back to the elevators, leaving the men's locker room.

"Any news?" Zara asks as I check my phone again.

"Nothing. I know DNA takes a while, but I was hoping Caruthers would have something by now."

"He'll get there," she says. "It's not like she's going anywhere."

"No, you're right." I lean back against the wall of the elevator, staring up as the doors shut us in. I take a deep breath.

"It's a lot."

"Yeah," I say before pushing back off and straightening my own blazer. "What about you?"

"Me?" she asks.

"Yeah, what was that notification? It isn't like you to ignore something like that."

"Oh," she says, pulling away, which makes me think it wasn't a simple spam call. "Nothing, just…Theo."

"Still MIA?" I ask.

"Not exactly. We talk, and he's made an odd appearance or two. But something feels wrong. He's been more reserved lately, cagy even."

"Cagy?" I ask.

She sighs. "Maybe a relationship with a supposed international intelligence agent wasn't a good idea after all. We're barely ever in the same country together, much less the same city."

"I'm sorry," I say. "I know you like him a lot."

"You've never really approved of him, though."

"I never said that," I say, defensive. "I mean, he did save our lives. I'll give him credit for that."

"But?"

"I don't know. There's just always something that seems… off about him. And I can't put my finger on it. But I don't have any evidence, and it's probably just my paranoia." I give her my best supportive smile as the doors open for us. "Plus, it doesn't matter what I think. I'm not the one going out with him."

"It *does* matter, though," she says. "It matters to me. I mean, would you be going out with Liam if I didn't think he was swoon-worthy?"

"No, probably not," I say. "But that's because you're a better judge of character than I am. You always have been. Which is why I trust your gut more than my own when it comes to Theo."

"You don't give yourself enough credit," she says. We push through the doors only to be bombarded by Nadia rushing up to us.

"We just got a hit on the phone line we set up for Liam's fake job. Someone asking for a reference," she says, slightly out of breath.

"And?" I ask.

"Went smoothly. I maintained the cover, acting as one of his employees. Elliott is managing the other hits. They're coming in quickly now."

"Someone is doing their homework," Zara says, and the three of us rush back over to the bullpen where we've set up shop. Elliott is there, a phone on one ear and typing at the same time.

"Yes, Mr. Burnett is one of our investors," he says. "It was his investment that allowed us to take the company public." He catches us from out of the corner of his eye and points to another phone line flashing.

Zara grabs it first. "Stockman, Hartwell and DeVoe," she says, putting on a sweet, southern accent. "Why, yes, Mr. Burnett is one of our clients. I'm sorry, I can't speak to that, but I know he's been with us since I started here five years ago. Why, yes, thank you as—" She purses her lips and hangs up the phone, dropping back into her normal voice. "Dick."

Elliott is still talking as Nadia takes up her station, monitoring the progress on all the sites we've set up for Liam's cover. "They are being very thorough," she says.

"Good," I say. "Better chance of this working."

"Okay, yes. Thank you. Yes," Elliott says before hanging up. "Where have you all been? We've been trying to field all these hits at once."

"We had to make sure he looked the part," Zara quips. "Plus, you guys have it in hand. Looks like everything is going to plan."

"They are not taking any chances," Nadia says. "They've already gone through half the business contacts on his LinkedIn page. And his work history."

"I guess this is what Okusaka was talking about," I say. "The final approval. Any idea when we'll get access to the site so we can make a reservation?"

Zara heads back to her computer, pulling up Liam's application page. "Nothing yet. Actually, wait, there's a call coming in through the false number. The one that's connected to his personal cell."

"Shit." I shoot off a quick text giving him a heads up. Hopefully he sees it.

"He's answered it," Zara reports. "I'll patch in."

"—urnett," Liam says.

"Mr. Burnett," an unfamiliar male voice says on the other end. "We understand you would like an invitation to our private club."

"That's right," Liam says, doing his best to neutralize his accent. He's doing a fair job of it. "Mr. Okusaka speaks very highly of your services."

"We only service the best," the man says. "If you are certain, there is a one-time entrance fee of ten thousand dollars. After that, you pay an annual membership of five thousand dollars."

"I see," Liam says. "Sounds reasonable enough."

Good job, I think to myself. *Don't let the numbers throw you.*

"Very well. We also like to meet our new clients in person. As you can imagine, we prefer a cash transaction."

"I prefer the same," Liam says. "When do we meet?"

"How is this evening for you?" the man asks.

"It won't be a problem," Liam replies.

"Good. You'll receive a text with the address and time thirty minutes before we are due to meet. We look forward to seeing you."

"So do I," Liam says. I turn and see him come into the bullpen with his phone to his ear. He hangs up and Zara ends the recording.

"Ten thousand dollars?" he asks.

"Okusaka didn't say anything about that," Zara adds. "Kinda pricey if you ask me."

"It's a test," I say. "They want to make sure he's not a flake, that he has a real stake in this little venture."

"So what now?" Liam asks.

"We get the money together, and you go in for the meeting," I say.

"With ten thousand of the Bureau's dollars? Can we just afford to let that go?" he asks.

"No, but we'll be getting it back. Plus interest, once we bust these people." I head over to Elliott's desk. "What are the odds whoever collects payment will be in a position to negotiate an investment?"

"Low," he says. "But they may be watching."

"As will we," I reply. I glance back over to Liam who is back in his regular clothes again. "Better go grab that suit again. We have a performance coming up."

Chapter Fourteen

"Kind of like old times, huh?" I ask. I'm sitting in one of the Bureau's unmarked black SUVs with Elliott as we watch out the windshield. The rain has been coming down for a solid hour and there's no indication it will be letting up anytime soon. Ahead of us is *CO.*, a new restaurant in Arlington, which is supposed to be one of the most exclusive spots in town, or so I've heard. The text came in about an hour after the call to Liam's phone, and Liam went in about thirty minutes ago with an envelope of cash tucked into his jacket pocket. Cash which I had to personally guarantee and will be responsible for if we don't get it back by the time all of this is over.

No one ever said this new job would be easy.

"Old times?" Elliott asks.

"Yeah, when we were working the terrorist case, going after Magus?"

I catch him glance over, but he doesn't fully turn his head. Elliott can be such a mystery to me sometimes. It seems, ever since that case, he's grown more reserved. Maybe that's due to what he considered was an inadequate performance during that case. Or maybe he just doesn't want to get into any more arguing matches with me. That was when Zara went missing while undercover, and I have to admit, I might have been a little overzealous in my pursuit of the case.

"What's your read on the situation?" I ask when he doesn't say anything else. It's like pulling teeth trying to get anything out of him. Still, I know I can trust him, and he's a good agent, which was exactly why I wanted him on my team.

"I think they're deliberately making him wait," he says. "Perhaps it's another test. Or perhaps they have no plans on showing up at all."

Nadia is around the back of the building, keeping an eye on things there while Elliott and I monitor the front. Zara has donned her best "going out" dress and is currently sitting on the other side of the bar, monitoring Liam from inside. The idea is for Zara to get eyes on whoever meets with Liam to see if she can't find out more about them while Liam attempts to charm his way in. Meanwhile, the rest of us are keeping watch in the event neither works, so we can at least tail whoever comes out with the cash.

"If they don't show up, we're dead in the water," I say. I don't have a better way of getting into this organization and we're still no closer to the identities of those two dead women. I'm afraid without any records from XRC, we're unlikely to ever find out who they were and have zero chance of notifying their families.

But more than that, we'll have a murderer on the loose, and until someone else is killed, we won't have any way of catching them. I've seen some pretty horrific things, but I can't imagine the kind of fear these women must deal with on a daily basis, just to make a little money. I know we're not going to curtail all violence against sex workers, but I would at least like to stop the worst of them. If I can't even do that, then what business do I have in this job?

"I think I've got something," Zara says over our comms. "Big guy, making his way over to Liam."

"Look sharp," I say to the team. "Is he alone or is there anyone else?"

"Might be a second man, can't tell yet," she says.

"You Burnett?" I hear a gruff voice say on Liam's line.

"That's right," Liam replies. "And you are?"

"Your ticket," the man replies. "I just need your fee."

"Here?" Liam asks. "Perhaps we should grab—"

"Payment now, or this doesn't happen," the man says.

"Jesus, he's an impatient fucker," Zara grumbles. "Completely bald. Looks a little like a jacked-up Bruce Willis."

"Okay," I catch Liam say. "How does this work?"

"He's just handed over the cash, discreetly," Zara says.

"Come with me," the other man says.

Zara is on the ball. "Okay, yep, the other guy is definitely with XRC. I've got images of both men, but it will take a while to see if I can find their identities."

"Where?" Liam asks.

"The boss has a surprise for you."

"Liam," I say, knowing he can't respond. "Go with them. We'll have your back. And get rid of the earpiece if you need to. We don't want them to find it on you."

"He's heading out," Zara says. Even through the rain, I see the big man Zara described exit the restaurant and stand under the large portico, followed by Liam and another man. A black Mercedes pulls up.

"They certainly are efficient," Elliott says.

"Zara, keep your position. Rendezvous with Nadia and start working on ID'ing those men. Elliott and I will follow the car."

"Got it," she says as Elliott starts the engine. Liam climbs in the back with the bald man while the other gets in the passenger seat. I can't hear anything, so I have to assume he's already ditched the earpiece. And even though I know Liam is a professional and can handle himself, my stomach drops a little at this unanticipated turn of events.

The Mercedes pulls away and Elliott follows, keeping a good distance behind. "Are you sure it was a good idea to ditch the earpiece?" he asks. "Now we have no way of hearing the conversation."

"It's better than them finding out he's a fed. I'd rather gain their trust first; we can continue to gather evidence later."

"And if they decide he isn't who he says he is?"

"Let's hope it doesn't come to that," I say. We follow the car through downtown Arlington before it heads into the suburbs. The whole time, I'm reporting my position to Zara so they can keep an eye on our location.

"They better reach their destination soon," Elliott says. "Otherwise, it's going to become painfully obvious we're following them."

He's right. The traffic has thinned considerably the further out we go. As we head out on the Lincoln Highway, the car turns off onto what looks like a deserted side street. I motion for Elliott to keep driving past and to pull over up ahead, out of sight. He cuts the lights and turns the SUV around to head back down to the side street. But when we get there, the Mercedes is nowhere to be found. My heart pounds, but I motion for him to continue down the street, slowly. There aren't any houses out here, only large, open swaths of land. As we near the end of the side street, another street juts off into what looks like a well-kept subdivision. The only problem is it's gated, and I immediately spot the cameras. I tell Elliott to back up the SUV, hoping we didn't get close enough to appear on anyone's radar.

"Now what?" he asks.

I don't know. We've lost both Liam *and* the money. I'm not used to being so out of control. Not to mention it isn't a good look for my first time running a team like this. "Head back to the main highway. We'll have to wait for them to come back out and hope Liam can handle himself in there."

"You don't think he can?" he asks.

"We're going to find out."

~

THE WHOLE TIME LIAM IS IN THE BACK OF THE CAR, THE SCENT of peonies fills in the air, and he can't figure out why. As best he can tell, none of the other men in the car are wearing cologne. Still, he tries not to let it distract him too much. They hadn't workshopped this exact scenario, but he believes Emily's call was right. It's best to take the chance while they have it. And it's his job to make sure whoever he's about to meet doesn't see any red flags.

Their client list must be small if everyone goes through such a rigorous set of requirements. Though he can't help but wonder what happens if someone fails? Presumably they give up the deposit. But what happens to the client? Is he about to see something that will make it impossible to leave this organization? Is that how they instill loyalty?

Or is this nothing more than a bunch of smoke and mirrors, designed to make it look like the money he just spent actually leads to some kind of bespoke experience?

"I don't guess it would do any good to ask where we're going," he says as the lights of Arlington have fallen far behind them. No one else in the car says anything. They could have at least offered him a water; he'd had to leave his drink back at the bar. He gets the impression if he pulls out his phone, it will either be taken from him, or smashed in the hands of the giant currently sitting next to him. The one with the FBI's ten grand in his pocket. Liam's head fills with scenarios of what he might have to do to get himself out of this should things go sideways. Em told him about the time she managed to wreck the car she was being held hostage in, but Liam doesn't think that's a possibility for him. For one, his seat mate isn't trying to get in his pants.

Finally, after what has been at least thirty minutes, they're far into the suburbs of DC and they pull off on a small side street. At the end of the street is a towering gate which opens as they approach, leading into a subdivision. All the houses out here are mansions, with wide, expansive lawns and fancy cars sitting in the sprawling driveways, the houses all lit by outdoor lighting designed to be as dramatic as possible. Whoever lives out here isn't hurting for money, that's for sure.

Liam sits a little straighter when they pull into one of the driveways and approach a house done up in a colonial style, with large columns out front. As the car pulls to a stop, the man in front of Liam gets out and opens Liam's door, holding an umbrella over the opening.

"Get out," the man beside Liam says.

Annoyed, Liam gives the man something of a snarl before stepping out into the weather. He's led by umbrella man up the stairs to the front door, which opens just as he arrives. Inside, another man in an identical suit stands by the door. The floor is all polished marble, and the staircase is black and white, like something out of a Tom Petty music video.

"May I take your coat?" the man asks in an almost identically gruff voice to the bald guy sitting beside him in the car. It's almost comical.

"No thanks," Liam says. "I'd like to know what the hell is going on here."

"Follow me," the man says. Liam takes a breath then follows him, realizing the umbrella man has stayed outside in the weather.

"Where are we going?" Liam asks. As he follows, he takes in all the details of the house. It's the opposite of modest, decorated with opulent furnishings, and spotless. In a way, it's very much like the crime scene where the women were found. He also doesn't like the menacing vibe he's getting from this place. Okusaka said nothing about anything like this, which doesn't bode well. They don't know how dangerous these people could be, and he might have just walked into a snake pit here.

The man leads him to a pair of grand, dark mahogany doors. It's strange, almost like they're putting on some kind of show. Still, Liam waits as the man opens the doors. He's hit by the scent of peonies again, except this time much stronger, and suddenly Liam realizes where it's been coming from.

In front of him, in the opulent room, stand half a dozen women, all of Asian descent, all with silky, black hair. Each wears a maid's outfit ranging from white to black and all the colors in between. They all smile upon seeing him, though he can immediately tell they are forced smiles. The first thought through his mind is how similar they all look to the two victims he's spent the last few days familiarizing himself with.

"Choose," the man beside Liam says.

Liam turns to him. "Is this something you do for all your customers?"

A smile plays on the man's lips, but he doesn't let it take shape. "We do this for our…special clients."

"And what makes me so special?"

"Not everyone is as…prestigious as you, Mr. Burnett."

Liam turns back to the line of women watching him expectantly. He can see the hope in their eyes—the hope that he won't choose them. Despite the plush surroundings, fear hangs heavy in the air. Whatever they've been made to do in the past, it hasn't been pleasant. It turns his stomach to even imagine it. He wonders if there's a way out of this that doesn't involve him choosing any of them. Not that it will prevent anyone else from inflicting trauma in the future, but at the very least it would spare them for a short time.

"You've overstepped," Liam asserts, trying not to allow too much anger seep into his voice. "This is not what I wanted this evening."

The man's face turns into a frown. "But you wished to join the—"

"On my own time. My own terms. And you just whisk me away from my night, bring me here with no explanation?" He can't help it. The anger is in full force now. But he can use it. "I have half a mind to demand a refund."

"We do not provide refunds," the man says, attempting to save face.

"Then maybe you should think about your customer care policy," Liam says. "I am currently undergoing a series of treatments that renders me...unavailable for the time being."

The man blinks, then bows his head. "I am sorry to hear that Mr. Burnett. We didn't know, we thought you would want—"

"You thought wrong," Liam barks. He needs to get them on the defensive. "I demand to speak with whoever is in charge of this so-called *elite service*."

"I..." He seems to think better of whatever he was going to say and closes the doors. Liam thinks he catches looks of confusion on the women's faces. "Unfortunately, there is no one to meet you this evening."

Liam huffs, his real frustration leaking through. "Then I guess you're taking me back to my car."

"I'm sorry sir," the man says. "Most of our members enjoy the power of our operation here. We thought since you—"

"I *don't*," Liam growls. This is not how he imagined this night going. But he can see these people are desperate to please him, which is something he can use.

The man shuffles his feet as the bald man approaches. "Take him back," the doorman says.

"Back?" the bald man says.

The doorman turns to Liam. "Again, I am sorry for the misunderstanding. We will endure to inform you of any schedule changes in the future."

"This isn't the same service Kenji spoke of," Liam says. "I am very disappointed."

The doorman bows again. "Our apologies."

Liam eyes the man a moment longer, then begins following the larger man back out. Apparently, Nadia and Zara were too good at their jobs, making him seem even more important than most of Red Sunset's clients, enough that they were willing to offer up what seemed to be a "freebie."

As they head back outside, Liam takes note of the house number. If nothing else, he's gained some valuable insight about these people, and learned they might not be as organized as Emily had initially assumed. Their methods have proved sloppy, not what he would have expected from an organization such as this. Which tells him they may not be as professional as they wish to appear.

Again, he's met with an umbrella outside the house and led back to the car. This time there's no one else inside but the driver. Without an order from anyone, the car pulls away from the house and they head back to Arlington.

Chapter Fifteen

"THAT'S IT?" I ask. "They wanted you to what, have sex with one of those women right there?"

Liam shrugs. "I got the impression I could have had all of them if I'd wanted. And if the apartment was wired with a camera, the house *definitely* was."

"I don't get it," Zara says, crossing one leg. She's still in her black dress from the restaurant. "So they feign kidnapping you in order to impress you?"

"Seems like that was the plan," Liam says. "Like a fantasy experience. But I got the distinct impression they hadn't done anything like this before. It all felt very...made up on the spot."

"You're thinking they took one look at the portfolio we built for you and saw dollar signs," Nadia says.

"That would be my guess," he replies. "Which may be why Okusaka didn't mention the ten grand, or the personalized limo service."

"Because those weren't perks he received." I shoot a look at Zara and Nadia. "You guys might have overshot your goal."

Zara shrugs. "Hey, you said make him look rich. He is supposed to be investing in this company, right?"

"Perhaps we can use that," Elliott says. "Turn their failure back on them. Liam could request a meeting based on the poor treatment he received."

"That's certainly an idea," I say.

Nadia stretches out, yawning. "We also have the license plate of that car, along with the house's address. It will probably lead to nothing, but at least it's a start." She yawns again. "But I have to admit, I'm fading."

I nod. "You're right, sorry. I know I'm keeping everyone late. Good work this evening. At the very least we got our foot in the door. We'll start on the rest of this tomorrow."

Looks like everyone else is just about as tired as Nadia. I check my phone and see it's already close to midnight. Liam comes up to me, still dressed in his new suit. "Sorry we couldn't get more. I hoped there was a bigwig in that house I could speak with right then and there."

I wave him off. "It's not your fault. You did great out there. And I'm just glad it didn't turn out to be something more serious. When they first got you in that car, we didn't know if they'd roll out the red carpet or leave you in a ditch somewhere in Pennsylvania."

"Neither did I," Liam says. "But I figured when they didn't take my phone and didn't bother searching for weapons, I was probably in the clear."

"I just hope the gate cameras didn't catch the SUV," I say, gathering my things as Nadia bids everyone a good night. Elliott follows wordlessly. "He and I were with you the whole time, right up until the end."

"I figured you were," he says, reaching down and kissing my cheek. "Thanks for being there for me."

"Hey," Zara says. "I know I'm probably interrupting a tender moment, but I can stay and work on those records if you want."

"Don't you want to go home and get some sleep?" I ask.

"Nope. You know I keep an emergency sleeping bag in the back office. I can stay, really."

I furrow my brow. There had indeed been a time when you couldn't tear Zara away from the office, but when she became a field agent, she started going home like a normal person instead of spending all her waking hours in the Bureau. Could her wanting to stay have anything to do with Theo?

"Z, I need you well-rested," I say. "It can wait until morning."

"Are you sure?" she asks. "I don't mind."

"I know, but we all need some sleep. We've been going all day."

Just as she nods, my phone vibrates. I pull it out, wondering who in the hell is calling me at this hour. But my eyes go wide when I see the name. "This is Slate," I say.

"Agent Slate," Caruthers says. "I thought I should call. I just got a line from DC Police. They've found Emily's car."

It's past two in the morning by the time Zara and I reach the abandoned lot lit up in the blue and red flashing of the DC police cruisers. She insisted it wouldn't be good for me to go alone, and I wasn't about to argue with her, but waiting the five extra minutes it took her to change into something with pants was excruciating. Liam agreed to head back home and take Timber out, but he wants me to keep him appraised of any new developments.

Even though I don't have any business being out here, I had to come see it for myself. It's another piece of the puzzle. And maybe something in the car could help us nail a "why" to my aunt. A reason for all this madness.

But when we pull up, my heart drops. Even in the rain, which has lightened considerably, I can tell the car has been incinerated. All that's left is the frame of the vehicle and not a lot else. In fact, it's a lot like my grandparent's house up in Ohio.

"Oh, dammit, really?" Zara says. "What is this pyromaniac's deal? She gotta torch everything she sees?"

"Let's just see if there's anything left," I say. "Maybe we'll get lucky."

The DC cops have already erected a large white tent over the vehicle to shield it from the rain. There must be at least a dozen people swarming all over the site. As we pull up, an officer in a wide-brimmed hat approaches, his hand up. "Sorry folks, active crime scene. You'll need to move on."

I hold up my badge, and his lips form a quiet *o* shape as he steps to the side, allowing us through. I park about twenty yards away from the car in another part of the lot. They're just now setting up large spotlights so they can get a good look at the car as soon as possible.

"When did they find it?" Zara asks.

"Caruthers says he found out about it around eleven thirty. So it wouldn't have been long before that. A few hours ago." We both get out of the car, looking around. Caruthers is standing under an umbrella near the site, his tall form unmistakable. We each grab an umbrella of our own and head over to join them.

"Thanks for the heads up," I say as we approach.

"Agents," he nods to us. "They're just finishing the setup."

"How's the reception?" Zara asks.

"Why do you think I'm standing over here?" He motions to another, smaller tent that's been set up beside the large one over the car. Under it, Detective Striker is coordinating with his team to begin inspecting the car. We make eye contact, but his body language doesn't change. The man is a master at keeping his emotions in check, I'll give him that.

We watch as he finishes handing out assignments before he heads over to meet us. "Agent Slate," he nods, and I return the gesture. "And you must be Agent Caruthers," Striker says, addressing the man beside us.

"This is my partner, Agent Foley," I say, indicating Zara.

Striker gives her a quick nod as well. "It's not every day I have three feds on my crime scene," he says.

"It's not every day you find the car that tried running us off the road," Zara says.

"Then you can positively identify it?" he says, skepticism tinting his words.

"I don't know about you, but I don't see a lot of Ford Granada's driving around," she says, her voice carrying that edge Zara sometimes gets when she thinks she's been insulted.

"The frame matches," I say. "The rest, we'll have to see. But Zara is right. I don't think I'd ever seen that type of car before last week."

"Hmm," Striker says, before sniffing and rubbing his nose absently. "Well, we'll check it. We're about to start taking evidence, what little we can find, anyway. Given the fire and now the rain, we're not optimistic."

"I'm assuming there wasn't anyone in the car when it was found?" I can see clearly from here that the passenger area looks to be empty of any bodies.

"Nope. Then again, it's obvious the car had been abandoned for a few days. Pure luck the patrol officer found it. He was investigating a burglary nearby and happened to chase the perp into this parking lot. He didn't realize what it was at first, he thought it was just another burned-out car. Funnily enough, it was the perp on the ground who ID'd the car as a Granada. Weird how that works, isn't it?"

"It wasn't burned recently?" I ask.

"Doesn't appear that way," he says.

"Then Emily could have been the one to torch it after all," Zara says, then looks at me. "Sorry, the other Emily."

"I will need both of you to provide a positive ID if you can," he says. "Then I'll have to ask you to stay back while we do our initial investigation. Once this rain lets up, I want to move it into a controlled environment. Hopefully there we can make some progress. Right now, we're just trying to salvage what we can."

I look over to see his people beginning to wrap parts of the car in plastic to protect it from any additional elements. "If you can pull a paint color, that will go a long way to identification."

"And plates," Zara says. "We issued the original ABP off those plates."

He nods. "I've got them. But I like to make sure. You never know, someone could have switched the plates."

"Any idea of the accelerant used?"

"Most likely gasoline. But we'll have a better idea once we get it into the lab." He looks at each of us in turn, but his gaze lingers on Caruthers for a half a second longer. "If you'll excuse me, I need to get back. I'll be in touch once we get it down to the station. Then if the two of you wouldn't mind coming down—"

"Be happy to," I say.

He nods before heading back over. He's completely soaked but doesn't seem to care. He continues overseeing the operation as his people take what little evidence they can from the site and while others keep wrapping the car.

"She burned it before she jumped in front of my car," I say. "She was trying to destroy evidence."

"Em, I don't mean to be insensitive, but your aunt is batshit crazy," Zara says.

"I'm inclined to agree with Agent Foley," Caruthers replies. "What little I've found hasn't been promising."

I'm in no position to disagree. Maybe that's why my mother decided to cut her off and lie to me about her existence. Maybe she knew she could be dangerous and didn't want that to be part of her life.

Was my aunt really suicidal, or is something more going

on here? So far, the evidence seems to be pointing to the former, but I can't believe she would have gone to all the trouble of the letters, of destroying that house, just to give up and throw herself in front of my car.

Then again, maybe it's like Zara says. Maybe she is just that nuts.

Chapter Sixteen

I FIND it difficult to concentrate as we head back. I drop Zara off at her place since it's closer than driving all the way back to the bureau before returning home myself. While the case has been a good distraction so far, these new developments with the car have my mind racing into overdrive with no stop in sight. Without even thinking, I find myself parked outside the hospital once more, staring at the large white façade, wondering if I'm ever going to get the answers I've been searching for so long.

But before I get out of the car, I stop myself. I'm bordering on obsessive behavior, even I know it. What would Frost say about me returning here day after day? Maybe if Caruthers hadn't called me about the car, I would have been able to go home and get a good night's sleep. Then again, when I've shut my eyes the past few nights, all I've seen is her face as she disappears under my car. It's like a bad movie being run over and over again in my head. And until she wakes up, I don't think it's ever going to stop.

"This is insane," I say aloud. And I believe it. Any normal person would just go back home and let this whole thing play out as best they could. But I'm not a normal person; I've always known that. And if this other Emily really is crazy, perhaps I inherited part of that from her. Is this what she would do? She obviously knows a lot more about me than I know about her, and it's clear she's been watching me for a while now. I almost laugh. I get rid of one stalker and immediately gather another. It's like some kind of sick joke. But this time it's not an international assassin hell-bent on revenge. This time, it's a member of my own family, someone who has been hidden from me my entire life. It's clear she wants something from me. And now, I want something from her too.

Somehow, I manage to resist the desire to go back in the hospital and check on her, and instead return home, coming in much later than I would want. For the first time, Timber is nowhere to be found and most of the lights are off, save for a lamp Liam has fished out of one of the boxes and plugged up in the living room, just sitting on the bare floor.

I set my things to the side and quietly make my way down the hallway, opening the bedroom door to find Timber stretched out in my spot in the bed under Liam's draped arm. It takes all my strength not to burst out laughing. Instead, I slip off my shoes and socks and get out of my work clothes before trying to carefully slide into the bed with them. Timber wakes up immediately, but with one sniff he knows it's me and lays his head back down, on *my* pillow. They're both so comfortable I hate to disturb them, but at the same time, I'm exhausted and we don't have the other bed in the guest room set up. In fact, this is *my* bed from my apartment.

"Em?" Liam mumbles softly.

"Sorry, I didn't mean to wake you," I say, slipping all the way in. Timber finally realizes he's not going to be able to keep his spot and gets up, turning around and laying down at our feet. Though he still takes up a good portion of the bed.

"What happened with the car?" he asks.

"I'll tell you in the morning," I say. "Go back to sleep." He turns over, and I hear him sigh before falling back asleep immediately. We're all exhausted. I'm pushing the team too hard. Maybe I'm not cut out for this. Not everyone is meant to be a leader. And I might just be better at following orders than giving them.

Though, if Zara was here, she'd probably laugh at that, given how often I like to skirt the rules.

I turn over, and despite feeling like I've been through the wringer all day, I can't shut my mind off. I keep seeing the other Emily, the look on her face as she slipped under my car. The absolute helplessness in her eyes. And now her car, burned and abandoned. The woman is an unending conundrum, and there's a very real possibility I won't ever get the answers I need. At some point after mulling the incident over and over in my mind, I fall asleep.

THE FOLLOWING MORNING, I GIVE LIAM THE RUNDOWN, BUT I leave out my impromptu trip back over to the hospital. I don't need him thinking I'm any more obsessed than he already does. He's as baffled as I am as to why the woman would try running me and Zara off the road, then decide to torch the car soon after. It's clear we're not going to get any answers until she comes out of her coma.

"Well," I say, stuffing the last bits of homemade waffle in my mouth. "We should probably get back. I'd like to get a jump on things this morning."

"Em," he says, using that impatient tone he always uses when he thinks I'm going too hard.

I shake my head. "Uh-uh, this is important. We're making progress. Yes, it's slow, but we're getting somewhere."

He smiles, walking around the island, and wraps me in a hug. "I know. But part of being a good boss is knowing when to pull back on the reins a little bit. Don't run your team so hard you exhaust them."

I want to give him a glare, but that's a little difficult when I'm smashed up against his chest. "Are you just saying that because you want your Saturday morning off?"

"I mean, I wouldn't *mind* it," he says. "And I'm sure no one else would either. In fact, I bet you'd be the hero of the office. There's no better feeling than having a snow day."

"It's not snowing," I say.

"Trust me. And everyone will be that much more alert when we regroup."

I huff. "Fine. Everyone gets the morning off. But I still want to keep going this afternoon. We have victims out there, and I don't want to find more because I let everyone hit snooze."

"You can't fix the world, Ms. Slate," he says, finally releasing me. "As much as you want to try."

I look up at him. "So what did you have in mind instead?"

He glances back at the dirty plates from breakfast. We still haven't unpacked our dishware, so everything we're using is disposable. "We could keep unpacking, considering we haven't made it very far and we've already been in this house over a week. I, for one, would like to sleep in a bed that's not on the ground."

"Uh-huh," I say, giving him a playful smack. "Among other things."

"It wouldn't be the worst thing in the world." He grins.

"Okay hot stuff. Bedframe it is. We'll see how things go from there." I shoot a glance over at Timber, who is half out of his dog bed, butt hanging off the end in his post-breakfast snooze. However, as soon as I take a step in the direction of the hallway, his head is up and he's behind me in less than ten seconds. "You're not missing anything," I coo. "We're just getting the house together."

"He just wants to help," Liam says.

After shooting off a quick text to the team letting them know they've got the morning off, it takes us a good thirty minutes to get all the parts of the bed back together and assembled properly. Then it takes another twenty minutes to figure out just how we want our new bedroom to look. It's something I hadn't even considered. When I moved into the apartment, I plopped things in one place, and that's where they stayed until I moved out, no thought process behind it. But now we have to map out the most efficient placement of the furniture considering both of us need to get ready at the same time. And honestly, all it's doing is giving me a headache. Not to mention, my mind keeps drifting back to the hospital.

"Hey," Liam says, drawing my attention. "Do you want the dresser here, or over here?"

"Oh," I say, trying to cover the fact I haven't been listening to him. "I guess...over there." I point to the far side of the room.

"What's going on?" he asks, leaving the dresser where it is. "Too boring? Why don't we do something else?"

"No, no," I say. "It needs to get done."

"You know, if you don't care where things go, I can always do this on one of the nights you're working late."

"No, it's fine," I insist. "Let's keep going."

He holds my gaze for a moment. "You're thinking about your aunt, aren't you?"

"I can't help it," I protest. "Especially after Striker found that car. I mean, I know I told him to keep me in the loop, but I didn't actually expect him to do it. He was the one who got in contact with Caruthers. He wanted me to see that car last night."

"Yeah, so you could ID it."

I screw up my mouth. "Maybe," I say. "Still, none of this makes any sense. Why is she even trying to do all this? And what didn't my mother want me to know? You'd think if my aunt was dangerous, my mother would have given me a heads up."

"When you were twelve?" he asks.

"I dunno. Or at least left a note or something."

Liam quirks the edge of his mouth. "You know, I don't think I've ever seen your mother except in some old pictures. Do you have any videos of her from when you were little?"

I nod. "Sure. But I haven't watched them in forever. Not since before Dad died. We'd watch them together sometimes."

"Maybe watching them will help you not feel so disconnected from her," he suggests.

"I suppose," I say. "But they're all on minidisc."

"Oh yeah," he says, tilting his head back wistfully. "I remember those."

I nod. "Too old for VHS and too young for digital uploads. My childhood fell right in the middle."

"Do you know where they are?" he asks. I lead him to the stack of boxes that were brought over from my apartment. It only takes two boxes before we find the stuff from my dad's house. This stuff has been moved from his place to my house with Matt, to my apartment, and now here. And in all that time, I let them just sit and collect dust because the last time I'd watched any of my old home movies, my father was there to watch them with me. And when he died, it seemed like a betrayal to watch them without him.

As I pull out the stacks of minidiscs, I realize I have no way to play them. "I don't have a DVD player anymore. Do you?"

"No," he says, removing the small camcorder Dad used to make all these memories. "But I think I can hook this up to the TV. You can just play them from here." He heads off into the living room. It's another thirty minutes by the time he finds the correct cable and gets the inputs right, but finally enough, the blue screen from the camcorder appears on the TV itself.

"There we go," he says. "What's up first?"

I glance at the stack of minidiscs. There's probably at least fifty in the shoebox from Dad's house. I flip through them, looking for any that might be particularly memorable. "Here. Folly Beach, 1999." I was seven.

"A family beach trip, perfect," Liam says, taking the disc and popping it into the camcorder. "Did you go to the beach often?"

"Not really," I say, thinking back. "In fact, I think this might have been our only trip."

"My dad used to take all of us out to the Chesapeake," he says as the menu boots up. "But we didn't get much time at the beach. Mostly it was tromping through the mud in some vain attempt to build character."

"Sounds like a blast," I say.

"It sucked." He laughs. "Literally. The mud would suck the boots right off your feet. I never liked those trips." He hits play, and the screen of the TV is immediately filled with the image of the ocean. It's a clear day with only high stratus clouds in the distance. But there are no shortage of people in the water, though the waves look mild. In the distance, a small form is on top of a boogie board, which "catches" a wave and takes it all the way in.

"Great job, Emily!" I'm immediately struck with how easily I'd forgotten my dad's voice. It almost sounds foreign at first, his accent odd.

The small form stands up, grabbing the float and running in as fast as her little legs would carry her. *"Did you get it?"* younger me says. I'm decked out in a purple swimsuit, and the salt water has plastered my dark hair to my head.

"Well, aren't you just the cutest," Liam says, grinning from ear to ear.

His grin is infectious. "Shut up."

"I got it. Are you going again?" my dad asks.

"We should eat first."

A chill runs down my spine. I haven't heard that voice in so long I had completely forgotten it. But unlike my father's voice, this one is exactly as I remember it. The camera pans to my mother, who is sitting on a beach chair beside a cooler full of food. Not only that, but as the camera has come around, it's easy to see the beach is *packed*. People take up almost the entire shore, from the dunes all the way to the water.

"Crowded day," Liam says.

"That's what happens when you go in the middle of summer," I reply. My mother begins unpacking the food while, in the background, I'm complaining about not being able to go back out for thirty minutes after I eat.

And it seems that my dad is intent on capturing every aspect of the meal. He continues recording Mom while she's unpacking. I come across the middle of the frame as I put my float to the side, just as another family is walking by. Mom happens to stand up just as they're beginning to pass, and I see something on her face. Something I've never seen before.

"Wait a second, go back," I tell Liam.

"How far?"

"About twenty seconds." He scrubs back twenty seconds to where my mother is sitting again. She stands, and I see her flinch away from the people passing. "Did you see that?"

"What?"

I narrow my gaze. "I'm not sure. Keep going." It seems Dad was relentless in his recordings. He's always either focused on me or Mom. Eventually, she tells him to shut it off so they can eat, and when the picture comes back, I'm running back toward the ocean, float in hand. My mother is standing out in front of my father, holding herself tight, like she might blow away. "That, right there, how she's holding herself."

"Maybe she's cold."

"Liam, it's South Carolina in the middle of summer. It doesn't get any warmer."

"What is it you're seeing?" he asks.

I've spent the last five years observing people as part of my job. I've been tasked with analyzing specific body language—

people tell you a lot by how they hold themselves. How they react to different stimuli. And in all of that time, I've learned to detect patterns, shortcuts that tell me what a person has been through in their lives.

I don't think I ever saw it before because the last time I watched this video, it was on a much smaller TV, and I had very little experience in the area. In fact, the last time I watched this video with my dad, I wasn't even an official agent yet. I was still in training at Quantico. Dad passed only a few weeks later, right before I graduated. And even if I had watched it again then, I wouldn't have known what I was seeing.

But after being in the field for the past five years and witnessing all sorts of horrors, there's no mistaking it. I've seen that look on a woman's face dozens, if not hundreds of times.

"I think…I think my mother is an abuse survivor."

Chapter Seventeen

I SPENT the better part of an hour going through the rest of the movies, looking for any other clues. And while Mom isn't often the subject of my dad's video shenanigans, when she does appear, I continue to see more and more signs that she endured some kind of lasting trauma and did everything she could to hide it.

"You don't think your dad—" Liam begins after we've reviewed another dozen videos.

"No," I say, shutting that down immediately. "He wasn't like that. He didn't have an angry bone in his body, and he was more caring than any other man I've known. Except maybe you."

"Still, that could have been for your benefit," Liam says. "I know you don't want to hear it, but you need to consider the possibility."

He's right. Generally, when someone is being abused, it's by the person closest to them. But when I search my memories, I can't find a single instance where my dad even raised his voice at Mom. In fact, it was rare they fought at all. When they would have disagreements, it would always be calm discussions; they never let their emotions get the better of them. Now I recognize that as people who had done some work on themselves. People who had managed not to throw blame carelessly.

"No, look, if that was true, we would see it in the videos. But she never shies away from him, and in fact, he seems to comfort her. Like in this one." I pull one of the ones we've already looked at back out and run it again. It's a video of me in a science fair in elementary school. Dad sets the camera down on the table so I can explain my experiment, and it catches both of them listening to me as I talk. You can clearly see my mother lean into my father without even thinking about it, and he wraps his arm around her shoulder. It's not hard to see they're both proud of me, and watching it makes my heart ache.

The video ends and I look away, wiping at my eyes while also trying not to draw attention to myself.

I feel Liam's presence behind me, and he wraps his arms around my shoulders, not saying anything. It's almost a perfect mirror to how Dad was with her. I guess it's true what they say, you really do seek out partners that remind you of your parents.

"I think you're right," he says, softly. "She's not showing any aversion to him. Even though it doesn't always show up, let's just say for the moment he's not the abuser. Then who is?"

"I don't know," I whisper. "How could I have missed this?"

"Because you were a kid," Liam says. "And kids aren't wired to look for that kind of thing. Even if you had been, would you have recognized it for what it was? It took years of experience and FBI training for you to even see it."

I let out a long breath. "Dad must have known about it. Even without training, your spouse would figure out something was wrong after a while. But he never said anything to me. Even after she died."

"Maybe he didn't want to burden you," Liam offers.

"And maybe she told him not to," I say. "Her doctor... Archer, he said she was adamant about me not knowing anything. Whatever Dad knew, he respected her enough to never reveal it. It must have been her parents, right? That would explain why she cut them all off."

"Your grandparents?" Liam asks.

"That's the next logical option," I say. "If it's not a spouse, it's parental. She could have grown up in a household of abuse, and by the time she was old enough to leave, she'd finally had enough and cut them all off."

"But we couldn't find anything on them in Millridge. At least, I couldn't," Liam says. "How do you find out?"

"By asking the one person who might have experienced it right alongside her." Now I have an even greater need for Emily to wake up. She and my mother were brought up together, she would know about any abuse my grandparents handed down. And she might be able to shed some light on my mother's life before she moved to Virginia.

As I'm removing the disc from the player, my phone rings on the other side of the room. I jump up, thinking it might be a call from the hospital, but I frown when I see Nadia's name come up on my screen.

"Nadia?" I ask. "Is everything all right?"

"Oh, yes," she says. "I got your text earlier, but I didn't have anything else to do so I came into the office anyway. And I think I've found something. Something big."

BY THE TIME WE GET BACK TO THE OFFICE, NADIA IS AT HER desk, going hard on the computer. Based on what she gave me over the phone, I thought it was important enough to bring the team back in.

"Been here long?" I ask as I approach her desk.

"Only a few hours. Agent Foley and I came in at the same

time. We've been putting our heads together, and I think we've made some excellent progress."

I furrow my brow as I spot Zara over at her desk. She hops up and heads over now that she sees us. "I thought you were going to get some rest," I say.

"I did. And as much as I appreciated the day off, I just couldn't get into *Monster Hunter Elite*."

I arch my eyebrow.

"It's a console game, and it's supposed to be really good. Great story, long campaign. But I just couldn't get into it. So I came back into work. Thought it would be better if I put in some more time on the case."

Even though she's as chipper as ever, the bags under her eyes tell a different story. Then again, I probably don't look much better. Since my discovery, my emotions have been riding on the surface and I've hovered on the verge of tears. Still, I need to be professional. This is my team and they're counting on me to keep it together.

"Okay," I say. "Let's see what you've got."

"Should we wait on Elliott?" Liam asks.

I check my phone. It's a little past two and I called everyone back in an hour ago. "I'm sure he'll be here in a few minutes. He can catch up on anything he misses."

The rest of them nod and we head back over to the bullpen beside my office. But when we get there, I take one look at that podium and my stomach twists. I don't want to stand up there, *lording* over the rest of them like Wallace used to do. This is my operation, and I can run it as I see fit. "Here, let's go do this in my office," I say. No one seems to argue as I unlock the door and lead them in. Because it's Saturday, everything is still quiet. Some departments will fill in as the day goes on, but it's never as busy as it is during the weekdays.

Nadia takes a seat on the couch, opening her laptop while Zara perches herself near my window. Liam takes one of the seats on the other side of my desk while I lean back against the desk itself. This feels better, more intimate. Less like a formal occasion and more like we're all on the same playing field. "Okay, let's hear it," I say.

"So we began by running the property records on that house they took Liam to," Nadia says. "It's owned by a similar shell company that owns Red Sunset and all its subsidiaries, but that wasn't always the case."

"The house was built in the early two-thousands," Zara says. "Where it was purchased by a Mr. and Mrs. Keith Underwood. They had the house for fifteen years, at which point they became empty nesters and sold the house to a man named Johannsen Bolo."

"Okay," I say, not following. "And?"

"Mr. Bolo was single at the time, with no children or extended family," Nadia says. "He's a foreign national from Indonesia."

Someone clears their throat, and the four of us look over to see Elliott standing in the doorway, a frustrated look on his face. "When did we decide on a new venue for our meetings?"

"Creative decision. You gotta get here early if you want to be on top of things," Zara says. "Some of us have been here since ten."

"Not all of us have lives that revolve around work," he says, coming in and taking a seat beside Nadia. I catch the briefest of smiles on her lips as he sits down.

"You didn't miss much," Zara says. "Underwoods owned the house where they whisked Liam off to for his six-woman tryst. Sold it to Bolo. National from Indonesia. Easy."

"So, who is this Bolo? And why is he important?" Liam asks, clearing his throat and doing his best to hide his reddened cheeks. He's cute when he's embarrassed, and it's not a side of him I get to see very often.

"Normally he wouldn't be, but I found it strange that a single person would buy a house that large. You saw it, property records indicate it has seven bedrooms and ten bathrooms, and it's almost eight thousand square feet. That's a lot of space for yourself."

I exchange a quick glance with Liam. "You said you didn't see any personal items in there, right? No photos, or anything that would indicate someone actually lived there?"

"No, it was more like a hotel. All of the art and furnishings were upscale, but I didn't see anything with a personal flare."

"Does Bolo still own the house?" I ask Nadia.

"No, he sold it in 2019 to the holding company which currently owns the property. A company called White Lion Holdings."

"I don't guess you found any link between White Lion and Red Sunset?"

"Other than adjective-noun names, not yet," Zara says. "But I'm still looking."

"Where is this Johannsen Bolo now?" I ask.

"He still lives here," Nadia says. "Over in Silver Spring. He's a partner with Morgan, Huang and Bolo, a prominent but small accountant firm in the area. They take care of some big clients."

"He's well-connected, and well-funded," Zara says, bringing her phone over and showing me Bolo's social media accounts. I scroll through the pictures and see the man in question with senators, congressmen, and people of power all over the city.

"Seems to have done quite well for himself," I say. "I'm assuming you're not doing all this work on him if you didn't suspect him of something."

"He's exactly the kind of person who would be behind Red Sunset," Nadia says. "Someone with a lot of money and connections. *And* looking for a way to provide an elite service to his clients. There's only so much money in accounting if you're following the law. And from what we can tell, they are. By the book."

Liam scoffs. "If that's true, they have a lot to learn about client satisfaction. I got the distinct feeling last night I was part of a bad play. Like they had tried to create 'an experience,' but it really just fell flat."

"It could have been their first attempt at something like that," I say. "They said it themselves; you were a *special* customer."

"More than congressmen?" Liam asks.

That's true, it doesn't really track.

Zara snaps her fingers. "Shit. I think I just figured it out." She crouches beside Nadia. "Remember when we were setting up Burnett's personal history?"

"Yeah?"

"And we manufactured all that stuff about his business investments in different cities? Remember Malaysia?"

Her eyes go wide. "Oh. Oh, Liam, I'm so sorry. I was building a profile for someone with more of an...edge. Someone who had familiarity with the prostitution business," Nadia says. "They would have had to have really gone deep to find this, but I created records showing that you had partnered with a company who provided similar experiences in Malaysia. Where high profile clients would be taken to a brothel of sorts for full...service."

"So?" he asks.

"So we insinuated that you had insisted on being the first person to test the...goods."

His face goes red again.

"Was that their way of showing Liam they could provide something similar? Not only an opportunity for sex, but also a bid for capability?" I ask.

"That seems to be the logical conclusion," Elliott says.

Liam wipes his brow, clearly flustered. "Which means they went deeper than we thought. Are you sure that persona was airtight?"

Nadia nods. "But I'm glad we went the extra mile. Otherwise, you would have been found out by now."

Liam crosses his arms. "Guess I should have studied my dossier better."

"Honestly, it wasn't anything they were *supposed* to find," Zara says, standing again. "We did it more to help form a base for some of the connections and contacts you had. To make them look more credible."

"I know it might seem like this is a failure, but I actually think this is a good thing," I say. "If they're trying to impress him, it means they already want to partner with Liam and that he's not just another client."

"Could they be hard up for money?" Nadia asks.

"More likely just greedy," I say.

"The other bit of good news," Zara says. "Is we now have access to the site legitimately, thanks to Mr. Okusaka. I can finally start digging deeper, see what we can pull out."

"That's great," I say. "Hopefully we can use that to help identify the girls being used here." I turn to Liam. "Work with Zara and see if any of the people on the site are the same they propositioned you with last night. That will at least help us confirm how they're using these women."

"Got it," he says.

"Meanwhile, the rest of us will keep working on this Bolo, but I don't want to get myopic. We don't know he's the one behind this, though he's looking like a good place to start." As we head out to get started, I feel a lot better about this kind of meeting environment. At least that was a good decision on my part; I swear never to use the bullpen again. And Nadia has made some excellent progress, but I have to admit how disappointed I was when it was her calling and not the hospital. I know I'm falling down a rabbit hole, and my obsession is rearing its ugly head, which is why I *need* to be here, to be distracted, so I don't start thinking of all the explanations or scenarios that could have left my mother in such a state. My logical mind knows that no matter how many different ways I run it, I'm never going to understand what really happened. Not until Emily wakes up. And who knows if that will even happen.

Until then, I just have to keep my mind on my work. It's my only choice.

Chapter Eighteen

"Good morning!" Striker announces as he enters the garage. It was a long night last night, but he was up bright and early, energized by the fact the car in his investigation may, in fact, have been found. He's cautiously optimistic, based on how Special Agents Slate and Foley reacted last night. The only reason he'd even coordinated with the FBI at all was because, not only were the two agents eyewitnesses, but the main one, Slate, had a hand in this. No matter how anyone looks at the facts, she ran someone over with her car. Someone she claims is a relative, previously unknown to her.

That's a red flag in any department. He doesn't care what her excuses are, he'll keep a close eye on Emily Slate until the details of this case become clear. Not only is she a prime suspect, but he also happened to receive a call from the other detective she mentioned, Michaels, up in Millridge. And while he didn't come right out and say it, Striker could read between the lines. He doesn't trust Slate either, and his primary suspect happens to be her fellow agent and apparent boyfriend.

All of that leads to some very interesting suppositions. But he's not about to go around accusing a couple of feds without some hard evidence. He had hoped allowing Slate to see the car last night would rattle her a little, but she's too slick for that. Her public record shows commendation after commendation for how she's handled some of her cases. However, there is also a heavily redacted section of the records he managed to get from a friend of his, something he finds curious. It would take more clout than Striker has built up over an entire career to read the original file, which means it's important. Just another peculiarity surrounding Agent Emily Slate.

"Morning Reg," Patterson greets, nodding. "Don't see you down in the garage much."

"I've got a special interest in this one, Ed," Striker says. "It's not our normal case."

Patterson nods. Striker has known him for almost fifteen years. He's been with Crime Scene Investigation for as long as Striker has been on the beat and is one of the best. He snaps on a pair of gloves. "You looking to get your hands dirty on this one?"

"Wouldn't be here if I didn't," Striker replies, grinning. "Were you able to pull anything last night?"

"Didn't bother," he says. "With the weather I was more concerned with retaining anything still there. Just a forewarning, this one isn't going to be glamorous."

"You ever seen one of these before?" Striker asks, motioning to the car. It's been unwrapped from the night before, and Patterson's team is already taking photographs from all angles.

"A Granada?" he laughs. "I think my uncle had one back in the seventies."

"You certainly don't see them much anymore," Striker says, getting close to the hood. Where there had once been a hood ornament is nothing but an empty hole. "Was the ornament removed before the fire or during?"

"Probably before," Patterson says. "Intentionally or not, I'm not sure, but I get the feeling this car wasn't kept in the best condition, especially if someone was willing to burn it."

"We don't know it was our perp who actually destroyed it," Striker says. "She could have just abandoned it and a couple of firebugs found it later."

Patterson concedes the point. "Where would you like to start?"

"Can you get the VIN?"

"Working on it now," one of the other techs says. He has the front door open and is trying to scrape away some of the soot from the metal plate on the inside of the door.

"Maybe we'll get lucky and can run down the registration," Striker says. "What I'd really like to do is get a look at the interiors. Glove box, trunk, hood. You know, the usual."

"Sure," Patterson says, leading him around to the side of the car and making a motion to his team. "Let's finish up these photos."

Two techs finish with all the photography before another comes in, opening the passenger side door. It squeals as the metal rubs against metal. The inside of the car is charred, but not completely burned away. Some of the upholstery remains, though it's all black or melted to the seat.

"Doesn't look like it burned very hot, or very long," Striker says.

"We'll have to do some comparisons." Patterson nods. "But yeah, I'd agree. More than likely that's from using gasoline as an accelerant. It doesn't burn as hot as some of the other combustibles."

The tech has to use a screwdriver and a pair of pliers to get the glovebox open. Inside are only a few papers, but they are in good condition having been protected by the firebox quality of the glovebox.

"Bag those," Striker says. "I want to check them for fingerprints."

"Yes, sir," the tech says, carefully removing the documents. What remains of the rest of the interior is unremarkable.

"Can you tell where the fire started?" Striker asks.

"My bet would be they just poured it over the outside of the car," Patterson says, "and lit it from there. Which is why the interior is still intact. Now if they had doused the interior of the car and let it burn from the inside out, that would have done a lot more damage."

"So we're not necessarily working with someone who has a lot of experience with this," Striker guesses, standing back up.

"Or they were in so much of a hurry they didn't have a choice," Patterson says.

Striker puts his hands on his hips, looking at the back of the car. "Does that mean we might have something in the trunk as well?"

"Given the condition of the interior, I wouldn't be surprised," he says. "It should be mostly the same. If it had burned out, the metal around the trunk itself would be warped more than it is."

"Then let's get to it, none of us are getting any younger."

The team first processes the back of the car for any prints, but the weather and damage burned off anything usable. They then attempt to open the trunk by just breaking the lock, but it seems to have melted shut. They resort to using a couple of sledgehammers to break the lock out and actually pry the back of the car open.

But even as they do, Striker can already see a dark shape inside the trunk. He instructs them to be careful as they use a pair of crowbars to finally break the remaining bolts and lift the trunk cover off the back of the car. As soon as they do, an acrid smell hits Striker's nose.

"What the hell is that?" Patterson asks as his people remove the metal covering and set it to the side.

"It looks like a burlap sack," Striker says. The edges are black and frayed, but it hasn't been burned. "I don't understand. Burlap should be like kindling. Even if the fire just licked it, it should have gone up like newspaper."

Patterson leans down closer and wrinkles his nose. "It

could have been treated. They do sell some specifically treated with chemicals so they don't burn."

"What kind of chemicals?" Striker asks. The smell only grows worse. It's a fetid, harsh odor that Striker doesn't think he's ever encountered before.

"I'm not sure," Patterson says. "There's bromine, phosphorus or nitrogen, graphite, silica or any number of different chemical treatments. Though I've never smelled anything like this."

Striker lifts one end of the sack with his gloved hand. But when he sees what's inside, he calls for the immediate ceasing of activities. "We have a potential biological situation here; I need everyone in protective suits."

Patterson begins backing away. "What's in there?"

"Bones," Striker says. "A lot of them."

Two hours later, Striker is standing in the building's adjacent garage, staring at what is almost a complete human skeleton. Only after everyone had donned complete protective equipment did they begin removing materials from the sack. Thankfully, it looks as though the bones are older than they first appeared. Striker's primary concern was that the body might still be in a state of decomposition, but now that the bag has been emptied and everything laid out, those fears have been put to rest. The bones aren't stark white, but instead a ruddy color, like they've been dunked in mud or brown paint.

"We're going to need a forensic analyst," Striker says as he studies all the bones laid out. They are all in approximately the right location, but someone with a degree will be able to tell him more. Specifically if this victim was male or female, and how old they were when they died. As to the cause of death, he's pretty sure it can be explained by the damage on the back of the skull. A contributing factor at the very least.

"Isn't Higgins an expert on this stuff?" Patterson asks.

"She is, but she's out of town," Striker says. "We need someone now. And we need to figure out if that car belonged to our mystery woman or not."

"My people are already on it. We weren't able to pull any prints from the car itself, but I'm encouraged we might get something from those glovebox papers." He pauses a moment. "Are you going to inform the FBI?"

He already decided he's not going to involve Slate or any of the others in this discovery. Giving them a heads up on finding the car was plenty. He's under no obligation to keep them up to date on the investigation. Especially not when one or more of them might be his suspects. Though, he thinks he might reach back out to Detective Michaels, in the event it turns out this car does belong to the woman in the hospital.

"Why should I?" Striker replies. "It's not their case."

Chapter Nineteen

IT TAKES the rest of the afternoon, but we finally make progress on the case. Zara is able to confirm the license plate on the car that drove Liam to the house is also owned by White Lion Holdings, and it was *also* purchased from a Johannsen Bolo almost a year ago. That is twice this man's name has come up in connection with this company, and I find it more than just a coincidence.

In transferring his assets over to this new start-up of his, Bolo left a trail of breadcrumbs for us to follow about a mile long. The connection was all there; it's just that no one else had spent the time to go this deep and find out what was really going on.

Still, it's all circumstantial, and if we're going to bring Bolo in for questioning, we need concrete evidence that connects him to Red Sunset.

There's a knock at my door and I glance up, deep into research into White Lion Holdings.

"Elliott?" I ask. "Everything okay?"

"I just got off the phone with CBP," he says, coming in. "I think we may have found the identity of one of the women." He lays a piece of paper on my desk. It's written entirely in

Chinese characters, but there's an image of a woman in the top right corner that looks remarkably similar to the Jane Doe down in the morgue. "Her name was Xiang Yu, and she was last seen in the Fujian Province."

"Which is where?"

"Mainland China. Close to Taiwan. CBP's theory is she bartered her way to Taiwan, then was either recruited from there, or came here undocumented and then recruited."

"What do you have on her?"

"Not a lot. Her family has been spending what little money they have putting these out." He motions to the flyer in front of me. "I wanted to check with you before I told CBP to notify the family of her death."

I hand the flyer back to him. "Go ahead. But we need to know how she got from Mainland China to Washington, DC. And is Red Sunset recruiting here or in Taiwan?"

"I'll start checking transport records," he says. "See if anything matches up."

"Good work," I tell him. "I don't know how you managed to find that—"

"I have a mind for faces," he says. "If it weren't for these flyers, I wouldn't have. My guess is the other woman's family isn't as desperate. From what little I could translate; Xiang is her family's only child."

I try to imagine what would have happened if I'd disappeared one day, having been shipped off to another country. My parents would have lost their minds and done almost anything to get me back—maybe I'd have my own flyers plastered with my face in the corner. "Hopefully we can at least give them some closure. Be discreet with the details."

He nods. "Of course."

One victim down. One to go. Though it still doesn't explain why they were both found dead in the same room, which has been sticking in my craw. It's possible there could have been two Johns in the room at once, but the odds that they would both be homicidal at the exact same time? And before they got what they paid for? Unlikely. I feel like something else killed these women, something…bigger.

I dive back into my research, determined to learn more about the actual crime itself. The hardest part about running a team like this is staying on the sidelines while everyone else does the work. Normally, I would have been the one to visit the apartment, to speak with the witnesses. Now I have to read reports on it and trust that my team can make the connections I'm used to making. It seems like everyone else is pulling their weight here and I'm just…what? Twiddling my thumbs, waiting for someone to give me an update?

It's not what I imagined this job would be like.

There's another quick rap on my door, but before I can say anything, Liam barges in, his phone pressed to his ear. "Yes, this is Burnett." He switches the phone to speaker and sets it on my desk.

"Mr. Burnett, I want to first profusely apologize for the treatment you received last night. Based on our research, we believed we were offering you a…unique experience tailored to your tastes. We like to try and anticipate our client's needs."

"Whom am I speaking with?" Liam asks.

"You may call me Mr. Black," the man says. I can't detect any semblance of an accent, so I'm not sure if this is Bolo or not. "I am your client liaison. And again, I would like to apologize. How can we make this up to you?"

"I don't like having my time wasted," Liam says, and I give him a thumbs up. "And I don't like being kept in the dark, especially where my money is concerned."

"No, sir, of course not," Black says. He's contrite, but unflustered.

"In fact, your little outing last night makes me wonder if I want to continue my relationship with your company. You are aware of my investment potential. I heard you were the best, and yet I received a sub-par experience."

"Of course, how can I make this right for you?" Black asks.

I mouth *play along* to him.

Liam nods. "You know I'm not the kind of man to sit around and let a prime opportunity pass me by. Your reputation among my colleagues is good, but it could be better. I'd like to meet to discuss…the future."

"I see." Now it's Black's turn to hesitate. "Usually we don't discuss our business with clients. However, given what happened to you and your…unique perspective on the market, perhaps a meeting would be in order. Are you available this evening?"

I nod.

"What time?" Liam asks.

"Around nine p.m. We can send a car to your house."

"No," Liam says before I can give him the signal. "You've already transported me once without my consent. You won't be doing it again. Give me an address and *I* will meet you there."

"We're not in the business of giving out our addresses, even to someone as established as yourself."

"Then meet me back at the house where I was taken last night," Liam says. "Or, we can forget all of it. I certainly have enough to keep me busy."

"No, I mean, we would be happy to meet back at the Kitlinger Mansion." For the first time, Black sounds on edge. They might be more desperate for investments than we'd anticipated.

"Good, I will arrive by nine," Liam says before killing the call.

"Nicely done," I say. "You've got them eating out of your hand. Whoever this 'Black' is, anyway."

"I'm sure it's nothing but a pseudonym. Red Sunset. White Lion. Mr. Black. See a pattern?"

"Not a very clever one," I add. "I guess you get to play dress-up two nights in a row."

"Lucky me," he deadpans.

~

BY SEVEN THIRTY, LIAM IS DRESSED BACK IN HIS SUIT, although this time Zara has paired it with a different undershirt and shoes to make it look as much like a different set of clothes as possible.

"It won't do us any good if they think you're too poor to own more than one suit," she says, straightening his collar.

"Maybe I'm just eccentric," he says. "Rich people can afford to be a little...off."

"You don't want to frighten them," Nadia says, tapping her ear. "Say something else."

"What, like *test?*"

She taps her ear again. "Perfect, clear as a bell."

"C'mon," I tell Zara. "We need to get going. I want to make sure we're in place long before nine, and it's a bit of a drive."

"Coming, coming," Zara says, putting the final touches on Liam's outfit. "Got the wallet?" He holds it out for her. "Watch?" He pulls back his sleeve, revealing a Hermes Quantieme, courtesy of the closed cases evidence locker. "Good to go?" Liam nods. "Okay," she says, gathering up her laptop. "Let's move."

I motion to Nadia and Elliott. "You have your assignments. Let us know over the comm if you run into any trouble."

"This should go smoothly," Elliott says. "Assuming there are no surprises."

"And you," I say, taking his perfect collar in my fist. "Be careful. No unnecessary risks."

"That's rich, coming from you," he says, grinning. I plant a quick kiss on his lips. "But I'll do my best."

"Good." Zara and I head out as Liam finishes getting ready. We've already procured a non-standard FBI vehicle from the motor pool, something closer to what Black and anyone else might be expecting.

However, one of the big unknowns here is just how many people Liam is going to be facing at once. No doubt the house will be guarded, and we already know there are at least three other men who work in this operation, all three who—according to Liam—could be bouncers due to their size. If he gets in trouble in there, we might not be able to get him out.

"You're thinking about it again, aren't you?" Zara asks as we head down to my car.

"About what?"

"Everything going on with your aunt in the hospital."

"Actually, I was thinking about how we're going to get Liam out of that house if things go wrong," I say.

"Oh, that's good. Progress." She smiles. "Seriously though, Liam is going to be fine. He knows how to handle himself."

"It's not that," I say. "I just…I'm already getting tired of being sidelined. It should be *me* in there."

"You're the boss now," she says. "It can't be you. That's not your job anymore."

"That's just the problem," I say. "I've been thinking about what you said. I need to be in it, not sitting back and watching everyone else do all the work."

"You get high on the action," she says, making a stern face and a fist, like she's going up to fight someone. "And you are every supervisor's worse nightmare."

"What?" I say, laughing as we come into the garage.

"You know you are. You go off on your own, do your own thing half the time, and you skirt the law more often than you want to admit. I think Janice did this to you so you would see what it's like from the *other* side."

"You're making that up." I open my door and slip in as she gets in.

"Hey, I overhear things," she says. "*Private* things. Things no one else should hear."

I can't help but laugh. "And what you hear is I am a terrible employee."

"Yep," she says. "An absolute nightmare. Hell on wheels."

"I'm glad to see you're feeling better. I was worried about you there for a little bit," I tell her as I pull out and through the security gate.

"I got word from Theo last night," she says. "He's coming back to the states. He says this time for an extended period. Though, knowing him, that could just be a week."

"Are you going to talk to him about it?" I ask.

"I don't think I have a choice," she says. "We need to figure out where this thing is going, and if it can last him being away and out of contact for such long periods."

"Has he admitted the MI6 thing is just a cover yet, or is he sticking by his guns?"

"He doesn't like to talk about it," she says. "Which only makes me more curious. But I promised him I wouldn't snoop. When he's ready, he'll tell me."

"Let's just hope he's not running around with someone like Hunter. I would hate for you to be in the same position I was in."

Her face goes stern. "I think if that were to happen, he knows I would absolutely kill him on the spot."

"Perfect," I say. "They say communication is key to a good relationship."

"Okay," Zara says. "Enough talk. Time for some driving music. We've got what, thirty minutes?"

"More or less."

"Then allow me to introduce you to the sultry sounds of *Kool and the Gang.*"

Chapter Twenty

My eyes snap open. Dark room. Dim lights.

Where am I?

To my right, a Blickman four-leg stainless steel IV stand, tube connected to my arm. Two hooks, seventy-pound capacity. One bag of half normal saline, forty-five percent, hangs from the first hook. The line goes directly into my arm, using a winged butterfly, nineteen gauge, three-quarters inch. Blue.

To my left, a Welch Allyn 300 NIPB and SO2 monitor with infrared non-contact thermometer beeps at a steady pace. Seventy-three beats per minute.

I'm alive.

The machines prove it. I should be dead.

I blink, the aqueous humor refreshing my dry eyes. My eyes still work. I attempt to lift my left hand. It obeys. I attempt the same with my right. The response is normal. I lift my head, looking down at the bed in front of me. I'm covered in a standard hospital blanket and am lying in what looks to be Madesite DP 81 hospital bed, but I can't be sure. Though the handles look familiar.

I attempt to wiggle my toes. The response is immediate

and gratifying. I can bend my knees and have full sensation in my legs. Good, I'm not paralyzed.

I should be dead.

The Welch Allyn beeps increase to eighty-one beats per minute. Eighty-six. Ninety.

I must calm down until I know more.

Deep breaths. Calming thoughts.

Eighty-five.

Eighty.

Seventy-five.

That's better.

The room is dark, but a small strip of up lighting surrounds the ceiling, providing enough for me to see. I'm in a private room, and the door is closed almost all the way, though a crack of light spills in from the hallway. A bathroom is to my right. An empty chair sits to my left, as well as a small table with a cup.

I'm thirsty.

I reach over, taking the straw in my mouth, and find luke-warm water, but it's enough to coat my dry throat.

Why am I still here?

The last thing I remember is...the car. The headlights as they illuminated the street in front of them. The asphalt, dry and gritty.

Pain. And then...nothing.

I reach up, feeling my head. A bandage covers the right side, the skin underneath tender. Road rash. I become aware of other points of pain as well. My arms, my hip. My back... aches.

I was hit by a moving vehicle. It was supposed to be the end.

And yet, I am still here.

I search every corner of my mind looking for an explana-tion. Only one thing makes sense. My job isn't finished. I lost my way, but now I have a second chance. A chance to be happy. Why else would it not have worked? Why else would I still be alive?

My course is clear. The job isn't done, but I must go through more trials if I want to find my truth. All these years, all these… obstacles, they have been for one purpose. There is no joy without suffering. No happiness without loss. No love without sacrifice.

I have sacrificed much. But I have been shown a way forward. A future where I am no longer alone. Where I am free.

But I cannot stay here. They wouldn't understand.

They never have.

I glance at the Welch Allyn, holding steady. If I disconnect without shutting the machine down, someone will notice.

I sit up slowly, noting the slight change in blood pressure. The machine has a retail mode, for use when the company is showing it off at trade shows. It even comes pre-loaded with a patient profile. My hands are shaking.

Calm down. Think of the future. Of what you're doing this for.

They steady. I force the machine into retail mode. The new, model patient has perfect vitals. Nothing that will throw up any alarms. I remove the pads from my chest and arm and take off the sensor around my finger.

Next, I disconnect the saline tube and tie it in a loose knot, looping it around the second hook. I'll leave the needle in until I have no other choice. I don't want to leave any extra blood behind.

Someone has secured non-slip socks on my feet. Other than that, I have nothing but a gown. Have they taken my clothes, perhaps destroyed them? Or the police may have kept them, for evidence?

Nothing in the cabinets. Nothing in the storage area. No personal effects. Nothing to leave behind.

The clock reads eight forty-five. They will have finished

dinner service by now. All the doctors will have gone home to sleep. They will need to be up early tomorrow for their rounds. A board on my wall indicates when the last nurse came in to check and tells me I have forty-three minutes before another comes back.

Though I stop, reading further down the board.

It's Saturday. Six days. It must have been an intercranial hematoma. I should expect dizziness, vertigo, headaches.

But I cannot let them stop me. The course is clear, the road ahead open. I just need to leave this place. Find my way back.

I move to the door, opening it slowly. The light from the hallway causes me to wince. It's so bright it hurts. But I look anyway. At one end of the hallway is a nurse's station. At the other end, a vending machine and a sign for a stairwell. I look up. The hospital has cameras.

They won't be monitored. Not all of them. And I have been given this chance. Why did I wake up if I can't leave? Eventually they'll see me, but not right now.

I believe it in my heart. I am free to leave.

Down the hallway. To the stairs. No alarm will sound.

I am in the stairwell. No one came running after me; they didn't see me. This hospital is large—bigger than I expected. I'm four floors up. But what I need will be on the first or the ground floor.

Posted on the outside of the door is a map of the current floor, arrows pointing to the fire exits. I head down to the first floor, taking the stairs one at a time. My balance has been affected, and I have to compensate. I examine the floorplan on the first floor. It doesn't have what I need. I move to the ground floor, which also has an exit to the outside. But an alarm will sound. Can't use that one.

This floorplan, even though the rooms aren't labeled, has what I need. I'd recognize it in any hospital. But I'll have to be cautious. It's next to the ICU. And no matter what time of day, an ICU of this size will have activity.

I peek out the door into the hallway. It's empty. I must be quick. A patient wandering the halls won't be ignored. I would not have ignored one.

My feet are silent on the linoleum floor, the socks giving them grip and purchase. I don't run, my head hurts far too much for that, but I move quickly. This isn't dissimilar from that time—

Can't get distracted. The ICU is ahead of me, its double doors sealing off the unit from errant wanderers. The room I need is close, on my left. But my ears catch the sound of a heavy *click*, indicating the ICU is about to be opened.

I duck to my left, the door to the room I need is marked *Authorized Personnel Only* and unlocked. Strange. It should require a keycard. Perhaps they are relying on the sign to keep people out.

Or, I may be incorrect, and this is not the room I'm looking for.

But as I enter and turn around the corner, I see I have made the correct assessment. Long lockers line both walls, and small benches sit in the middle. I walk down the row, checking each door and finding most of them locked. But I come to one that hasn't been fully secured.

Someone was in a hurry.

I'll use it.

Inside are jeans and a plain blouse, the nurse's change of clothes for when their shift ends. I put the clothes on quickly even though they aren't a great fit. The pants are too tight, so I leave them unbuttoned but keep the shirt untucked so it covers them. The shoes are also tight, so I remove the socks and go without.

I must hurry. There isn't a lot of time left. Every minute I stay here risks exposure.

Inside the small bag at the top of the locker is a wallet and set of keys. I take the keys and remove what little cash is in the wallet. Sixteen dollars. It will have to do. The keys have a fob for a vehicle.

That's all I need.

Before I leave, I take an extra towel from the shower area, wrapping it around my head and neck like a headscarf. It won't pass close scrutiny, but I won't need that.

I check the hallway once again. Whoever came out of the ICU is gone, and the hallway is again empty. I quickly head down the corridor until I emerge into the main atrium.

A man sits at a desk not far away, reading something on his phone. I don't look at him, don't wave. Don't call any attention to myself.

Instead, I walk purposefully towards the elevators that will take me to the garage. The wait is excruciating.

But the guard doesn't move.

I get on the elevator, which takes me to the underground. There is a small glass atrium down here as well, and a car running just outside. A woman in her eighties sits in the passenger side. As I pass, I wonder where the driver is.

My finger presses the fob, listening and watching for any vehicle that will respond.

None do.

I must go deeper. But I don't return to the elevators. I take the stairs down a level to employee parking. I use the fob down here, and a gray Toyota chirps back at me.

I am inside the car, feeling the warmth of the vents as the engine heats up. I pull out of the garage, into the night. The lights are like starbursts, shining too bright. But I can see the lines. The car has three-quarters of a tank. Sixteen dollars in my pocket.

It will have to be enough.

What will happen when they find me gone? They will notify the authorities, there's no question of that. But will they notify...*her*? I saw her, in those final moments. I saw her face clearly. It was as close as I'd ever been to her. And she looked just as I imagined she would.

They will tell her. They'll have to.

Then…she'll come. She has no choice. After all, she's a good daughter.

One who would never disobey me.

Chapter Twenty-One

"HERE HE COMES." Zara is looking through her binoculars at the house she's dubbed the "sex mansion," approximately five hundred yards away. We're parked on a small hill that sits opposite the side road leading to the house. It's not ideal, but it's the closest we could get without getting on the cameras. Nadia and Elliott are on the other side of the subdivision, beyond the tree line and out of view.

Zara hands the binoculars to me and I squint. It's difficult to make out in the dark, but I see Liam's car approaching the turn off to the side street. He turns, then makes his way down to the gates. "Approaching slow from the south," I say.

"Here we go," he says over the comms. He doesn't sound nervous; instead he's focused, ready. Liam has this way of radiating a quiet intensity that really only shows up in his work. It's something I first noticed about him when we met in Stillwater, and it's probably what makes him so good at his job. He can always maintain his cool.

The gates open after he presses the small button on the keypad next to the door and announces himself. He pulls the FBI's Maserati in, and the gates shut behind him.

"If we have to go in there, we're going to have a problem with those," Zara says.

"Is there anything you can do?"

She gets up and manages to squeeze herself into the back-seat of the SUV, opening her laptop. "Let me see if they're using a wavelength signal. If we're lucky, it will be on a remote. If it's hard-wired under the ground, that makes things more complicated."

I keep watching as Liam navigates the driveway until he's right in front of the large house. Because we're at an angle, I don't have a good view of the front of the home, but I can just barely see his car over the roof. He gets out as a man comes into view, presumably from the front steps.

"Mr. Burnett," the man says. "Welcome back."

Liam doesn't reply as he walks past the man and into the shadow of the house where I can't see him any longer. I put the binoculars down as I hear a door open.

"Glad you could make it," I hear a voice say. "I'm Mr. Black. We spoke on the phone."

"Leo Burnett," he says.

"Yes, we know," Black says, but there's something in the way he says it that sends a chill down my spine. Like he knows *more*. Is it possible they could have gotten past Nadia and Zara's background? I turn to her, a worried look on my face.

"He's just posturing," she reassures me. "Someone would have to be at least as good as me to know it's a cover."

While I don't doubt Zara's abilities, there's no telling who this man has on his payroll. And given we had trouble with the site until we were granted access by Okusaka, it doesn't leave a good feeling in my gut.

"Please," Black says. "If you'll come with me. May I get you a drink? We have a fully-stocked bar. Any kind of rare liquor you could imagine."

"No," Liam says. "This isn't a social call."

"Of course not," Black replies. "I'd like to personally apol-

ogize to you for our...oversteps." I can imagine the two of
them walking side by side down the hallway Liam described. I
don't know why, but I picture Black on the shorter side. A little
weasel of a man whose primary job is to kiss the asses of his
clients.

But what I really want is the boss man. Whether that be
Bolo or someone else entirely.

"This way," Black says.

"This is a different direction than yesterday," Liam says.

"Yes, we've sequestered the...entertainment...in the west
wing for the time being. So we do not accidentally repeat our
previous mistake. I'm sure you understand."

"Good," Liam says, confident.

"Here we are," Black says. "The library. I must admit,
every time I come in here, I am in a state of awe."

I look through the binoculars again and see that he's
talking about a room in the back of the house, one with large,
plate glass windows that run from the ground up two floors to
the ceiling. I can see Liam inside, taking it in. The walls are
lined with rows and rows of shelves full of books. And in the
middle of the room is a large signature desk, surrounded by
plush chairs.

"Make yourself comfortable. Our host will be with you
soon."

"Who is my host?" Liam asks. "I thought I was meeting
with you."

I catch sight of Black. He's not as short as I had thought,
but he's thin. Wiry, and his hair matches his name. From this
angle, I can see it's been slicked back. And he's got a thin
moustache. If I'm not mistaken, the man is of Asian descent.

"No, you'll be meeting with our owner, Viridian."

Viridian? I mouth to Zara.

She shrugs. "Maybe he'll get to meet Azure, Roan, and
Puce next."

"Only if we're lucky," I say as I hear the door to the

library close. Through the binoculars, Liam walks around the library, looking around for anything that might be helpful, just like I would be doing in his position.

Finally, I hear the door open, and Liam turns to meet his host. "Mr. Burnett," the man says with a slight accent. I can't place it, but it could be Indonesian.

"You must be Mr. Viridian," Liam says. I can't see the other man yet, but Liam doesn't raise his hand to shake or make any other move toward him.

"Just Viridian, please," the man replies. He walks into view, but I can only see his back as he circles around the desk and sits down, indicating Liam take a seat across from him.

"That's an interesting name. I don't think I've ever heard it before."

"I would think you of all people could respect the need for a pseudonym," Viridian says.

"Shit, has he been made?" I ask. "Anything on those gates yet?"

"Nothing," Zara says. "I'm still looking."

"Look harder."

"Why do you say that?" Liam asks, his posture unchanged. If he's rattled, he's not showing it.

Viridian holds out one hand as if to make a generalized gesture. "You've been in this business long enough. Surely you know not everyone appreciates what we do. What we bring to the table, as it were."

"I don't hide behind pseudonyms," Liam says. "And I don't play games. I'm here to talk business. Particularly yours, because trust me, you're bad at it."

"Nice," Zara whispers.

I can't tell if Viridian is squirming yet as I can't get a read on him. But Liam can be intimidating when he wants to be, ad he hasn't even sat down yet.

"I know Mr. Black has already offered our apologies. How can we make this up to you?"

I can't see it clearly, but I can hear the placating smile in Liam's voice. "Allow me to do something for *you*."

"For us?" Viridian asks, clearly confused.

"You seem to be in desperate need of a consultant. Someone who knows this business inside and out. And who can help you navigate the dangerous waters you've found yourself in."

"I can assure you; we have all the *advice* we need."

"Do you?" Liam demands. "Because that's not what I saw. I saw a piss poor attempt to create an experience for someone who you thought you knew. I saw your men stumble over themselves in an attempt to service their customer—and fail spectacularly at it." He approaches the desk and places both of his hands on it, staring directly at Viridian. What I wouldn't give to have a glimpse of the man's face, just to see if we could match it to Bolo. "You wasted my time. And yours. And by any other measure, you would have lost me as a client."

"But your entry fee—"

"Do you really think I'm going to lose sleep over ten grand?" Liam asks. "It's a wonder you've retained any of your clients."

Viridian clears his throat. "Most of our clients are…well, I must admit they aren't as established as you are."

"You mean they aren't as knowledgeable."

"And what would you want in return for your services as a consultant?" Viridian asks.

"A stake in your company," Liam says. "And a voice at the table. If for no other reason than to prevent fuck-ups like this in the future."

I can just imagine Viridian going red in the face. Liam's entire posture is designed to throw the man off guard, to crack him so Liam can worm his way inside.

"As much as we *appreciate* the offer, I don't think we'll be needing your services at this time," he finally says.

"Yeah?" Liam asks. "What about those two dead girls? How's that going for you?" We had discussed the possibility of bringing this up if he wasn't getting anywhere. It's another gamble, but I trust Liam to know what he's doing in there. If he thinks it's necessary, then we go with it.

"I'm afraid I don't know what you're talking about," the man says, but there's a waver in his voice.

"That's interesting, because I happen to know both women worked for Red Sunset and were listed on your site. See, believe it or not, I wouldn't be here if this was over something as trivial as a fake kidnapping dolled up as a sexual fantasy. I'm here because if *I* know about those two women, so do the authorities."

I catch Viridian clear his throat. If only he would turn around, we could get a clear shot of him. Zara has climbed into the front seat again and has the long camera lens in her hand, ready to take a picture, but his high-backed chair is preventing us from getting a good bead on him.

"What is your suggestion?" Viridian finally asks.

"No, you don't get my services for free," Liam says. "Agree to my terms, and we'll talk."

Viridian lets out a long breath. "Will you excuse me for a moment? I need to speak with some of my colleagues. In private."

"Of course," Liam says. The other man gets up and leaves the room, but we still don't have a good shot of his face.

"This is infuriating," I say. I click the radio on. "Liam, I have eyes on you. Stay sharp."

"Wait a second," Zara says. "I've got an outgoing call on one of the phone lines." She taps a few keys on her laptop, and I hear a dial tone.

"Speak." I don't recognize the voice, but it's harsh and unyielding.

"I'm with Burnett." It's Viridian. "He knows about Xiang and Yachi." I write down the second name.

"How?"

"I don't know. He wants to *consult*. He says to prevent something like that in the future."

"Fuck him," the unknown voice says.

"But the money——"

"We don't need the money. Are you so greedy that you're blind to what's in front of you? Do what needs to be done." The line clicks off.

"Shit," I say, opening the line to Liam again. "Heads up," I say. "I think they're coming for you."

"I've got multiple radio transmissions," Zara says. "Just one word. *Rapture.*"

"This is Kane," Nadia says over our secure line. "There's some movement over on the east side of the building. I've got security personnel moving about, quickly. One of them is heading for Liam's car. The others are entering the house through the back."

"Everyone, move in," I say, starting the car. "I hope you have that gate code," I tell Zara.

"Still working on it," she says, putting the camera away in the back as I pull out onto the road. I slam on the gas and tear down the pavement until we reach the side street.

"Mr. Burnett," I hear Viridian say over Liam's radio. "I'd like to thank you for your offer, but we will have to decline at the present."

"Sure you know how to wield that thing?" Liam asks. "That's a Baretta 9-millimeter isn't it?"

"Shit, shit, shit," I say, speeding up even faster. We reach the gates, but they're still closed. "Z!"

"I can't get them, I think they're hard-wired," she says.

"We'll do it the old-fashioned way, then." I press my foot to the floor. "Brace!" We both hold on as the vehicle slams into the metal gate. At first, I don't think it's going to work, but as the thoughts fire through my brain the gates give and fly off their hinges as the SUV roars through.

A siren blares over Liam's radio along with what sounds like grunting and struggle. Behind us, Elliott's SUV is close on our heels. I pull up to the front of the house to see a startled-looking man in a black suit who is just about to get into Liam's car.

"FBI, freeze!" I yell, jumping out and leveling my weapon at him. But instead of doing as he's told, he pulls out a gun from his jacket and begins firing directly at us.

"Christ," I swear, jumping behind the door of the SUV in time to feel a bullet slam into the other side. "Take cover!" I poke my head out and back for a quick assessment and see he's situated himself behind Liam's car door, effectively blocking him from our fire. Another round hits the windshield, shattering the safety glass. In my ear, I can still hear Liam and Viridian struggling for the gun, along with the siren that won't shut up.

I check the cover again and this time fire off two rounds that go into the side of the Maserati.

"Second shooter!" Zara calls out, and I do another quick check, seeing the second security guard who has taken cover behind one of the person-sized concrete planters that sit on the front porch.

More bullets slam into the SUV. One of us is going to get killed if we don't do something, quick.

"Cover fire!" I yell out. I hear multiple rounds coming from Zara, and I presume Elliott and Nadia. I check again and see both men have ducked down behind their respective covers. I stay low, advancing as quickly as I can until I'm up on the Maserati. Before I can think too hard about it, I circle around the door, surprising the man behind and slam the butt of my gun on his hands, causing him to drop his weapon. He grapples for me, but I manage to elbow him in the stomach, and he doubles over. I have him on the ground and a zip tie around his hands as he curses me out in a different language. I may not understand the words, but their meaning is clear enough.

I level my weapon at the man behind the planter, of whom I have a clear shot now, though he's looking around the other side, probably trying to figure out where the others are.

"Drop it!" I yell. He turns to me, and I see the rage plain on his face, so I squeeze off a round which embeds itself into the concrete six inches from his head. "Now!"

I can see him processing the decision, but he finally lays the weapon on the ground, holding his hands up. "Move in!" I call out.

Elliott is the first on him, wrestling him down with Nadia's help as Zara comes up behind me. "Is he secure?" she asks. I nod. Somewhere in the fray, I've lost my earpiece, so I have no idea what's going on in the house.

"C'mon, we need to get to Liam."

She's right behind me as we make our way inside, checking each doorway before we enter. The house is a potential land mine; there's no telling how many security personnel are here. But before we can make it very far, two figures emerge from one of the back doorways. I raise my weapon at first, then drop it when I see Liam has the other man in custody and is leading him in our direction.

"It's clear," he calls out. "*Viridian* here has assured me he only had two security guards working this evening."

I holster my weapon, coming up to meet the man in person. He's about my height, and I catch a whiff of something floral when I'm in his presence. "Well," I say, looking into his green eyes. "Pleasure to finally meet you, Mr. Bolo."

Chapter Twenty-Two

A FURTHER SEARCH of the house revealed Mr. Black hiding in the basement, who Zara recognized as one of Bolo's partners in his accounting firm, a Martin Huang. However, that wasn't the only thing we found down there.

Apparently, the basement was where they kept all the women who "lived" at this house. We counted seven small beds, but only six different women, all of whom spoke only very broken English. When we called for backup, we made sure to loop in CBP and the local DC cops so we could get an interpreter. The women were skittish, not understanding what was going on, even as we showed them our badges and tried to explain to them that they were safe. I had to tell Liam to leave because they were all shooting him glances, I'm sure because they recognized him as a "client" from the night before.

"It's a mess down there," Zara says. She's right. The basement was segmented off with curtained divisions, one room for bathing and showers, one for beds, one for prep, and there was a small table for what looked like meals. These women lived in squalor when they weren't "on the job."

"I can't wait to get Bolo into an interview room," she adds. "I hope he saved some money for a lawyer."

"Him and his goons," I say. Though, we know there are more out there. Whoever he spoke with on the phone is still at large, which is why I'm trying to keep as much of a lid on this as I can. But I'm sure he's going to be more difficult to find. Not only that, but we know they have more properties and more women held somewhere. These six only represent a small number of those available on the website.

Finally, an interpreter from CBP arrives and begins explaining the situation to the women. Because these women are all undocumented immigrants, we're going to end up handing them over to immigration, but my hope is we can at least get them into some regular clothes and a few hot meals before they're sent back to their families in Taiwan or China.

"This isn't going to go over well," I say as Zara and I investigate the rest of the house. Nadia took charge of the arrests of the two security guards and Bolo, all of which are being transported back to headquarters as we speak.

"I can't wait to turn in my firearm for IA to do their investigation," she says. "That's *never* an inconvenience."

"Hey," I say, looking around the impressive library where Liam managed to overpower Bolo. "You could have always just stayed in the car."

"And let you get shot? Not likely," she says, looking at an errant bullet hole in one of the books. Bolo tried discharging the weapon twice while he and Liam were struggling. It's a miracle neither of them were hurt. "By the way, what are you going to tell the motor pool when you have to return that Maserati full of holes?"

I run a gloved hand over the books, finding a few that don't seem to match the others. I press on them, but instead of slotting back into the bookcase, a false door pops open, revealing a medium-sized safe.

"Oh, I think accounting will let me get away with it.

Remind me when we interrogate Bolo that we need the combination for this thing. I'm sure my missing ten grand is in here somewhere."

"Good find," she says, coming over. "You know, get me a stethoscope and I could probably crack this baby."

"As much as I know you'd love to try, we have other work to do. We need to lean on Bolo and Black as soon as possible. I don't want to lose what momentum we have." We head back down the hallway as I pull off my gloves, passing a couple of CSI techs in their white zip-up suits as they head in the direction of the basement.

"Can we at least grab something to eat first? I'm starving."

"As long as you make it quick."

WE LEAVE OUR RUINED SUV AT THE HOUSE AND TAKE another unit back to the bureau, stopping to grab some late-night fast food on the way. Liam insists on something healthy, but given it's close to eleven at night, our options are limited. We manage some chicken sandwiches that aren't completely fried to death and the entire way back, Zara goes on and on about how good the fat is and how much she *loves it.*

Frankly, I don't think the events of the evening have fully sunk in yet. All three of us were in mortal danger not two hours ago, and yet here we are, yukking it up like a bunch of college kids as we head back to the bureau. I think part of that is needing to let go of all that adrenaline from the shootout, while the other part is my preoccupation with how this interrogation is going to go. By the time we get back, Nadia should have all of them processed and ready to go.

Before we even reach the elevators, we're met by Internal Affairs. Normally, it would have been Janice's job to inform them that agents discharged their weapons in the line of duty, but that responsibility fell to me and was one of the first things

I had to do as we were securing the site. They relieve me and Zara of our firearms, but seeing as Liam never discharged his, he's allowed to keep it. We go through the standard interview following fire in the field and fill out the proper paperwork before they let us go. I was hoping they would wait until morning, but apparently I'm not the only one who keeps late hours.

By the time we're finally done and back in the office, it's past midnight, all of us having finished off what was left of our "dinner."

"I called in some additional help," Nadia says, meeting us at the doors. "I hope you don't mind. But I figured we'd need all hands on deck for this one."

"No, it was a good call," I tell her. "Where are we?"

"The guards, Samuel Ignacio and Milos Harakal have both been detained downstairs. Bolo has called for a lawyer, and Huang hasn't said a word since he arrived. We've kept them all separated and haven't allowed them to interact."

"Good work," I tell her. "I want to start with Bolo."

She looks around us. "Elliott didn't come back with you?"

"He stayed on site," Zara says. "He's coordinating the investigation from there and making sure everything is catalogued."

She smiles. "That sounds like him. Here, Bolo is down on three. But I'll warn you now, he's not talking."

"Let me speak with him," Liam says. "Maybe I can get something else out of him." I nod, and the four of us head downstairs where FBI personnel are working on background checks of all four men. I have to admit, this investigation has become a lot larger than I'd originally anticipated. I'd hoped to just find the culprit behind the deaths of two young women, but now we've ended up with a multi-departmental investigation, spanning two, maybe three countries.

We check in with the team keeping an eye on Bolo through the monitors hooked up to one of the interrogation rooms. "How long has he been in there?" I ask, watching the man on the screen. He's sitting at the far end of the table, a small cup of water at his side. His hands are bound by handcuffs, which are attached to the nearby wall.

"About thirty minutes," one of the techs says. "He's keeping pretty quiet."

"You're up," I tell Liam, who nods. I head in behind him. Bolo doesn't react when we come in, and I take up a position in the back of the room, leaning against the wall as Liam sits down across from him.

"How's your evening going?" Liam asks.

"I want my lawyer," Bolo says.

"Mine's not bad, thanks for asking." Liam smiles. "Let's get started. First, I'd like to congratulate you on being such a massive fuck-up that you decided attempting to kill an FBI agent was an appropriate way out."

Bolo grimaces.

"So, we have you on attempted murder. Also on sex trafficking, conspiracy, aiding and abetting, immigration, kidnapping—the women, not me—assault and finally, tax evasion."

"Tax evasion?" he asks, incredulous.

"I'm assuming you haven't been reporting all your income from your little Red Sunset operation to the IRS. Correct me if I'm wrong, though."

Bolo just stares the man down.

"I see here you gained your American citizenship in 2009. Congratulations. Consider that revoked."

"You can't do that," he protests.

"You don't seem to understand your position here. I don't care if you have the best lawyer in the world," Liam says. "You are fucked, my friend. Your only hope to see the sun again one day is to cooperate fully and completely."

Bolo's eyes are wild, scanning the room. He flits his gaze to me for a second, but I don't give an inch. Liam is doing a fine job on his own; he doesn't need any help from me. "W-what do you want?"

"First? The name of the person you spoke with on the phone. Name, address, relationship to you. Everything."

"You heard that?" he asks.

I can't help myself. "You really aren't very bright, are you?" We're used to working with people who know our methods a little better. Criminals who aren't stupid. "Do you not realize we can tap your phones? Listen to your conversations?"

"I thought—I thought you needed a warrant—"

"Who said we didn't have one?" Liam asks. "Huang *showed* me women who had clearly been trafficked. Me, a federal officer."

"Who was on the other end of the phone?" I ask.

"What...um, what do I get in return?" he asks, his voice shaky.

I don't want to give this creep an inch. And if he were smart enough to shut up until his lawyer arrived, I'm sure they could negotiate a better deal for him. But he's here, talking to us now. And I want to pump him for every ounce of information he's stupid enough to cough up. He deserves to be in prison for the rest of his life as far as I'm concerned. What he's done to those women, what he's put them through. It deserves multiple life sentences.

"We won't pursue the death penalty."

Liam turns around so Bolo can't see his face and shoots a questioning look at me, eyebrow arched. Generally, we don't pursue the death penalty anyway in these kinds of cases, but I'm betting Mr. Bolo doesn't know that.

He's visibly sweating now, and I can see him working it through. The thought of a needle in his arm being the last thing he ever feels can't be sitting well, at least not for someone whom I would describe as used to a certain amount of comfort. I'd be happy if he got a life sentence with no possibility of parole, but I'm also not going to lose any sleep over fibbing to the man.

"He's uh, his name is Therron. Therron Crowley," Bolo says.

"Who is he to you?" I ask.

"I met him at Brown," Bolo admits. "We've stayed in touch. He was…I mean, we were—are friends. We got along well."

"What does he do now?" Liam asks.

"He does something with climate regulations," Bolo says. "With the US Congress. He was in private practice for a while, but then started lobbying."

I cross my arms, already guessing which side of the fence the man is on. "How did you get into business together?"

"We approached him, Martin and I. When you're in our business, you tend to find out all of your clients' dirty little secrets and the ways around them. We were doing it so often we figured why not set up a business where our clients could… act in a risk-free way."

"You mean illegally," I say.

"We figured if we owned the company and the transaction, it would be easier to cover up," he admits.

"And you decided shipping in people from another country was a good way to keep your overhead costs low," I say.

He gives us a sheepish look. "It was a win-win. We didn't have anyone asking questions about where these women were, Martin speaks Mandarin so he could interpret, and we got to keep a greater percent of the profit."

"So why bring in Crowley?" I ask.

"He had access to another client base," Bolo says. "He could attract people with bigger pockets."

I shake my head, unable to believe what I'm hearing.

"I guess you didn't plan on how…*rough* your clients could

be with your *assets*. Considering what happened to two of them," Liam says.

"That...wasn't a client," Bolo says. "That was Crowley."

Liam and I exchange a stunned look. "What?" Liam asks.

"One of the reasons he agreed to join the business model was free use of the gi—women at any time. In the beginning, we didn't see a problem with it. But then they started showing up with bruises, marks that were hard to hide for our other clients. I tried telling him to cool it, but Crowley isn't the kind of man who takes orders." Bolo drops his head. "We never thought he would take it this far."

I lean forward. "What happened?"

"I don't know exactly. All I do know is he called us, saying we needed to clean up the apartment at Westwood. Martin and I didn't know what he meant until we got over there. But when we found what he'd done...we just left. I didn't know what to do about it."

"He never gave you a reason?"

"No, and Xiang and Yachi were his favorites. I don't know what happened."

"Where can we find Crowley?" Liam asks.

My phone buzzes but I ignore it as Liam continues to press Bolo. He seems reluctant to give up Crowley's location, though I don't know why. My phone buzzes again and this time I pull it out, seeing that it's Caruthers.

"I'll be right back," I tell Liam as he lays into Bolo, doing everything he can to get the man to release the information.

"Slate," I say to Caruthers. "What's going on? It's late."

"Agent Slate," he says, and I can already hear in his voice that something is wrong. "I'm afraid I have some bad news."

Chapter Twenty-Three

I STORM INTO THE HOSPITAL, scanning the people working at the front desk. A security guard standing close stiffens and reaches a hand toward his weapon. I pull out my badge. "FBI. Where is Striker?"

The guard relaxes as the worker at the information points down the hallway. "At the end of the hall. Personnel lockers."

I don't bother thanking them, instead I seethe my way down the hallway, the man in the dark coat my primary target. He spots me coming and takes a step back, holding up one hand. "Hang on there, Agent, not so fast."

"You must be kidding," I growl as I approach him. "How could you let her go?"

"We didn't *let* her go," Striker says. "She must have woken up and left on her own."

"You didn't think to post a guard outside her room? Or handcuff her to the bed? How could she have left without anyone seeing?" I'm practically rumbling with rage, and not being shy about it.

"We're trying to figure that out right now," he says. "One of the nurse's cars is missing from the parking garage. I've already put out an APB for it."

"I swear to god, you have to be the most incompetent—"

"Careful, Agent," he warns. "I've been open to including you on this investigation up until now, but don't try my patience."

"What patience?" I demand. "All I see here is incompetence."

As Striker and I are about to come to blows, a large but thin figure appears in my periphery. "Agent Slate, I see you made good time." I turn to see Caruthers, looking out of breath for the first time since I've known him.

"I don't know what either of you think you're doing here," Striker says. "This is a DC police matter. And until I say otherwise, it's going to stay that way."

"I wouldn't be so sure," I say, my anger seeping through my veins. "If she's left the city, which I'm sure she has, this becomes a federal matter."

"I will *not* have you inserting yourself into an investigation in which you are a suspect," Striker yells.

I swear my restraint can only hold so long. I'm still running on the adrenaline from the shootout and then the interrogation and I only have so much self-control. "Let's take a breath, here," Caruthers says. "We aren't going to find her by pointing fingers."

"Why wasn't she locked down?" I demand.

"There wasn't a need. She was in a *coma*. I just learned this evening there had been some mild improvement yesterday and they'd taken her of the ventilator to move her to another room. I wasn't aware she was on the sixth floor until they called and told me she was missing."

"For *fuck's sake*," I seethe.

Striker straightens, and it's almost as if his shoulders grow broader. "Now that I have you here, maybe you can tell me why we found an entire skeleton in the back of the car you identified."

"What?" I shoot a glance at Caruthers, but he seems as surprised as I am.

"It was stuffed in a burlap sack that had been treated to be fire retardant."

"Whose skeleton is it?" I ask.

"We're working on that. My team is trying to gather DNA to be sent off for analysis. Other than that, we don't have any information. However, we were able to confirm the make and model of the vehicle. It was a brown 1979 Ford Granada, same as the one you issued the alert for last week."

"I don't understand," I say. "She was driving around with a skeleton in her trunk?"

"It appears that way," he says, hesitating. "If you don't mind me asking, where have you been since six p.m. this evening?"

"Oh, you *can't* be serious," I say.

"I have a job to do, Agent. I would think you, of all people, could appreciate that."

I grimace, not wanting to give him the satisfaction. "I've been heading up an undercover operation. And if you must know, I was almost just killed in a shootout in someone's front yard. So yeah, I've been busy tonight. Though I guess I could have found time to come over here and help my aunt escape. It's not like I wanted to sit down and ask her why she's been stalking me for the past three months." I glare at him.

"I can confirm," Caruthers says. "Supervisory Special Agent Slate headlined the operation all evening."

"Wait, a shootout?" Striker says. "Not that thing up in North Potomac?"

I nod. "That's the one. We requested backup support from DC police."

"I heard it come over the callbox," he says. "Sorry. I didn't realize. But you can't blame me for being suspicious. I know the two of you are operating your own investigation. And I know about the blood sample you're analyzing."

"Call it a backup," I say. "In case someone decided to alter the evidence."

"You really think I would do that?" he asks, defensive.

"I've already had one detective try to pin something on me and my fellow agent that wasn't our fault. I'm just being cautious."

He studies me, as if trying to figure out if I'm telling the truth or not. "Okay. If you get your test back before we do, will you share your findings? I think I can firmly say you're not a suspect in this now."

"Thank you," I tell him, shooting a glance at Caruthers. He nods. "Agent Caruthers here will coordinate with your office once the tests come back."

"I appreciate that," Striker says, his voice having softened a bit. "Things don't always move fast for the smaller departments."

"They don't move fast for anyone," Caruthers says.

I look at the locker room, which has been partitioned off with police tape. "What happened in there?"

"Apparently, she stole the nurse's clothes, then her car. We're reviewing the tapes to see exactly when she left."

"When did they notice her missing?"

"Nine o'clock rounds."

"And where are the security tapes?" He motions for me to follow, and we leave Caruthers talking to one of the CSI techs at the scene. A couple of other officers mill about, some of them shooting me looks.

"I'm sorry, Agent Slate," Striker says. "When we first met, I didn't know if I could trust you or not. This isn't your normal case."

"For any of us," I say, some of the heat leaving me. Striker is just doing his job; he's not malicious about it like Michaels, and I need to cut him a break.

"Whoever this woman is, whether she's your relative or not, she apparently had intimate knowledge of this hospital in order to get around so effortlessly." He leads me into a small security room where another officer is sitting with a hospital employee, running through the tapes.

"Evening Reg," the officer at the desk says. "I think we might have figured this out." He nods to the hospital employee, who rewinds all the feeds and pulls up one image on the screen. "This is the hallway." On the screen, Emily steps out of her room and, without even looking behind her, walks confidently down the hallway toward the stairs.

"No one saw her?" I ask.

"We don't actively monitor the cameras," the hospital employee says. "We don't have the manpower for that. It's just for record keeping. This isn't a prison." The next image shows a stairwell as Emily heads down at a slightly quicker pace, but she's holding tight to the handrail. As best I can tell, she's a little unsteady on her feet.

"Well, at least she's not completely insane. She knows she's under a clock to move." The image flips again, and this time it's of the hallway Striker and I just came from. Emily exits the stairwell, makes a straight path to the door, and enters the employee locker area.

"Not locked?" I ask.

"We don't keep it locked in case someone accidentally leaves their keycard inside. It's happened more often than you'd think," the employee says. "And there are no cameras inside, for privacy."

A few minutes later, Emily comes out, dressed in somewhat loose-fitting clothes. "Is that a towel on her head?"

"To cover the bandage," Striker deduces. She makes her way down to the elevators where she gets on and the footage ends.

"Is that it?" I ask.

"We don't have cameras in the parking garage, except at the exit. That camera caught a still image of the car leaving, but that's all."

"As I said, we already have an APB out on the car," Striker reiterates. "We'll find her."

"She won't stay in that car," I say. "She's obviously too smart for that." I check my phone. It's been almost four hours since she went missing.

"Do you have any idea where she might go?" Striker asks.

A pressure has built up inside my head, one that feels like it might actually erupt if I'm not careful. This woman has been chasing me down for the better part of three months, and now she's back out there again. But she's not just going to sit around. And now she knows I've seen her. She's baited me for the last time. I need to end this.

"No. But I have a feeling with enough time, I can figure it out."

Chapter Twenty-Four

I PICK up the laminated menu, flipping it back and forth, though nothing looks good. My stomach is unsettled. A cup of coffee sits on the table in front of me, quickly losing what little heat it had since the waitress last warmed it up. I should eat something, but I am ninety percent sure anything that goes down will just come back up. Anything but coffee, that is. I've done something terrible, and in my heart of hearts I know it. I've broken the trust of the people I love the most. And the worst part is I didn't have a choice. Or did I? Am I just that stubborn? Or can some part of me not accept something good when it comes my way? Am I doomed to sabotage everything I hold dear for the rest of my life?

As I turn and look past the faces of the people in the diner, at the morning sun as it falls in slats across the tables, I'm reminded of how fragile it all is. Of how quickly it can all disappear.

My phone buzzes for what has to be the fiftieth time in two days. I pull it out and see I've missed another call from Liam. I also have over a hundred texts from Zara pleading with me to call her back or Liam, or anyone. She's worried about me. They all are.

I'm worried about me too. After learning that Striker had nothing to go on, I knew this investigation would be starting over from scratch. It was glaringly obvious, almost as if the past couple of weeks hadn't even mattered. And I was faced with a decision: let other people determine my fate or take it by the reins and do something about it. Ever since my promotion, I've felt like I've been sitting on the sidelines, unable to control what's been happening around me. And while maybe I could accept that for a case where I don't have a personal connection, this is different. This is my *family*. This is my life.

Emily is cunning. She's dangerous. She wants me. And I'm going to make sure I deliver, without any collateral damage. Liam has already risked his life trying to find her. Zara barely survived one megalomaniac who drove her to the verge of sanity. I'm not putting this pressure on them. Even though I know they would both be here in a heartbeat, they have both risked more than enough for me. I won't put them in the crosshairs again. Especially not when it has to do with *my* family.

It's been two days since I left D.C. My phone has basically been ringing nonstop since that night at the hospital. And all I have with me is my emergency bag of clothes and toiletries. I had to stop and pick up another phone charger somewhere in Pennsylvania. I shouldn't have left them all there, but I know the team can handle Bolo and the fallout. They are good at their jobs, and they don't need me there telling them what to do. Meanwhile, I need to take care of this on my own. To see it through to the end. Because until I confront her, she's never going to stop.

When Detective Striker asked me if I knew where she was going, I flat out lied to him. There's only one place she would go: back home. Which is why I'm just outside the Millridge, Ohio city limits. She's in there somewhere, waiting. And I think she knows I'm coming. My only explanation for her being able to leave the hospital so naturally is that she's had experience in the field. She may have even been a hospital employee once. The point is, I don't know. I don't know anything else about her, but I am determined to find out at any cost.

I've been keeping up with any updates on the case by monitoring the local chatter between here and D.C. The car she stole was found abandoned in the middle of a field in West Virginia. Even though it's not exactly on the route to Mill-ridge, I know that's where I'll find her. She's chased me all this time, now it's my turn.

My phone buzzes again and it's filled with a string of expletives from Zara, along with a long string of emoji's I don't cognitively understand, but I can feel their meaning. I'm betraying her and I know it. She may never forgive me for this, but if I had told her she would have insisted on coming along. And right now, anyone close to me is in danger. The way Emily tried to run us off the road is proof enough of that. She doesn't care who gets hurt in her pursuit of me. So until I can contain her, this is a solo act.

The waitress approaches, pencil in hand. "Decide on something for breakfast?"

"I'll just stick with the coffee, thanks," I say.

She takes the laminated menu. "You visitin' family from out of town?"

"Something like that," I say.

"Well, if you change your mind, just flag me down." She heads back in the direction of the kitchen. My phone buzzes again, but this time it's from Nadia and is nothing more than a link to a news story. I tap it and see the headline: *FBI Brings Down City-Wide Sex Trafficking Ring*. I smile as I read through the details of the story, about how several suspects have already been charged and that the FBI is still searching for more victims. There's a picture of Liam and Elliott, both removing a large man from what looks like an apartment building. The article identifies the large man as Therron

Crowley, a well-known lobbyist in political circles. It also mentions Bolo and Huang as accomplices, and states that all three men are being indicted with federal charges of kidnapping, sex crimes, and in Crowley's case, murder in the first degree.

"Way to go," I whisper. I knew they could do it. While I want to respond to Nadia, to at least thank her for the link, I've decided a communications blackout is best for now. I don't know how I'm going to explain all of this to Liam and Zara, but I'm sure Elliott and Nadia will understand. They haven't known me as long and don't rely on me, not in the same way my boyfriend and best friend do.

My stomach clenches again and I push away the coffee. What's worse is I've also left Timber behind without so much as a goodbye. I've been away from him for long periods before, but it's never easy. I knew if I went home before leaving, I wouldn't have had the guts to go through with it. Liam would have been there, and I couldn't have left while looking in his eyes.

The fact is, I'm a coward. Because only a coward would leave the people that love them and not say a word. But I am not going to let Emily slip through my hands again. I am putting an end to this, once and for all. Ever since Matt died, I have been watched under a microscope by one group or another, by an assassin, or by a family member I didn't even know. I'm tired of wondering who or what might be waiting for me when I walk out my door every morning. I deserve peace. And if this is the price I must pay, then so be it.

I pull out a five-dollar bill and place it on the table before getting up. I head out into the morning sun and get in my car, backing out and merging back onto the road before I can convince myself to turn around and go back home. As I pass the city limits sign for Millridge, I narrow my gaze.

This ends now. One way or another.

Chapter Twenty-Five

IT'S SURPRISINGLY easy to get around the town, considering I was just here with Liam not more than a few weeks ago. That, and Millridge isn't a large place. It's what I would call an industrial town, one that had its heyday back in the thirties and forties when manufacturing was still a large part of the American workforce before those kinds of jobs were automated or outsourced. Towns like this are becoming more and more scarce as people search for jobs in larger metropolitan areas or as its residents die off. I pass more abandoned factories than I can count.

I try to envision what it would have been like when my mother lived here as a little girl. Even in the late sixties and early seventies, it was probably a bustling place, full of life and activity. I imagine it was the kind of place where everyone knew each other, a town which thrived on bake sales, swap meets, and the ever-important Sunday Service. But as I drive down the pot-holed streets, I barely pass another vehicle. Most of the shops around the downtown have been closed up, more than likely run out of business by the big box store two towns over.

But there is one building that's still in operation: the Millridge Police Department. I may not be willing to bring Zara and Liam in on this, but I have no qualms about enlisting the help of Detective Michaels. He's made my life enough of a hell that I think he owes me that much, at the very least. I've also determined that if I am going to make any headway in this case, I'll need his assistance. He'll have access to records I need, records Liam and I couldn't access before, seeing as we were both suspects. I just hope I can convince him to work together.

I pull up and park, taking a deep breath even as my stomach does another bad turn. I ignore it and get out. It's cooler here than in DC, but not by a lot. The trees are still beginning to bloom and winter has already released the town from its icy grip. Still, I pull my coat collar up around my neck as there is a breeze that's just a little too cold for my liking. I make my way around the building, up the steps, and head inside.

An officer sits at a desk right inside the door, glancing up as I arrive. "I'm here to see Detective Michaels," I say.

He raises his eyebrows. "FBI?"

"Yeah, how—"

The officer motions to the door behind him. "Head on back. I'm sure he's expecting you."

I pause but decide not to linger on it and head through the door. How can he be expecting me? I didn't tell anyone I was coming, especially not him. And while Michaels may be a good detective, he's not *that* good. Not unless he's somehow learned how to predict the future.

The door to his office is open and I head inside without knocking. Michaels is sitting at his desk, though his chair is turned to the side so he can rest his feet on a couple of case files beside his desk. He's reading a newspaper, looking as relaxed as a dog sunning on a porch.

"Detective," I greet, hesitant.

He barely glances over. "I was wondering when you would get here," he says.

"I'm sorry, were you…expecting me?" I ask. That's when I hear the toilet flush in the adjacent room, and a moment later, the door opens, revealing Zara, wiping her hands on a paper towel. I'm frozen in place, unable to comprehend how she's here. She takes one look at me then tosses the towel in Michaels's waste basket.

"We need a minute," Zara says, her voice completely cold.

"Mm-hm," Michaels says. He folds the paper back together, shoots me a smirk, and heads out, closing the door behind him.

"Z—" I begin.

"Don't," she says, her eyes already beginning to water. "Don't try to explain." She wipes her eyes quickly, then walks around to the other side of Michaels's desk, putting it between us.

"What are you doing here?" I ask, softly.

"How could you just leave?" she asks. "After everything we've been through? After that entire mess in Vermont? After *Magus*? We have *always* been there for each other. And you just up and leave? Without telling me? Without telling Liam?"

"I know," I say. "But it was the only way—."

"I don't want to hear it," she snaps. This is the first time I have seen Zara truly angry. As in the deep anger that comes when someone has cut you to your core.

A tremble seeps its way into my skin, and my fingertips have gone numb. I'm on the verge of losing my friend and I don't have anyone else to blame but myself. "You deserve a better friend than me."

"Don't *do* that," she yells. "Don't try to play the pity card."

"I'm not!" I say. "I honestly believe it. I'm not a good friend to you. I'm not a good girlfriend to Liam. I always put my work first, my own needs over everyone else. Trust me, I *know* how selfish I am. I have to live with it every day."

"You are not selfish," she says. "Putting your work first, that's the opposite of selfish. You help people at your own expense. And you do it more than anyone else I know."

"That's just because it's all I know how to do," I say. "I've never been very good with people. If you weren't—if you didn't try so hard, you would have—" I can't even form the complete thought. I drop down, collapsing on the sofa.

"What?" she asks, though it's still tinted with anger.

"You're the one who keeps our friendship alive, not me," I say. "If you didn't try, I would have drifted away a long time ago. Not because I don't love you, but because I am shit at relationships."

"That's not fair," she says. "To you or me. Do you think I would stay friends with someone if they weren't giving me anything in return? I've been in one-sided relationships before; that's not what this is. Your problem is you just haven't had enough close relationships to tell the difference."

"Maybe there's a reason for that," I say. "Who else do I have in my life? Who else am I close with? Liam? I think I may have just killed that too."

"I'm not going to stand here and list out examples of why I value our friendship," she says. "That's not my responsibility. If you can't see how important you are to me, that's your problem. But it doesn't give you the right to completely disregard me when hard things happen. You're supposed to lean on your friends, not push them away."

I shake my head, vehemently. "No, you'll get hurt. Maybe —" I wince as I say it. "Maybe if I push you away and make you angry enough, you'll be out of the way when the hammer finally falls."

"Is that what this is?" she demands. "You can't protect me. Or Liam. Or any of us."

"But," I say, weakly. "But I can live with it. Even if you never speak to me again, I'll know you're still alive. That I wasn't the one who put you in danger."

Zara circles the desk again, sitting beside me. "Remember when you agreed not to make decisions for me? For anyone else?" I nod. "Is it possible I could be hurt or even killed? Yes. But I deserve to make that choice for myself, not you. And even though I would be really sad if that happened, I would be even sadder knowing I had lost my best friend for the rest of my life. If something is going to happen, we need to face it together. Because a life without friendship is not a life worth living."

I can barely contain the tears and have to look into the florescent lights on the ceiling to try to keep them from falling. She's right. *Again.* I need to stop pretending I'm in this alone, and that I can stop the bad things from happening. "Z, I'm so sorry."

"I know. But there is only so much we can control in life. And we never know when our last moments will be. Stop trying to live for *what-if.* Live for right now." She places her hand on my arm and that does it. The dam breaks. She pulls me into a hug, and I find myself crying silently into her jacket. When I finally pull back, she stares directly into my eyes. "As soon as Liam said you hadn't come back home, I knew. You are so stubborn it's almost predictable."

"You know what happened at the hospital?"

She nods. "We all do. Caruthers called me. I hoped you wouldn't do something this reckless, but then again, you are who you are and sometimes we just can't change that. I guess…just like you can't make decisions for me, I have to accept there are some things I can't change about you. And I have to decide if I'm okay with that or not."

I glance over. "What have you decided?"

"I'm not sure yet." Her voice is deadly serious.

I nod, swallowing hard. "How did you know I'd come here?"

"Because it was the only place you *could* come," she says. "That and I kept pinging your cell signal and figured out your projected route. Oh, and I took a flight to get here, which you *approved* before I left."

"I did?" I ask, wiping my own eyes.

She smiles. "With an expertly forged signature. Even Janice won't be able to tell the difference."

"How long have you been able to forge my signature?"

"I was saving it," she says, "for an emergency."

"Z," I say, my voice cracking. "I know words don't mean anything anymore coming from me. But I want you to know I'm really sorry."

"I'm not going to lie, this really hurt," she says. "But I know you did it because you were scared, and you thought it was the right thing. I'm still trying to understand you, sometimes. But no matter what happens, I will always be your friend. And I will always love you."

I smile, weakly. I don't deserve a friend like her. "I love you too. You are the sister I never had."

"Aww," she says, some of the lightness coming back in her voice. I may have irreparably damaged our relationship, but she came here anyway, and that says something. Despite my best efforts, she didn't give up on me. She smiles and squares her shoulders. "Let's do what you came here to do. We'll deal with the rest later. Head into the bathroom. You don't want Michaels seeing you like this. I'm assuming you're here because you think he can help?"

I nod, wiping my eyes again. "I wasn't willing to risk you or Liam, but I figured Michaels was expendable."

She chuckles. "From what I've seen of the man so far, I haven't been impressed." I get up and head into the connected bathroom to splash some cold water on my face. My eyes are puffy and my cheeks are red, but the water helps temper it some. I spend a few minutes taking calming breaths, which helps more than the water.

When I emerge, Zara is still on the couch, though she's

scrolling through her phone. "I think I owe you big time when we get back," I say. She glances up. "Karaoke?"

Zara smiles. "Lady, you owe me a *lifetime* of karaoke. Whether you hate it or not."

"I don't hate it," I say. "I just need someone there to help warm me up."

Her eyes light up. "Seriously?" I nod. "Oh, I've got the perfect place. It's this little hole-in-the-wall dive bar with this tiny stage. It'll be perfect."

"Thank you," I say. "For coming after me. Even though you had every reason not to."

"You're welcome," she says. "But you need to call Liam. He deserves that much."

"I know," I say. "Let's get this locked down with Michaels and I will. I'm afraid…I'm afraid I might be pushing him too far away."

"Just be honest with him," she says, standing. "I didn't give up on you. I don't think he will either."

I take a deep breath, nodding. "Okay. Let's get this over with. I don't want to be here any longer than I need to be."

"You really think he can help?" she asks, going for the door.

"I think at this point, I'm willing to try anything."

She opens the door, and we find Michaels leaning back in another chair at a desk across from his door. He's still reading the paper and looks up at the two of us. "Finished?"

"We need to talk," I say.

He folds the paper together and heads back to his own his desk. "That's funny. I didn't have a meeting with two FBI agents on my schedule today." He glances over at Zara. "Though, that one wouldn't tell me what was going on until you arrived."

"I told you we found your arsonist," I say. "She also burned her car down in DC. Apparently with a body in the trunk."

He settles himself, then gives us an examining glare. "Yes, I heard from Detective Striker that a burned-out car had been found. Though, last word was they didn't know *who* burned it or why. And there was no mention of a body."

"It was her," I say. "I'm sure of it. And you may also not have heard, but our suspect escaped the hospital two days ago. We think she headed back here."

"Why would she do that?" he asks.

"Because she has nowhere else to go," Zara says.

"I'm not in the habit of letting someone else dictate how my investigations are to go," he says.

I step forward, closer to his desk. "Do you have any other leads?"

He watches me a moment, then finally sits back in his chair. "No."

"Then if you want to catch your arsonist, and potentially a killer, you might want to change your attitude," Zara says. I smile. How could I have thought I could do this without her?

Michaels's gaze flips from me, back to Zara, then to me again. "I can see you won't take no for an answer. So where do we begin?"

Chapter Twenty-Six

WE BROUGHT in a couple of chairs from the other room while Michaels left for a fresh pot of coffee. I imagine we're going to be here a while. As Zara pulls out her laptop, I excuse myself to make a phone call. I find I have to take deep breaths to keep my hand from shaking as I press the first contact on my speed dial list.

"Em?" His voice is tinged with worry and I hate that I've done that to him.

"Liam, I'm sorry," I say before I can utter anything else. "I've been a shit."

"Are you okay?" he asks.

"I'm fine. I'm in Millridge. I think the other Emily came back here." I hear the hesitation in his voice. "What is it? Do you want to yell at me?"

"No," he says. "I'm just disappointed. I thought we could trust each other."

"We can," I say. "At least, I trust you. I don't know how much you can trust me."

"Then why didn't you tell me you were going?" he asks.

I take a deep breath. "You've already sacrificed so much. And it almost cost you your life. I couldn't ask you to do that again. I knew if I told you what I was doing, you would insist on coming with."

"I feel like we've had this conversation before," he says. And he's right. It's like with Zara. But I also have to accept I'm not perfect, and I'm not always going to get it right. I've spent most of my adult life on my own, or with someone who I never really knew. And getting out of that mindset is going to take some serious work. I see a lot more sessions with Dr. Frost in the future.

"I know. I'm trying," I reply. "Zara is here. She's doing her best to set me straight."

"I'd be there too, but we've had our hands full," he says.

"Crowley. Nadia sent me the story. Congratulations."

"Couldn't have done it without your help in the interrogation room," he says. "Once we put the pressure on him, he confessed in exchange for a plea bargain."

"A plea bargain?"

"He's copping for two counts of second-degree murder down from first, without the possibility of parole. They're giving us their entire client list. Along with all the footage the company has kept."

"Wow," I say. "That's…amazing."

"He claims he was just…having a bad day when he went to the apartment. Xiang just happened to be in his way. And unfortunately, Yachi happened to come out of her room at the wrong time. That's his story anyway. We're still working on that particular footage."

"I'm glad you nailed him," I say. "You deserve all the accolades. I hope Janice recognizes just how much you've contributed on this case." Liam really has been the lynchpin in this one, and he's delivered in every way possible. I'll be surprised if he doesn't receive a commendation. In fact, that's something I plan on recommending when I get back.

"Speaking of which, Janice is looking for you." I grimace.

Leaving the team in the middle of a takedown was probably not the smartest move.

"How much trouble am I in?"

"I don't know. But I'd be cautious."

"Liam, I know I screwed up. *Again*. I just can't seem to help myself." I pause. "No, that's not true. I knew exactly what I was doing."

"We'll talk about it when you get back," he says, though I can hear the exasperation in his voice. He's tired of putting up with this, I can feel it. I may not have lost Zara, but I haven't known Liam nearly as long. I may have pushed his patience to the breaking point. Already I've been given far more leeway than any reasonable person could expect.

"Okay," I say. "I love you. Tell Timber hi for me."

"Be safe," he says and hangs up. I wince again. *Not good, Emily. Not good.*

When I return to the office, Michaels is back. Zara looks at me expectantly, but I just give her a small shake of my head. She mouths, *It'll be okay.*

"All right, what's so important it's required both of you to interrupt my morning paper?" Michaels asks.

The printer behind him starts up and he turns, surprised. "I'm printing off all the files we have on who we believe to be Emily Katherine Brooks," Zara says.

"When Agent Coll and I were here last time, we spent some time in your town archives," I say, "and found out I had an aunt named Emily, born in 1969. She stayed in Millridge until at least 1983, but that's when we lost track of her."

"Lost track?" he asks.

"She only appeared in the freshman yearbook of Millridge high," I say. "After that, nothing."

"So she moved away," he suggests.

"And yet my grandparents and my mother stayed in town." I nod to Zara, who prints out another document.

Michaels grabs it from the printer. "It's a story about a missing girl. *Her*."

He frowns, reading the story from his own town's newspaper. "You said the woman in the hospital came back here. How do you know she's the same missing girl?"

"Blood and DNA samples show a familial relationship with Emily," Zara says, "*Our* Emily." She turns to me. "That's the other thing. The DNA came back on those bones in the back of the car. It was inconclusive, but some of the markers were similar."

"Similar to what?" I ask.

"The DNA results from Emily's blood. And yours. They couldn't say definitively, but there's a possibility whoever that is, they're also related to you."

I *knew* it. At least my instincts are still working. "What are you thinking?" I ask.

She shrugs. "I dunno. A daughter maybe? She's about the right age, and Caruthers did confirm it was a female. Something might have happened. Grief does strange things to people."

"Wait, wait a minute," Michaels says, reading over all the pages Zara has printed out. "Just so I understand. This woman, Emily *Brooks*…" He glances at me. "Lived here, in that house, then burned it down when Agent Coll investigated."

"That's what we believe," I say.

"She then proceeds to drive to the nation's capital, with a body in the trunk that you assume is her dead daughter, because who else could it be, then attempts to drive the two of you off the road, fails, and ends up burning her car and whoever was inside."

"Analysis showed the bones in the car weren't fresh," Zara says. "The person hadn't died recently. Also, the sack containing the remains was treated with fireproofing, so she didn't intend the bones to actually burn."

"So…she was just driving around with a protected bag of bones in the back of her car?" he asks.

I shift in my seat. "It appears that way."

He bites his lip like he can't believe it. "*Then*, after burning her car, she attempts suicide by stepping in front of you." I nod. "Survives, then wakes up and escapes the hospital. Only to end up right back where she started."

"Yeah. That about covers it," I say.

"It sounds like the most ridiculous thing I've ever heard," Michaels replies. "Why would anyone do that?"

"That's what we'd like to find out as well," I say. "My mother died when I was twelve. I never knew I had any living family on her side. She told me they were all dead. When Agent Coll and I were here last time, we couldn't find anything on my family other than a few yearbook photos. Which led us to *her.*" I point to the picture printed out with the files. It's of Emily, still hooked up to the ventilator when she was first admitted.

Michaels lets out a long breath. "Let me see what I can find out." There is an old computer that sits off to the side. One that looks like it hasn't been turned on in the past ten years. He rolls his chair over and boots it, which takes a considerable amount of time. Zara's leg is bouncing as we wait; I know this kind of thing infuriates her. She likes her technology to be quick and efficient.

The Windows 98 logo appears on the screen and Zara groans. It's another good five minutes before the computer is up and running and Michaels opens a database. He types the name *Emily Brooks* into the search bar, and it returns with one result. A case number.

"It's still open," he says.

I lean forward, looking for any other information. Whatever program he's using is simple and only shows the case number, name and supposed location. "Can we take a look?"

"I'll go get it," he says, impatience seeping into his voice.

"Give me a minute." He gets up and leaves again as Zara blows out a frustrated breath between her teeth.

"I don't know about this guy, Em. He doesn't seem like he's on board."

I don't disagree. "I know. But I think he wants to get to the truth as badly as we do. He just doesn't show it. He's one of those cops who keeps everything buried deep inside. We just need to convince him she's here."

"Do we know that for sure?" she asks. "She could have gone anywhere."

"No, she's not done yet. Otherwise, why leave the hospital? She's got something planned; I just don't know what. But I do know somehow it involves me."

Michaels returns after about fifteen minutes, holding a brown accordion folder that's been tied together. There's a fair amount of dust on the edge, but I see clearly the case number matches the one he found on the computer.

"It has a four-zero prefix," he says, setting it down on his desk. "That's missing persons."

"Which lines up with the newspaper article," I say. "When was the last time the file was accessed?"

He unties the string and pulls the files out. There's a record card on the top. "Looks like 1989."

"No one has looked at this case in over thirty years?"

"Doesn't seem that way." He opens the rest of the file. It's surprisingly small. "Initial report, interview with the parents, girl disappeared on October 12, 1983."

"May I see that?" I ask, holding out my hand.

He scans the report, then hands it over. The initial call was taken through the call center then recorded and sent out to patrol vehicles. Later the same day, a Detective Lloyd Oberth took a statement from my grandparents. "Did you know him? Oberth?"

Michaels nods. "Retired about fifteen years ago. Good cop. Put the job first."

I read the report from Detective Oberth. *"Parents state that missing girl went to visit her sisters' house and never came back."* My eyes linger on the word *sisters*, but I dismiss it and read on. *"Also state she would often visit and return on her own, and the girls didn't live far away enough from the parents that they considered it a dangerous walk.* Wait a second. The *girls*? Is that a typo? Or is he talking about Emily and my mother?"

"Oberth was as thorough as they come. I think his wife was a schoolteacher. Not the kind to let her husband get away with not knowing his grammar," Michaels says, taking and scanning the page again. "No, I think that's correct."

"What does that mean?" Zara asks.

I take the page back and continue to read. It's filled with more of their statements, but nothing useful.

"Here," Michaels says, causing me to look up. "Here are a few more. I've got two additional statements from the relatives. A Margie Brooks." He holds up a piece of paper to read, and I recognize the handwriting as the sun shines through the page, making it partially transparent.

"That's my mother," I say, and he hands the page over. It's a statement written in her own words about the last time she saw Emily.

"And this one," Michaels pulls out another piece of paper. "From a Laurie Brooks."

"Laurie?" Zara asks, her brow forming a *V.* "Is that your grandmother?"

"My grandmother's name was Janet," I say.

Michaels hands over the paper, and I almost drop it. The handwriting on it is almost identical to my mother's. Right down to the way she repeats the first stoke in the A's.

Michaels gives me a nod. "Looks like you have more family than you realized, Agent Slate."

Chapter Twenty-Seven

No, no, no, this can't be right. As I look at the two statements side by side, they're almost identical. I don't even see the words; all I can see is the handwriting on those *fucking letters* that kept showing up at my apartment.

"Em, are you okay?"

I'm practically shaking, and I don't know how to make it stop. "I need...I need to see the birth records," I say. I point to Michael's ancient computer. "Tell me that thing is connected to the hospital."

"No," he replies calmly. "But we can request the information. It usually takes a day or more."

I squeeze my eyes shut. "Contact...Kingsley. Melanie Kingsley." I feel Zara's hand on my shoulder, rubbing it softly.

"Em, it's okay," she whispers. But I can't stop the ringing in my head. I feel like I'm about to throw up. My mind is barreling through the possibilities, but I don't want to admit it. I don't want to admit it could be true.

"I'll write up the request and—"

"No," Zara declares, and I hear her pick up Michaels's phone. "Call her. Right now." I open my eyes to see him staring at her, stunned.

"Listen to me, I only have so much patience and—"

"We don't have time for your ego," Zara says, more authoritative this time. "She's out there. And she's a danger to this town and its citizens."

He snatches the receiver from her hand and dials a number. "Yes, this is Detective Michaels over at the Millridge Police Department. Melanie Kingsley, please. I have a records request." He shoots a glare in our direction, but it doesn't even register with me.

Two letters. *Two* daughters. *And* Emily. Can it really be possible?

"Yes, Kinglsey. I'm here with Special Agents Slate and Foley with the FBI. Yes, the same one. We need you do perform a birth records search for us." He holds out the phone to me. "Tell her what you want."

"Kingsley?" I ask, my voice shaky.

"Agent Slate, good to—are you okay? You don't sound so good."

"I'm fine," I say. "Thanks. Do you remember that search we had you perform? On Emily Brooks?"

"Vaguely," she says. "That was a few weeks back."

"I need another one. This time on a Laurie Brooks, same parents. But it would have been about five or six years earlier."

"Okay," she says, "Give me one second." It's as if time slows down as I listen to her type in the background. The whole time I'm trying to figure out how I could have read this so wrong. "Here we go. Lauren Abagail Brooks, born to Janet and William Brooks, April 14, 1962. Oh, and it's listed here she's a twin. The related file is for a Margaret Brooks, same birthdate obviously. Do you need the weights and heights?"

"No," I say, my voice as small as a church mouse. "That's all, thank you."

"You're welcome. Take care, Agent Slate."

I hand the phone back to Michaels and turn to Zara. "My mother had a twin sister."

"*Two* sisters?" Zara asks.

How could she never have told me? How many more family members did she hide from me? Who else is out there?

"So then where is this Laurie Brooks?" Michaels asks.

"*She's* the one we've been chasing, not Emily," I say. "That explains why she looks just like her. Why she *writes* just like her. I was right when I thought the woman I hit was too old to be Emily." I ball my fists, as my head feels like it's going to explode. I can't believe this. We've been chasing the wrong person this entire time? How is this even possible?

"Check your system," Zara says. "Look for any open cases on Laurie Brooks."

As Michaels types on his ancient computer, I try resolving it in my brain. But as I turn things over, they just don't make sense. It's not lining up. "The picture," I say. "There was only the three of them in the picture Liam found. My mother, my pregnant grandmother, and my grandfather. That's it. There wasn't anyone else."

"What if the girl in the picture wasn't your mother?" Zara says.

"What?"

"If they were twins, couldn't that have been Laurie?"

I don't know what to think anymore. I rub my temples with both hands.

"We'll figure it out, Em," Zara says.

I need to detach myself from this. It's the only way I'm going to get through this without losing my mind. Treat it like just another case, pretend like it isn't my own family and that everything I've known is a lie. I take a deep breath and grab the statements from my mother and "Laurie" to read them again, this time paying attention to what they're actually saying.

The last time I saw Emily, she was headed

back home. She'd come over to bother us like she always did, but nothing seemed wrong. She was normal. She left around four thirty, and that's the last time I saw her.

Then the other.

Emily came over around noon to help me pack. She was always coming over to the house, wanting to hang out with her big sisters. We shared some snacks, talked about some boys, then she went back home around four thirty. I didn't see her after that.

"No open cases on Laurie Brooks," Michaels says. "I do have one closed case, but it's sealed."

"Sealed?" I ask.

"Juvenile record," he replies. "I can't get into it. We'll need a court order."

"She wasn't in the yearbook either," I whisper, remembering going through the records with Liam. Laurie should have been there, right beside my mother's picture. "It's like she never existed."

"How long will it take to have a juvenile record opened?" Zara asks.

"Judge Porter is usually pretty quick," Michaels says, checking his watch. "But he's also very by-the-book. We're going to need hard evidence and good cause to unseal that record. And right now, I don't see it. You can't prove she's the one who has been following you, you can't prove malicious intent—"

"She tried running us off the road," I say.

"Was she stopped at the time?" he asks. "Arrested? Charged? Do you have footage? Did you see her *actually* driving the car?"

"Liam saw her, at the house," I say.

"Doesn't mean she started the fire," he replies.

"Michaels, come *on*."

He gives me a stern glare then plants his index finger in the middle of the file on his desk. "We need actual, tangible evidence connecting her to a crime that would justify opening those records. You don't have it. We need to find something else."

"Ugh," I say, sitting back in the chair. "You're infuriating."

"I'm following the law," he says. "Even if we find her, you can't just arrest her. What are you going to charge her with? Escaping a hospital?"

"Suicide is illegal," Zara says. "We could charge her with attempted suicide for stepping in front of Em's car."

"A misdemeanor at best, assuming you can find a judge willing to prosecute," Michaels says.

"He's right," I admit. "We don't have much of anything except a lot of pieces that happen to point in one direction. And unless Striker can find something on the vehicle that connects her to it…"

"So what about the bones?" Zara says. "Should we look for birth records that list Laurie as a mother? I mean, why else keep the bones with her?"

"It would have shown up," I realize as I'm saying, "As Kingsley did the search. So if that is her daughter in the trunk, she didn't birth her at that hospital."

"*Or*," Zara suggests, "she was using a different name."

Michaels looks up, intrigued. "A different name?"

"You've never heard of her, right? And you've lived here your entire life. Where she's been the entire time, right under your nose. How else could she have done that other than adopting another identity?"

"Contrary to belief, I don't know *everyone* in town," he says.

"No, Zara's right," I say, thinking. "If she was laying low, she wouldn't use her own name. Her family name. We need to look deeper."

"Again, why is she laying low?" he asks. "What crime has she committed?"

"That's the question," I say, standing. "Why did she wait until now to try and find me, and why did she try to run us off the road? And why try to pretend to be my mother? There is definitely something more going on here, and we need to find out what."

"Where are you going?" Michaels asks as Zara gathers her stuff together.

"To find some help."

~

"THIS PLACE?" ZARA ASKS, LOOKING UP AT THE OLD STONE building.

"Trust me, the inside isn't any better. But it's the best chance we have." We head in through the large oak doors to find a familiar face sitting at the desk right inside. He's leaned all the way back in his chair with a news cap over his face, snoring softly.

"Um…" Zara says.

"Mr. Amos?" I ask, gently. There's no reply from the man. He's deep in it. I tap the little bell on his desk, and he shoots straight up, his cap falling to the ground.

"Huh?" he says, startled.

"Mr. Amos, it's me, Agent Slate. We met a few weeks ago?" I say as the man gathers his bearings.

"Oh," he says, blinking a few times. "Right, the pretty one. I remember you. You're Liam's squeeze."

I clench, trying to remember Amos is probably in his

nineties and comes from a different time. "We need some help with the town records."

He glances at Zara, then at me, then back at Zara again. "Both FBI?"

"That's right," I say.

"Don't guess I need to ask for your badges," he says. "What do you need?"

"Automobile records," I say.

"Oh, for that you'll have to check with the Ohio DMV," he says.

"Not for this one. It's an older car, late seventies. I kind of doubt the registration has been paid in a while. But I want to find out who originally purchased the car."

"Seventies, huh?" he says. "Bought in Millridge?" I nod. "We should have a tax record, even if it was a private sale." As he stands, his bones make a series of audible cracks. I catch Zara's eyes go wide as she bites her lip. "Okay, let's see what we've got. And pray I don't break something on the way down."

We follow Mr. Amos through the building back to the stairs and into the stacks where he assisted me and Liam in finding anything we could on Emily Brooks. Had I known at the time we were looking for someone else, maybe we could have avoided a lot of headache and pain. "Has anyone else contacted you about an Emily Brooks?" I ask him. "Anyone from DC?"

"No, no, it's been quiet here. Should they have?"

I quietly curse Striker. I *told* him the answers to this case were here, and he ignored me. "No," I reply. "Just checking."

Zara and I split the work, looking through boxes and boxes of documents, all of them forty years and older, looking for any kind of record that might point us in the right direction. Amos tries to help, but eventually he returns upstairs, leaving us to it. I move with the speed of someone who can feel the fire licking at their heels because I know as soon as we find what we're looking for, we'll have her.

"Did you and Liam check the property records of the house that burned down?" Zara calls out from across the room. She's at least four or five aisles over from me, and I can't even see her in the dim space.

"It was in my grandparents' name," I say. "And Liam never found any mention of a will, but we couldn't confirm if they were dead or not." Without a will, the house would have passed to their next of kin and would have required little more than an ID and a signature from whoever that was. Assuming it was Laurie, the title of the house *should* have passed into her name, but when we looked for the property records last time, it was still listed in their names.

What I still don't understand is why all the subterfuge? Why go to all this trouble to keep herself concealed from the world? Not showing up in the school records, not showing up *anywhere* as far as I can tell. And only coming out of the wood-work now? Something isn't right here, and I *need* to get to the bottom of it.

"Finally," I say, when I come to a vehicle record that matches the '79 Granada. "I think I've got it!"

"You got it?" Zara asks.

"May of 1984," I read from the document. "A brown 1979 Ford Granada sold by Eloise Harper to Francis Knox." I check the signature at the bottom of the tax document, paid by Francis Knox once the title was transferred. The hand-writing is similar to that on the statements from Michaels's file. "I think this is her."

"We need to look for anything else in her name," Zara says. "If that's the name she used—"

"—then that's the name she lived under while she stayed here." I nod, removing the document and taking it over to the copier from the decade before I was born. When I get a copy, I take a photo and text it to Michaels.

"I need to check something," I tell Zara as she continues to search.

"Where are you going?"

"Back over to the hospital. I need to talk to Kinglsey again, but I don't want to do it over the phone. This is too sensitive. I need to find out if *Francis Knox* ever had a child, because if she did and something happened to her, we might be able to explain who the bones in the back of that car belong to."

"I'll come with you," she says, her voice apprehensive.

"I need you here, looking for anything else in that name. Or anything about my grandparents. You're a better searcher than Liam, though, don't tell him I said that. Just...anything that might help us. I'll be back in a bit." She eyes me. "I know. But I'm not going to run off again. I've already seen that's an exercise in futility. Plus, I can't see that look of disappointment on your face. It would kill me."

She gives me a hesitant look, but finally relents. "Okay. Just keep me in the loop."

"I will."

As I head out, I thank Mr. Amos, telling him Zara is staying. He reminds me they close at four and it's already closing in on three in the afternoon. Hopefully she can find something else useful. Some other connection that we've missed.

Because we're running out of time.

Chapter Twenty-Eight

"MELANIE KINGSLEY, PLEASE," I say as I approach the main desk at Hickory County Hospital.

"Regarding?" the man at the desk says.

I show him my badge. "An active case."

He pinches his features before picking up the phone and dialing a three-digit number. He speaks too softly into the phone for me to hear before hanging back up. "She'll be with you in a moment."

"I know the way," I say. Despite his protestations, I head down the hallway to the records area, where I catch a flustered-looking Melanie Kingsley coming out of the door. She seems to be muttering something to herself but stops upon seeing me, her entire face transforming into nothing but a pleasant visage.

"Agent Slate," she says. "I—uh, how are you?"

"I'm fine, thank you," I say, noting this is the second time she's asked about my health in the same day. "Is everything all right with you? You seem—upset."

"Do I? Oh, no it's nothing you need to worry about. Just hospital politics. What can I do for you?"

"I need another search, this time on a Francis Knox."

"Wow, you really must be interested in birth records," she says.

"I'm trying to determine the identity of someone who—before a few hours ago—didn't exist for me. And there are a lot of moving pieces to this puzzle."

"Very well," she says, and uses her keycard to get into the records room, holding it open for me. That strikes a thought in my mind.

"Do you have an employee locker room in this hospital?" I ask. She nods. "Do people need your keycard to access it?"

"Oh," she says, giving me a brief laugh. "No, we stopped that long ago. Maintenance had to come by every day to let someone in who forgot their keycard or left it inside. The hospital tried instituting a policy that people wear them from the moment they got out of their vehicles to the moment they returned to them, but you know how people are: slow to change and quick to complain."

"So you just leave it open? For anyone?"

"Well, most people don't even know it's there," she says. "You'd have to know about it to know what's inside. We have *Authorized Personnel Only* signs. And it's not like there's anything sensitive in there like patient records or expensive equipment. There are a hundred other doors in this place that are locked for that very reason. Why do you ask?"

"Just curious," I say.

She sits down at one of her terminals. The room is empty today, no other doctors looking through patient records.

"You want a birth record on Francis Knox?" she says.

"That and I want to know if there is a record of birth that lists her as the mother," I say.

"Okay," she says absently, typing it into the computer. A couple of lines come up. "Here we go. Francis Knox, born January 25, 1924. Wow, that was back when the hospital was a single building in downtown Millridge." She smiles before opening the file. It shows the birth record along with the hand and footprints of the baby.

That can't be right. That would make her close to a hundred by now.

"Here," Kingsley says. "This other record—oh, wait, this isn't a birth record. It's an employment record."

"Employment?" I ask. "Open that one."

She hesitates a moment. "I'm not sure I can do that. It could be a HIPAA violation. We keep those sealed by federal law; I'll need a signed warrant to open it."

"Can you at least tell me when she was employed?"

Kingsley scans the line of code, which shows a string of numbers. "Wait, this can't be right," she says. "It has her listed as a registered nurse from 1996 until 2008. But the hospital wouldn't have hired a nurse in her mid-seventies."

"Why not?" I ask.

"Because it can be such a physically demanding job," she says. "And the hospital doesn't want the liability of someone older who might injure themselves, maybe permanently."

"So the record is wrong," I say.

"Hang on." She opens the record and before I even realize it, I recognize the face staring back at me. It's the face of my mother, almost the same age I last saw her when I was a teen. Her dark hair is vibrant, though her face is sallow, having lost some of its vigor. In fact, if I didn't know better, I would say this picture *was* my mother. But that can't be possible, because my mother died in 2004, four years before *this* woman stopped working here, apparently.

"Doesn't look seventy to me," I say. "In fact, she looks like she's in her mid-thirties."

"I don't understand," Kinglsey says.

"That isn't Francis Knox," I say. "It's someone using her name."

"I'll need to notify the administrator," Kingsley says. "This could lead to a lot of problems for the hospital. We do rigorous background checks; how could she have slipped through the system?"

"She's a master at manipulation," I say. "Is there anything else you can give me? I don't need medical history or anything like that, but it would be helpful to know if she has any children."

"I'm really sorry, Agent Slate, but if I did, it could cost me my job."

Damn. I guess I can't blame her. But at the same time, I can't help but glance at what little information is shown on the screen. "What does code eight-seven-one mean?"

"Oh." Kingsley's face falls. "That's an internal hospital code, noting why she was let go. It means someone has acted inappropriately with a patient on the job."

"Inappropriately how?"

"There's no standard definition. But I can tell you something like that would have taken a lot of evidence. That's not a common reason someone is fired."

"I don't guess you could tell me what evidence they had, either?"

"Unfortunately, no." She turns back to the computer and clears out the search, my mother's picture disappearing from the screen.

"This is just hypothetical, but in the event someone was let go for that reason, would there have been a criminal investigation?"

She shakes her head. "They wouldn't have wanted the bad press. Any time something like this happens, they keep it quiet. I'm sorry Agent Slate, but I think you're going to need a warrant if you want to find out more. I've already probably shown you too much."

I nod. "I appreciate all you've done. I know this is a little out of the ordinary. But I wouldn't be here if it wasn't important. At least, it's important to me."

"I'll be happy to help more, if I can." I thank her again

and head out, returning to my car. I'm back to my original problem, which is I don't actually have a *crime* here to charge the woman with, except maybe identity theft and impersonation. Why would Laurie have registered to work under a name belonging to a woman double her age? And not only that, why buy a car in that name as well?

As I head back to the Millridge town records building, I note the time is only ten 'till four. Amos will be closing soon, but I'm not sure I can wait for him to open back up again tomorrow morning. I pull out my phone and call Zara.

"You better not be in the middle of Pennsylvania or something," she says.

"Okay, I deserve that. No, I'm headed back to you."

"Did you find anything at the hospital?"

"I did. Laurie used the name Francis Knox as a pseudonym to work there for almost twelve years. Explains how she knew how to get around the hospital in DC so easily."

"No birth record?"

"None that we could find, but she could have used another pseudonym," I reply. "I won't get back before Amos closes back up. See if you can find any property records for Francis Knox. I want to see how deep this rabbit hole goes."

"Way ahead of you," she replies. "I already have an address."

"Great, I'll swing by and pick you up."

"You want to go now?" she asks.

My knuckles turn white as I grip the wheel harder. "Z, I need this to be done. We need to find this woman. And this is the best lead we've got."

"Then I'll meet you outside."

I PULL UP TO THE RECORDS BUILDING JUST AS ZARA IS COMING down the stairs, talking animatedly with Amos. He says something that causes her to laugh out loud before tipping his hat and making his way down the sidewalk. He gives me a quick wave as he hobbles past—I'm still amazed at how quick he can move for his age.

"What was that about?" I ask as Zara gets in, two files in her hands.

"He was just commenting that I was a fair sight better than the last agent you brought with you."

I grin. "Liam is going to be heartbroken. He thought he and Amos really got on well."

"We don't have to tell him," she mock-whispers.

"I think that's best. What are those?" She hands me the first file, which I open to find a set of property records, going back almost seventy years.

"I found Mrs. Knox's house. It sits out on a little inlet that connects to the river. It was *built* in the fifties and is still in her name, to this day."

"And the other?"

She hands it over. "Everything else I could find on Francis Knox. Whoever this woman is, she is *not* your aunt. She attended Millridge high in the late forties and early fifties, married young to a man named Wilbur—of all names—and settled down with two children. Both children, as far as I can tell, moved away from Millridge in the early eighties. One of them, Brian, died in Desert Storm, and the other, Amber, is living out in California somewhere, but information on her is scarce."

"So there is no connection to my family at all?"

"None that I can find, other than both families lived in Millridge around the same time. But I couldn't find much on your grandparents. At least, nothing that confirmed if they were still alive or not."

"And what about Mrs. Knox? Is she still alive?"

"No death certificate anywhere, but I'll admit I was pressed for time and it was *a lot* of paper to sort through."

I take a deep breath. "Okay. Then I guess we need to go speak with her. And find out what her relationship is with my aunt. Maybe she'll know where to find her, even if she doesn't realize it."

"Assuming she's cognizant," Zara replies.

"Hey, Amos is still kicking around pretty well and he's in his nineties," I point out.

She grins. "Are you saying Millridge is the fountain of youth?"

I pull away from the curb, heading for the address in Zara's file. "No, but there is definitely something in the water here."

Chapter Twenty-Nine

As we drive out to the property, my mind is buzzing with the ramifications of what my aunt has done here. How did she even meet Mrs. Knox? Not only that, but is Mrs. Knox even aware of what's happening? We could have a case of elder abuse here, where Laurie has taken over Mrs. Knox's life and has been using it for her own needs. At the very least that and the identity theft requires investigation.

I don't have a good feeling about what we're going to find in that house, and we must be ready for anything. It's possible Laurie could have returned to the home when she came back to Millridge, especially if it is where she's been living. She had to have gone somewhere after she destroyed my grandparents' home. And despite what Michaels says, I'm going to nail her for that too.

The woods around the road leading to the turn-off grows denser the deeper we drive, even though this is a main road. It's like the woods are closing in around us, and a foreboding grows in the pit of my stomach.

"Did IA return your sidearm?" I ask Zara.

"No, they're taking longer than usual," she replies. "When you left, you didn't help things any. Why, you think there's going to be trouble?" I explain to her my suspicions about Laurie, and about what we might really find in that house. "We should call Michaels."

"I agree." Because just like her, my weapon is also with IA. I do have another, unregistered handgun in my glove box, but I really don't want to use it if I don't have to. The amount of shit I would get from the Bureau for carrying an unregistered weapon would be enormous. Not to mention using it in the line of duty.

But at the same time, after Camille, I swore never to be caught off guard ever again. And I wanted something that couldn't be traced in the event things went really bad. I have to be prepared for anything.

I pull off the side of the road just before a small gravel driveway forks off to the left and call Michaels.

"Go ahead," he says, and I put him on speakerphone.

"I'm giving you a heads up. We're investigating the home of Francis Knox. Laurie Brooks was using the name as a pseudonym and even went so far as to use the name on her employment record with the Hickory County Hospital."

"Okay," he says. "What do you want from me?"

"Backup would be nice," Zara says.

"Backup for what? You're investigating the home of an old woman."

"And Laurie Brooks may be here," I say. "She had to flee somewhere, and she obviously couldn't go to the house she burned down."

He sighs. "Give me the address." I rattle it off for him. "Keep me updated. If you run into anything, call and I'll send someone out there."

"Or, you could stop being a *dick*, and come out here yourself, right now," Zara says.

"I get it. This is personal for you. But as far as I can tell, you don't have anything yet. Nothing concrete to connect this woman to any crime. Except escaping custody, and that's iffy at best."

"Identity theft," I point out.

"Which I'm sure two federal agents can handle on their own," he replies. "Let me know what you find out." He hangs up before we can get another word in.

Zara slumps back in her seat. "Wow, you really picked a winner here."

"*I* didn't pick him, he took the arson case," I say. "Trust me, I would have picked just about anyone else." I motion to the glovebox. Zara opens it to reveal the handgun. "Keep it on you."

"What about you?" she asks.

"I'll be fine without it. Hopefully this is nothing more than an informal interview with an old woman."

She scoffs and I pull back out before getting on a gravel driveway, which the GPS tells me leads up to the Knox property. It's a long, bumpy driveway through dense woods, but it eventually empties out into a clearing with a small house sitting off to the right. In front of us is the inlet, which connects to the Rappahannock river, and a long dock which stops about halfway out. There's an old boathouse connected to the dock, but it looks like it hasn't seen any maintenance in a while as the roof is caving in.

The house itself looks a little better. It's a red siding home with white trim, one floor and a car port instead of a garage. The house can't be bigger than fifteen hundred square feet, which I guess was big back in the fifties when it was built.

"No vehicles," Zara observes. She's right. If Laurie is here, she hasn't left a vehicle around. The woods around the property look too deep to hide anything within, though they do create an idyllic environment, tucking the house away from any of its neighbors or any nearby roads.

I pull the car close to the house and we get out. The scent of the river hangs in the air and I swat at a mosquito looking for an easy meal. "I'll take point," I tell her and Zara pulls back.

"You sure you don't want this?" she offers the handgun.

"I'll be fine," I say, though I would feel better if we were both armed. I don't like going into a situation like this without some sort of guarantee, but at the same time, I'm not willing to wait. Not after everything I've been through. At least Zara is here to back me up. She's right, I should never have come out here alone seeing as Michaels doesn't want to lift a finger to assist.

As I come up to the entrance, the main door looks to be heavy wood, sitting behind a rusting metal contraption that used to be a screen door once upon a time. Without opening the metal frame, I give the door a solid knock. Zara gives me an exaggerated thumbs up, to which I roll my eyes.

There's no response on the other side.

"Mrs. Knox?" I call out. "Are you in there?" Still nothing. I motion to Zara. "Check around the back of the property. See if you can see anything inside." She heads off and I turn my attention to the door again, knocking harder this time. The wood seems to bend under the force. Upon further examination, the home doesn't look well-cared for at all. The grass is overgrown, and the bushes that once sat up against the home are all dead and dried up. The paint on the red siding is peeling and windows are caked with grime and dirt.

"Mrs. Knox," I call out again. "If you can hear me, open up. This is the FBI." I wait but hear nothing. I try the handle, and it's barely holding itself together in the door. By jiggling it a little, it unlatches and the door swings on its hinges. "I'm coming in," I say, hoping the announcement won't startle anyone inside. But I don't know what I'm about to find in here. The ghost of my sidearm hangs heavy at my side. I've never before been in a situation like this without it.

Inside the house, it's dark and musty. The air is stale, like it hasn't been breathed in a long time. A small shape skitters away from me across the dark carpet. It looked like a mouse, but could have been something bigger, it's hard to say. "Z?" I call out. "Any luck?" There's no response. The back door may have been locked tighter than the front. And sure, I probably shouldn't have entered on my own. I probably shouldn't be doing a lot of things, but I have been pulled and dragged along this roller coaster for long enough. If the FBI wants to ding me for entering a home without authorization, let 'em. It's far from the worst thing I've ever done.

The living room is little more than a few dusty chairs, a small table and an old television. I head around the room into the small kitchen, which contains appliances from another age, complete with a linoleum floor and a Formica countertop. But it's not as dusty as the living room. I check the fridge, which is still running, and there are recent provisions inside. *Someone* has been living here. "Mrs. Knox?" I call out. It's possible she's bedridden and doesn't get out much. Maybe Laurie has been staying here, taking care of her in exchange for free room and board. But I don't like the way that living room looked. And I can't see out of any of the windows; they are that dirty.

I head back around through the living room to the other side of the house where the bedrooms are located. A small bathroom is the first door and sports a pink tile motif that has long gone out of style. But there are clear signs of recent usage, and even a toothbrush on the counter. Continuing, I reach one of the bedrooms, which is obviously in use. The bed is unmade, but there are clothes strewn around the room. I check for any articles that could identify the owner but come up short. It's just a place to rest and nothing more. The only lamp in the room is switched on, and the bulb isn't very warm yet. Whoever is staying here, they're close.

I head back out to the hallway to the final door. It's shut tight and I press my ear up against the wood grain. There are no sounds inside. And judging by the lack of any light coming through underneath the door, it doesn't seem occupied. But I need to check anyway, just in case whoever was in the other bedroom fled here. I should have grabbed something to protect myself with from the kitchen.

Carefully, I open the door. The room is completely dark inside, and there's a stale odor to the air itself. The windows are shut, though what little light comes through bathes the room in a strange, bluish hue. I reach over for a light switch and flip it with a soft click.

I'm so startled I take a full step back.

In the bed is a rotting skeleton.

I pull my shirt up over my nose and enter the room, checking the corners. As far as I can tell, there's no one else in here. And given the layer of dust on everything, it doesn't look like anyone has been in here for a *very* long time.

Approaching the body, I take short, shallow breaths. Even though my mouth and nose are covered, I can still taste death on the air. The body has been in a state of decay for some time, the bed around it having turned black from mold. What little skin remains is stretched thin over the skull, and whisps of white hair lay discarded on the dark pillow. The person is still wearing a nightgown, which makes me think it was a woman, probably of advanced age.

Mrs. Knox. That answers one mystery. And it leads me to assume Laurie has been squatting in the house since the woman's death, having subsumed her identity as much as she can. But where is she?

Using my jacket sleeve, I pull the door closed. We're going to need a full hazmat team out here. I need to call Michaels. But first I need to inform Zara. I head to the door that leads out to the back of the property and the boathouse, expecting to find it locked. Only, it's cracked open a little. "Z?" I call out. "You there?" When I open the door, I find myself on a back covered patio, complete with an old swing that looks like it will collapse if anything more than a bee puts its weight on it.

Zara's nowhere to be found.

"Z!" I call out, heading back around to the car. She's not there either. It's then I see the tracks in the overgrown grass. They're not regular tracks either. Instead, they look like they were made by someone being dragged. And they lead directly to the boathouse.

Chapter Thirty

MY HEART IS PUMPING as I rush to follow the tracks. Laurie was in the house the whole time; she must have gotten the jump on Zara when she came around the side. If I hadn't wasted so much time poking around in there, I might have realized it earlier, I might have found her. And now I'm unarmed, headed into a hostile situation.

This isn't anything like the shootout at the mansion. There, I was calm and collected. But here, all I can think about is Zara in danger. Has she hurt her? Has she already killed her? I have no way of knowing. And I'm completely out of options.

The boathouse has what looks like two entrances. One from the grass side of the property, which is accessible via a door, and another, which connects directly to the dock, and as far as I can tell, is just an open entryway. Regardless, I will have an easier path inside that way, though I won't have the cover of the door itself. I quietly come up on the dock, trying to make as little noise as possible before reaching the boathouse itself. My back is flat against the wood as I try to figure out how to approach this.

My main priority is Zara. I need a way to get her out of there, assuming she's still alive. Only then can I focus on—

"*Emilyyyyy.*" The word sends a shiver down my spine. It's the voice of my mother, as clear as the last time I heard it. Where she sounded familiar on the home video, here the voice sounds ethereal, almost like it isn't real. But in the same sense it is, and it digs at the memories in my brain. I catch my own breath. "I know you're out there," she says. "Come to Mama."

I take a deep breath. "Where is my partner?"

"Come on in and I'll tell you." Her voice is as soft and comforting as I remember. Though there's an edge as well, like her voice is hiding a blade that will cut me as soon as I let it in. But I can't worry about myself.

"If you give yourself up now, and don't harm Agent Foley, things will go much better for you."

"Who says I haven't already harmed her, *Emily*? You were always so careless with your friends. Leaving them lying around like discarded toys. I always had to pick up after you."

That's not true. She's baiting you. "You are *not* my mother. My mother died seventeen years ago!"

She chuckles. "Did she? Or perhaps it was Laurie who died? Perhaps Margaret is still alive."

I'm trembling with rage so badly I've lost all sensation in my body. If I go barreling in, there's no telling what kind of a trap I'll be falling into. I could doom both me and Zara, and right now, I'm her only chance.

"Let your hostage go, and we'll talk. That's what you want, isn't it? Isn't that why you sent me all those letters? You wanted my attention. Now you've got it. So let's go."

"Tsk, tsk," she says. "Always trying to take the shortcut. The *easy* way out. No. You come in here, and *then* I'll consider letting her go. Or you could just shoot me. But you wouldn't do that to your own mother, would you?"

"*You are not my mother!*"

Her voice abruptly changes. "Make a decision, Emily.

You're out of time." Gone is the teasing, the softness. She's all business now.

"What does that mean?" There's no response. I don't have a choice. I'm going to have to go in unarmed and hope I can find a way out of this for both of us. *Damn* Michaels for not listening. If he'd just come when I'd called the first time—

I pull out my phone and shoot off a quick text to him. I don't have time to explain everything, but hopefully he understands the urgency. Still, it will take him a while to get here. This house is at least half an hour from downtown Millridge.

"Okay," I say. "I'm coming in."

"Slow," the woman says. That edge in her voice is back again. I know it—or a version of it—well. The few times my mother got upset had a hint of that edge, but never anything like this. It's almost *malicious.*

I turn the corner and find I'm staring into darkness. The boathouse has no lights, only the slats of the roof which have broken apart and caved in, creating slivers of blue light that barely penetrate the space. The sun is approaching the horizon outside, and very little of that light is getting inside. But as my eyes adjust, I can make out two figures. One is lying on the dock itself, not moving. The other stands behind her, with what looks like a metal pipe in her hand.

It's her. Even before I make out her face, I know it. I can tell by the way she holds herself, the silhouette against the darkness. It's the woman who stepped in front of my car, whom I followed to the hospital.

And she's *grinning* at me.

"Good girl," she says. She tilts her head, the bandage having been discarded. A dark bruise marks the corner of her temple. "No gun?"

"I'm unarmed," I say.

Her eyes bore into mine. "I've been waiting so long."

"Let my partner go," I demand.

"No. Not until I get what I want," the woman replies.

"Until then she stays right where she is." She waggles the pipe. Though there's barely any light in here, I see a brief reflection on Zara's head. Blood. There's no telling how badly she's been injured.

"Please," I say. "Let me get her help. Then we can talk."

"You should have come yourself," she replies.

"What?"

"The letters were for you. *You* should have come to the house. Not some *man* who wasn't invited."

"Liam," I say. "It *was* you who burned down my grandparents' house."

"It was my house," she says matter-of-factly. "They left it to *me*."

"Then they are dead," I say.

"Twenty-eight years," she whispers. "Two months, twelve days, nineteen hours, fifty-six minutes." She wiggles the pipe a few more times. "It was…tragic."

"You killed them." My voice has gone cold, emotionless.

"No. I *helped* them," she says. "People shouldn't waste away like that. No one should…suffer." Her gaze goes a little glassy.

"You never transferred the deed, why?" I ask. "And why were you impersonating Francis Knox? *And* my mother?"

The woman pins her gaze on me. "Because. People can be cruel. And I only ever wished to be *kind*. But no one wanted my kindness. They wanted to pretend like I didn't exist. I learned to live with that. Embrace it, even. Do you know what it is like for no one to know who you are? You can do… *anything*."

I grimace. The woman is obviously mentally unbalanced. I'm feeling a little unbalanced myself. "What do you want?"

She doesn't respond for a moment, instead just stares at me. *Through* me. "You are so much like her. The genetics are unmistakable. I knew your face the moment I saw you."

I glance at Zara's unmoving body, not sure how much time

she has left. Does she have a concussion? Or worse? I need to get that pipe away from Laurie, but I'm too far away and I can't guarantee that she won't slam it into Zara's face the second I try to reach her.

"Look like who?" I ask, hoping if I buy into this woman's delusions, maybe I can get the upper hand.

"Like my sister." She says it softly, drawing out each word like letting air out of a balloon. And for a brief second, I see the woman I knew as my mother. But this woman is not her.

"Did you know she died?" I ask.

"I suspected," she replies. "But I didn't confirm until I found out about you."

"She died when I was twelve," I say.

"She left when I was twenty-one," the woman says, matching my tone and cadence. "She abandoned us both."

I grimace. "She didn't abandon me. She got cancer."

"Did you know…memories, traumatic events, they can manifest themselves in real, physical ways. There are studies showing certain types of trauma can…transform. Your mother had a sickness because of a secret. It manifested itself…," the woman replies. "Brain cancer. Maybe if she'd never left us…" She steps to the side, away from Zara. In the dying light, it's more difficult to make out her features, but my eyes continue to adjust.

"Are you seriously suggesting her brain tumor was caused by leaving Millridge?"

Her eyes snap shut for a split second and when they open again, a rage burns behind them. "When you cut off everyone and everything you know, it leaves a mark. It creates a rift."

She's further away from Zara, almost far enough away that I might be able to get to her first. I'm still unarmed, but I'm willing to bet I can take a woman thirty years my senior. I make a move towards Zara, only for the woman to pull out Zara's gun from under her loose button up shirt and point it at her.

"You will lose her forever," she says. "I don't want to do this, Emily, don't make me."

I wince, my adrenaline spiking. "Just let her go! She needs help!" I pause. Zara is here because of me. After everything, she's in danger because I didn't protect her. "She's my best friend."

"I had a best friend once," the woman says. "We were as close as two people could ever get. But she left me. And went and started a family. Had a niece I never knew about."

"Finally decided to stop pretending you're my mother?" I ask.

She narrows her gaze. "There are some people in this world who can be manipulated. Some who are easily led astray by their emotions. It's clear by now that you are not one of those people."

"Whatever you want with me, please just let me help *her*, and then you can have it."

Laurie takes the first deep breath I've seen, then sighs. "I want to believe you. But you're too much like her, Emily. You will take any opportunity to gain the upper hand. I don't believe I can convince you."

"Then what are we even doing here?" I demand. "What do you want from me?"

"I want my sister back," she says.

"Yeah, well I'd love to have my mother back too, but it's not happening. That's life."

"Ironic, because life seems to have given me a new opportunity," she says, stepping back closer to Zara. "One I didn't know existed four months ago. The day I saw you on television, standing behind all those agents at the FBI, being congratulated for all your hard work, I realized Margie had borne a child. A child who had grown up to be just like her mother. Courageous, determined, brave, and kind. And I knew in that moment, I needed you."

I screw up my face. "So you decided to start sending me

234 • ALEX SIGMORE

letters in her name? Why not just contact me? Why not just call me up and tell me who you were? I think if I'd received a phone call from an aunt I didn't know existed I would have been more receptive to meeting you. Rather than all...this." I motion to everything around us.

"As you've proven, there are no guarantees, especially where family is concerned," she says. "You needed...molding. In the same way I molded your mother. I was too sloppy with her, too inexperienced. I didn't realize...she could leave me. I couldn't take that chance again."

"What are you talking about?" I say, cautiously. None of this is making any sense.

She turns away, then looks back at me, her eyes glistening in the darkness. They are almost wild with what I would call desire if I didn't know better.

"She never would have spoken of it," Laurie says. "She wanted to forget all of it. Pretend like it didn't happen. But it did. You can't forget. You can't erase."

"Just tell me what happened!"

"The day she rejected me was the day she broke my heart," Laurie says. "It was the day I died."

"Rejected you?"

"So much...I went through so many...alone for so long that I thought...but she didn't share my feelings. We were supposed to be inseparable, mother used to say there was no stronger bond than a sister's love."

All sound and thought stops. I can't hear my heartbeat in my ears. I can't feel the tips of my toes or my lungs taking in breath. I can't even speak.

"Emily, your mother and I were lovers."

Chapter Thirty-One

It as if the world has fallen away from me and I'm free-floating in space. My brain has shut itself off, trying to protect itself from receiving this information. But there's no putting the genie back in the bottle. The words have been spoken. They cannot be taken back again.

"You—you're lying."

"*I can't be a part of this. I can't stay here. You're sick and you need help.* Her last words to me." Laurie steps over Zara's body, closer to me. "But *I* wasn't ashamed. Because I knew our love was pure. What could be more real than the love of two people born of the same cells? What could be more natural? We were already two halves of the same being, all I wanted was to bring us together again, the way we were meant to be."

"You—you're crazy," I whisper.

"*I am NOT crazy!*" She roars, and I take a step back. "That's what my parents used to say. And the teachers. And the children at school. That's why I spent my entire youth in that…place—that *home* for *special* children." Her voice pitches around the words, mocking them, but her words come out as a snarl. Where she was almost emotionless before, now it is *all* emotion, all coming out at once. "They thought they could just shove me in there and it would solve all their problems. Everyone thinks they can just push me to the side and go on with their lives, and I'll just go away. But that's not how it works. You can't just forget about me, as hard as you try."

I'm still trying to grapple with all this information. "They put you in an institution?" I ask. I recall the juvenile record Michaels found. "What did you do?"

"Cut off from everyone I cared about. Mom, Dad, Margie. In a home where no one visited me, where they left me to disappear. It took me a few years, but I finally figured it out.

"The trick about places like that is they want you to be someone else. You can't change who people are, not really. But they tried. They tried over and over. What I realized was, you just have to *pretend* like you've changed and all of a sudden everyone starts treating you better. All I had to do was learn how to create the mask everyone wanted to see. And then it was 'you're making great progress Laurie,' 'glad to see you're improving Laurie,' and I would have them eating out of my hand. I learned then, that life is all about saying the right things to get what you want. No matter if you believe them or not. And that people, especially people with hope in their hearts, are easily manipulated.

"But I was still too naïve. Because guess what I found when I came home? Guess what surprise awaited me, once I had finally figured out that no one wanted *me*, they just wanted the mask I wore?"

I'm not sure how to respond. But she's lying about Mom. She *has* to be.

"A brand-new sister," she snarls. "A *replacement*."

"Emily," I say.

"That's right. Funny how your mother told you about her. But given your name—"

"She didn't," I say. "I didn't know about Emily until Liam and I investigated the fire. We thought *you* were Emily."

"Me?" she says, as if she's genuinely confused. She cocks her head at me and I can't tell if she's really intrigued or just pretending. But the way she looks at me reminds me so much of my mother it hurts. "Your mother really never revealed anything, did she?" She sighs. "When she told me she'd never be back, I didn't want to believe her. I always thought we'd see each other again. That I might..." She begins to approach, but pulls back, seeming to remember herself.

"She said all of her family was dead, that there was no one left for her to go back to," I say.

Laurie looks as if she's been slapped. She winces once, then twice, almost as if I'm hitting her myself. "I had hoped... I had thought..."

It's the same haunting look I saw in my mother's eyes in the video. And then it hits me. I had thought she might have been a sexual abuse survivor from my grandfather, or some other person of authority. But could it have been from Laurie?

"What did you do to her?" I demand.

She turns to me, fire in her eyes. "*Do* to her? I *loved* her."

"You forced yourself on her," I say. "I may not have known about you, but I've been around enough sexual assault survivors to know when they've been hurt. And I've been around enough predators to know one when I see one."

"You don't know anything," Laurie spits. "You just think you do."

"I know you're sick in the head, and anything you did to my mother wasn't consensual," I say. "No matter what story you tell yourself."

She laughs, but this time it's mirthless. "You think your mother was so perfect? You think she was a paragon of virtue? You don't know her as I did. As the girl who slept around, who wouldn't say no to whatever was being passed around, who put herself in danger because she was reckless. I tried to save her from all that."

"You're lying."

"Am I? You think your mother was such a saint? Then tell me, where is your *other* aunt right now? The one whose name you carry?"

A cold shiver runs down my spine. In everything that's happened, I had neglected to consider her. We'd been so focused on finding Laurie that Emily had fallen to the wayside. Laurie is staring at me with a penetrating gaze. One that reaches down into my very soul.

And then I remember.

"You never had a daughter, did you?" I don't need her answer to confirm, I can see it in her eyes. "The bones. They're hers. They belong to Emily."

She frowns. "And it's all your mother's fault."

"No," I whisper.

"Your mother came back distraught. A bad breakup with *another* guy. There were so many I couldn't keep up. But I was there to soothe her. It was the first night we were really together. But neither of us realized Emily saw everything."

I shake my head, unable to believe what she's saying.

"Margie was close to Emily, I'd never known her well. I told Margie she needed to convince Emily never to say anything. That people wouldn't understand. People like you. She invited her out to this very inlet; Emily loved the water. She said she was going to explain everything. But Emily wouldn't listen. And the only way to keep her quiet, was to silence her forever."

"No."

"Your mother killed her and left her body at the bottom of this lake, where she remained until *I* came and retrieved her."

I'm going to be sick. My stomach is turned in a hundred different knots.

"It was an efficient solution to the problem," Laurie says, tilting her head in an offhanded manner. "Most people just thought she'd run away."

I recall seeing the articles about Emily going missing.

And her missing photograph from the yearbooks. Now it all makes sense. She died because of my mother's terrible secret.

"What did you hope to gain? With the letters?" I ask, trying to distract myself so I don't puke right here.

"Your trust. I wanted you to come and find me here. But I needed you…desperate. Willing to accept an impossibility. I didn't count on you being so…resilient."

"Why did you try running us off the road? Why step in front of my car?"

She takes a deep breath and some of the fight seems to go out of her. "I lost my way. Thought I'd failed again. The letters weren't working. You didn't show up like I'd hoped. But when I woke up in that hospital, I realized my work wasn't done. I had another chance to put it right. I knew you would still come for me. I just needed to be patient. You may not be moldable, but you are predictable."

Despite it all, I have to remember this woman is a master manipulator. I can't trust a word she says. For the first time, I see a vulnerability I might be able to use to my advantage. I chance a look at Zara, who still hasn't moved. Laurie is a few steps in front of her now, almost within my reach. I just need to get to those weapons.

But before I can, she tosses the pipe down, creating a loud clanging sound as it hits the metal part of the dock and rolls to the side. She snaps her fingers a few times for good measure. "I need your full attention!"

"I…was just thinking how awful that must have been for you," I say.

She groans. "Your sympathy is transparent," she replies, the gun still hanging in her other hand. "You'll say anything to save your friend."

"You don't know anything about me," I tell her. "I know what it is to be alone. To have the person you love the most leave you behind. Only for you to find out they weren't who you thought they were in the beginning. I know it in my heart. I have *lived* it. You didn't deserve that."

She pinches her features before they relax, and it's almost as if she's looking *through* me again. "You are so much like your mother. So kind." She reaches up with one hand, moving closer to my face. "I knew you would be. I knew I chose well. If I couldn't have Margie, I knew you would be a suitable replacement. That I could still find what I needed."

I snatch her hand the second before it touches my skin, wrenching her arm back. She cries out, firing the gun wildly as I wrestle it out of her other hand. I manage to grab her wrist, but she drops the gun before I can reach it. I hear it splash into the water somewhere. She's surprisingly strong for someone her age, and she manages to elbow me across the jaw, causing me to stumble back.

She races forward to Zara.

"No!" I yell, before I see her grab Zara's leg and tips her up and off the dock into the water. Without a thought, I dive in after her, but the water is pitch black and I'm barely below the surface before I hit something hard. It has to be a pylon of some kind, but it's slick and smooth. I feel around for Zara, as my eyes are completely useless in the murky and stale water. I'm sure Laurie is on the run, but I don't care. All that matters is finding Zara, but she could be anywhere. I flail with both arms in all directions, trying to find anything that might be a leg or an arm.

Images flash in my mind. Images of my mother, standing on the dock above as her sister sinks slowly to her death. I can't believe that's the truth. I *won't* believe it. Not until I find proof. And I won't let what happened to Emily happen to Zara.

I reach the inlet's bed, but still without being able to see I know I'm running out of time. I went in right after her, she should be here! I can't lose her. She has been my rock and despite everything she has never given up on me. And I'm not about to give up on her. I swim forward, hitting another pylon. Then another, searching wildly.

I feel something flutter against my hand. At first I think it might be a fish. But I reach out and feel it's a piece of clothing. I grab hold, finding an arm connected to a torso. I get both hands under her armpits and push off the floor, trying to get us high enough to break the surface. Up I swim, the anticipation building like a crescendo.

Finally, we break the surface and I take a big gulp of air. Zara coughs in my arms, water flooding her lungs as she begins to struggle.

"Hang on, I'm getting you to shore," I say. We've come up under the dock and have to make our way to the grassy bank. Zara is still coughing in my arms, which is a good sign. She's not dead, though I still don't know how serious her injuries are. Finally, I get us both up on the grass, and I roll Zara to her side as she spits up murky water. She opens her eyes, looking up at me. The wound on her head has begun to bleed again, and the trickle of blood is headed for her eye. I press my hand to her forehead to stem the flow.

"Em?" she asks.

"I'm here," I say. "I've got you."

She smiles, but her eyes go wide. I turn just in time to see the metal pipe coming straight for my head. I manage to duck, and the pipe digs into the dirt right where my face was. I kick out, driving my sopping wet shoe into Laurie's midsection.

Crying out, she stumbles back, though she's still holding the weapon. I scramble to my feet, only for her to charge me again, burning rage in her eyes. Blocking her swinging arm, I deliver a quick blow to her chest, then a second to her neck, causing her to drop to her knees as she grapples for air. The pipe rolls harmlessly to the side.

"See how you like it," I say as I return to Zara. She's holding her own head now, wincing at the pain.

"She caught me off guard," she admits. "I didn't see her coming."

"That's okay," I say. "I think we have her neutralized." I catch the sound of sirens in the distance. Sounds like Michaels got my message, albeit later than I wanted. I turn back to Laurie, the woman who has caused me so much trouble, so much strife, has been turned into a helpless old lady, gasping for air in the mud. Part of me wants to just roll her into the water so she can never say any of those vile things again.

But I know there is no going back. You can't bury your problems, hoping they'll go away. Because somehow they always find their way back to you.

"Are you okay?" I ask Zara after I get Laurie's hands bound behind her with zip ties and I'm sure she's not going to choke to death.

"I will be," she says, sitting up and holding her head. "I was in and out of consciousness. I heard what she said. About your mother. You don't think it's true, do you?"

I furrow my brow, thinking about the bones Striker found in that car.

I don't know what to think anymore.

Chapter Thirty-Two

WE'RE BACK at Hickory County Hospital. I have spent far more time in this place than I care to admit. First when Liam was admitted after the arson, then during the investigation into Emily *and* Laurie, and now, with Zara as they patch her up.

As I'm waiting, Detective Michaels appears at the end of the hall. One of the nurses points toward me and I stand, getting his attention. He approaches, removing his hat. "How is your partner?"

"She's being treated for a concussion," I say. "And she needs eight stitches."

"I wanted to apologize for not believing you earlier," he says. "We've just finished interrogating Laurie Brooks. The woman is as crazy as a soup sandwich."

"Yes, I found out firsthand."

"I received the authorization to open her juvenile record. It seems she was a resident of Meadowview Home for Children from 1967 until 1980. She almost killed a preschooler when she was that age. Lashed out at the poor girl, nearly tore her scalp off."

"She never got better," I say. "All that place did was teach her how to lie to the world. Make it seem like she was okay."

He nods. "We also found traces of rat poison in Francis Knox's remains, which Laurie must have slipped into her food unknowingly. Though I doubt she'll ever confess. We think she probably learned some of her skills from working in the hospital. I'm actually here to speak with the administrator about why she was fired."

"So you believe she is responsible for the arson?" I ask.

"It's looking that way. As for the other house, even though the deed was still in Knox's name, we believe she was living there, at least part-time. It looks like she first met Knox in her twenties, then proceeded to cut off communication with her friends and family and make Knox totally dependent on her."

"How?" I ask.

"We're not sure yet. You've seen how well versed in emotional manipulation she is, though. She didn't start using the woman's name until after all of that, when she figured she was safe to assume a new identity. Apparently, she didn't want anyone looking into her past."

"What about the bones?" I ask. "Can you confirm they belonged to Emily?"

"Detective Striker is still working on that. Until we can find a DNA sample from Emily herself, it will be hard to make a positive match. We're still working on it."

"Any idea why she carried them with her?"

"Apparently something happened back in the eighties where a couple of kids found a human skull on Knox's property out there. I found where they reported it, but when I read the investigation notes, the officers who responded couldn't find any trace of what they'd been talking about. It was dismissed as nothing more than kids playing a prank."

"She stole them," I say. "For safekeeping."

"Seems that way."

"Because she didn't want an investigation?"

Michaels pinches his features together. "That's a possible reason. Agent Slate, she's given her statement. And in it, she places the blame for Emily Brooks' death squarely on the shoulders of your mother. Given the woman's history and her propensity for lying, we're taking it with a grain of salt. At least until we can come up with something more concrete."

That should make me feel better, but it doesn't.

"As soon as the two of you are done here, we'll need your statements down at the station."

I nod. "As soon as Zara is okay, we'll come in."

"I wish I had better news, Agent," he says. "I really do. You've been through more than your fair share with this case."

"Thank you," I say. He nods, then heads back to the nurse's station, presumably to speak with the administrator. I'm not sure how I'm supposed to feel. And I don't know how much of what Laurie told me was fact, and how much was fiction. Or something in between. All I do know is *something* happened to my mother that caused her to cut off her entire family. It's very possible the trauma of what happened *with* Laurie and *to* Emily was the source of it all.

I think back to my conversation with Frost. About how my mother might not have been as perfect as I'd always believed. But there is a big gap between not being perfect and being a murderer. Am I ready to accept that possibility? Am I ready to deal with the fallout? If my mother could kill her sister and cover it up her entire life, did I ever really know her at all?

But if she killed Emily, why would she name me after her? That doesn't make sense, unless she was somehow trying to atone for it. And the worst part is, I can't ask anyone about it. Even if Dad knew, he never left anything behind that would indicate something about this. And it's obvious my mother never wanted me to know.

I feel so lost. It's like a black cloud has stretched out before me, obscuring everything. And there is absolutely nothing I can do about it.

"Agent?" I look up to see the nurse appear at the door. "She's done. You can see her now."

I head into the recovery room where they've brought Zara. She's on one of the beds, a large bandage wrapped around her head as she's being hooked up to an IV. "Hey."

"Hey," she smiles. "How bad is it?'

"Um," I say, staring at the bandage. "I can't tell."

"They said they had to shave part of my head," she says. "Guess I'm going to be off duty for a while."

"Maybe that's a good thing," I say, taking her hand. "Are you okay?"

"I will be. I'm actually looking forward to taking some time off. As long as that's okay with my boss." She winks.

"I'm not sure how much of this I can handle, Z," I admit.

"How much of what?"

"All this," I say. "This is exactly what I was afraid of. Not to mention we were both in a shootout less than three days ago. Here you are, in the hospital. *Again*. And I still don't have all the answers."

"That's kind of how it goes, isn't it?" she asks. "This is the job we signed up for."

"I didn't sign up for my aunt to try to hunt me down. I still don't understand all her motives. And she specifically said she found out about me when we took Hunter down. She saw me on TV. If I had never been on there, she never would have... and I wouldn't know..."

"Hey," Zara coos. "It's okay. I'm here for you. So is Liam. So are the others. You aren't going to have to go through this alone. I know it's hard and it sucks, but we have your back. No matter what happens."

"Even if you can't fully trust me?" I ask.

"I've decided if I'm going to be in your life, I have to live with the fact you will try to protect me, in your own dumbass way." She smiles. "I can't change that about you. But I'm not giving up on you either, I'm not going to stop following you into the fire. I wouldn't be a very good friend if I did."

I sigh, feeling like an elephant has just climbed off my back. "That's more than I deserve."

"No, it isn't. Stop trying to convince yourself you're not worthy of people who care about you."

"It's just been…so much. I don't know how much longer I can do this. I need a break. A vacation."

"So take a vacation," she says. "You have more than enough time saved up. And you're right. You need it. That's something you actually deserve."

I smile. "You're not just saying that so I'm not bossing you around, are you?"

"Unless you haven't noticed, I'm in no shape to return to work either. I think a vacation sounds like the perfect thing. For *both* of us."

I chuckle. "Too bad Liam hasn't accrued any time yet."

"Seriously, if you do nothing other than go to the park with Timber every day, it will be good for you. Especially now that you don't have to worry about crazy train anymore."

"Yeah," I say, though I can hear how distant my own voice is. I don't like leaving things unresolved. But I guess I'll just have to accept I may never know the truth about my mother.

"What is it?" she asks. "You have that look."

"What look?"

"The one that says, *I'm upset but I'm not going to talk about it.*"

My lips form a line. "I just wish I could talk to my mother about what happened. About what *really* happened. But there's no one left who can tell me the truth."

"Well, maybe there still is," Zara says. "And you know exactly where to find them."

~

I'M STARING UP AT SMALL SIGN PLASTERED ABOVE A DOOR THAT reads Dr. Ruben Archer, PhD.

"You don't have to do this," Liam says.

I turn to him, smiling. "I think I do. Honestly, I'm surprised you're still even talking to me."

He turns to me, his face serious. "Em, you know that's not how I deal with things. I'm not going to shut you out and I'm not going to give you the cold shoulder. I think I know you well enough by now to know why you did what you did. You have a lot of trauma in your life, and you're not always going to respond to things in the way I think you should. But that doesn't mean I should get mad at you about it. Just like I'd hope you wouldn't get mad at me for the same reason."

"Sometimes I feel like I ask too much," I say. "Or I expect you to deal with too much. I know my life is…a lot."

"You mean *our* life," he says.

I can't help myself, and I find that I'm in his arms, my head against his chest. "I wouldn't have made it this far without you. Or Zara."

"I know," he says as we pull away. "You sure you don't want me to go in with you?"

"I need to hear this on my own first," I say. "I promise to tell you everything."

"You don't need to do that," he replies. "I was just making sure you didn't need the moral support. I know this is a private matter. We never have to talk about it again if you don't want to."

I take a deep breath and face the building once more. "No. We will. Whatever I find out, I'm not keeping it to myself. I get in trouble when I bottle things up." At least, according to Dr. Frost.

"Okay, I'll be over in the car if you need me." He reaches down and squeezes my hand. "Good luck."

I squeeze it back. "Thanks." He returns to the car while I head inside and find a small waiting area. There's a door at the far end of the room, cracked open, with a small sign on a side table that says, *Please Be Patient, I'll be With You Soon.*

But before I can sit down, Dr. Archer appears in the doorway. His face is pinched with worry, and I'm wondering if he's decided not to help me after all. How many times did he bail on me before? So many that I had to track him down and almost force him to speak with me. "Agent Slate."

"You can call me Emily," I say. He beckons me inside and I follow to his office. There's a long couch in the room, along with a desk pushed up against one of the other walls. He takes a seat in his chair and indicates I sit wherever is comfortable.

"How have you been?" I ask.

He works his jaw. "Better. After you called and told me about Laurie…" He trails off, then takes a sip of water from a glass on his desk. "I wanted to apologize for what happened during our last meeting."

I swallow, hard. "We were both under a lot of stress. I shouldn't have pushed you so hard."

"And I should have told you the truth from the beginning. But I got cold feet. I'm not the kind of practitioner who reveals the confidentiality of his patients on a regular basis. That, and the threatening letters from your aunt didn't help. God…I can't believe she's under lock and key. I never thought…when those letters arrived at my house, I thought for sure she was coming after me. I thought she had found out what your mother had told me, that she would silence me in— well, that doesn't matter now."

"How did she know you had contacted me?" I ask.

"I don't know for sure, but my feeling is she knew more about your mother than she revealed. Despite what she told you, I wouldn't be surprised if she'd been watching your mother for a long time. Long enough to know she was seeing me. And we know she was watching you."

"But why threaten you?" I ask. "What was she afraid of?"

He takes a deep breath. "You have to understand. Your

mother had a lot of demons. Things she kept buried deep inside. We worked together to bring a lot of that out so she could heal, but if I'm being totally honest, we really only scratched the surface."

"Then you don't know what happened between her and my aunt?" I ask.

He leans back, and his gaze finds the room's only window before returning to me. "No. I know."

"And Laurie was afraid you'd tell me."

"You said she wanted to manipulate you so she could seduce you. While that should be surprising, it's something she's tried before."

"It's true then. They were involved." I can hardly believe it. My mother...incestuous? It's...it's something no child should have to imagine.

"Perhaps not in the way you think," he says. "When your aunt was first released from the institution, she didn't move back home. Instead, she moved into a halfway house of sorts and stayed there until she got her own apartment. Margie, ever the caregiver, attempted to make up for lost time by moving in with her. However, we found out through our sessions that, really, Laurie had pressed for it, and had lured her there with the promise of freedom from your grandparents.

"Over the course of a few months, Laurie introduced your mother to the kind of life she'd already become accustomed to: alcohol, drugs, older men. Laurie convinced your mother their life together was better than anything they could ever have anywhere else and I believe was planting seeds in your mother's mind, attempting to permanently bind the two of them together. See, Laurie is the kind of person who will do anything to find the connection she needs. And for her, that was her sister, the one person who had been ripped away from her at a young age.

"Margaret, on the other hand, still had her parents and a

new baby sister to dote on her. So the two of them grew up very differently. And when Laurie was released, she latched onto your mother like a leech. Your mother recounted a particular night when she had broken up with her boyfriend, returning to the comforting arms of your aunt. Your aunt gave her something to sleep, but when she woke up the next morning, your mother knew something was wrong. That something had happened. Through some hypnotherapy we managed to uncover some of it, but I'll spare you the details."

"I can guess," I say. "She assaulted my mother."

"We believe she did. And she was so enraged, she declared she was moving out the following day. However, what neither of them knew was fifteen-year-old Emily, who had bonded with your mother and followed her around like a puppy, had been at their place that night. She'd snuck away, perhaps tired of being the little sister left behind, and had seen what your aunt did to your mother. In an effort to protect your mother, she confronted Laurie, telling her she was going to the police."

"That lines up with what Laurie told me," I say, feeling that pit in my stomach deepen.

"What I'm sure she didn't tell you, was that Laurie saw Emily as an obstacle between her and your mother. Your aunt is a true psychopath, she doesn't form emotions the same way other people do. She saw your other aunt as expendable. *Laurie* was the one who invited Emily up to the lake, and your mother found out about it. Your mother found Laurie struggling to throw Emily in the water. Emily, who didn't know how to swim."

Immediately, I'm thrown back to being four years old at our local pool, swimming back and forth as hard as I could, my mother cheering me on. I remember how she said it was so important to know how to swim, and that I was her little fish. That I had taken to water like a salmon. She had been teaching me to swim since I was six months old. "What happened?"

"Your mother confronted Laurie. In the struggle, Emily slipped and struck her head the dock before she fell into the water. Your mother went after her, but the blow had already been fatal."

I recall the damage to the skull found in the back of the car.

"She told me over and over how she tried to revive her, but there was so much blood. And when your mother tried to go for help, Laurie threw Emily back into the water, where she slowly sunk to the bottom. Your mother wanted to call the police, but Laurie said that would only invite questions. And that Emily's death was *her* fault. If she'd never come there, Laurie would have convinced Emily to leave them alone. Of course, we both suspected Laurie was trying to kill your aunt even before your mother arrived.

"But your poor mother…she was so conflicted she didn't know which way to turn. Though I will say this for Laurie, I think in that moment she knew she had lost your mother. That there was no coming back. She told Margaret if she never told anyone about Emily, if they pretended she just ran away, that Margaret could leave, and Laurie would never try to find her."

"So that's what she did," I say.

He nods. "Your mother decided to start over." His eyes fall a little. "She named you in honor of her. Of the sister she lost, and betrayed. Even though she did everything she could to try and save her, eventually your mother used the opportunity to get away from Laurie, from everyone in her family. And it wore on her. She carried that guilt as if she was carrying the world on her shoulders."

"I can't believe it," I whisper. I take a few minutes to try and digest the information. To understand. Never in my wildest dreams would I have imagined my mother capable of something like that. But I understand now why she often looked so sad, especially when she was looking at me. "She didn't name me to honor her. She named me so she would never forget the shame of what she'd done." I know because it's what I would have done.

"Your mother was a complicated person," Archer says. "Like I said, she had a lot of demons."

"Would you be willing—" I'm having a hard time breathing, but I swallow, attempting to focus. "Would you be willing to testify to this information? If for no other reason than to rule Emily's death an accident? I don't want my aunt thinking she can get away with accusing my mother with murder, even if she didn't make all the right decisions."

"Since you are her only living heir, if you authorize me to, I can," he says. "I still have the notes from our sessions."

"It's a start," I say, getting up. "Things would have been a lot easier if you had just been honest with me from the beginning."

"I know," he says, dropping his head. "That was my intention. But when I received the threats, I knew who was behind them. And one of your mother's final instructions to me was to never get involved, that it wasn't worth it. Laurie was dangerous, and I needed to stay as far away from her as possible. She wanted the exact same for you. This was never supposed to be your burden to bear."

I take a deep breath. "If I have learned anything, it's that the things we most want to control in our lives have a way of disobeying us."

He nods.

"I'll be in touch," I say and I head back outside into the sunlight. As soon as I'm outside, I close my eyes and take a deep breath. She may not have killed Emily, but she didn't do right by her, either. I'm going to fix that. I'm going to do what my mother never could.

I'm going to set it right.

Chapter Thirty-Three

TWO WEEKS LATER

"FEEL FAMILIAR?" Liam asks as he finishes the final touches on the buffet he's meticulously been working on for the past few days.

"Familiar?"

"Yeah, does it feel like home yet?" Timber is right by his side, watching every hand movement as he adjusts the appetizers. His eyes haven't left the table since Liam began setting it up an hour ago. I grab the throw blanket we've been using to unwind in the evenings and fold it, laying it over the back of our brand-new couch. Only a few things in the house are new, as we were able to mesh most of our stuff together without too much trouble. The couch was one of the few exceptions. Neither of us had a couch big enough for this new space.

"Well, I—" Before I can answer, the doorbell rings and Timber finally tears himself away from the table and runs to the door. He's whining before I can get it open, and I can see Zara through the glass wiggling her hand in front of Timber's face. As soon as I open the door, he slams into her, and I have to take the plate out of her hand before she collapses from laughing.

"Boyfriend!" she giggles. Finally, Timber lets her up and I happen to look at the plate she's brought.

"Rolls?" I ask.

"Rolls with ham and butter," she corrects. "Trust me, they are like *crack*."

I smile and hand the plate to Liam, who adds it to the table. Timber follows Zara in, and I close the door behind her. The bandage around her head is gone, but there is a small patch where she still has tape and stitches covering the shaved part of her head. She's pulled the rest of her hair over on one the side to cover it, but it will be less noticeable when the stitches are out.

"How's it feeling?" I ask.

"Almost healed. Stitches come out tomorrow. Then I'm back to fighting shape."

"And back to work after some time off," I say.

"Look who can't wait to get back to her new office," she says, winking before spotting the table full of food. "Holy *shit* guys, I did not realize you invited the entire bureau."

"We didn't," I say. "*Someone* just likes to go overboard. Timber has been slobbering over the floor all day."

"I'm about to join him," she says.

I glance absently at the door. "Anything from Theo?"

"He's just landed," she says. "He said he'd be here as soon as he can. And that he has a surprise."

"What's a surprise in Theo-world?" Liam asks.

"Beats me; I'll find out when you do. What can I do to help?"

"You can get yourself a drink and relax," I say. "This is our housewarming; guests are to do nothing."

"Does that sound like me?" she asks, putting one hand on her hip and cocking it out.

"No," I admit.

"Good, then put me to work."

"You can monitor the grill," Liam says, motioning to the door leading to our back patio deck. "It's already warmed up. I was just waiting for a few more people to arrive."

"C'mon," Zara says to Timber. "Maybe Auntie Zara will give you a burger. Would you like that, a burger? Yes, you would." Timber follows her outside.

"Just one!" I call. "You're going to make him fat!" She completely ignores me and slams the door behind her.

As Liam and I continue to make our final preparations and finish cleaning the house the best we can, people begin arriving. Nadia and Elliott come together, something I'm not even sure Elliott is aware is a big deal for Nadia, though I can see the excitement in her eyes. Caruthers arrives next, which gives me a chance to thank him for all his help with the case regarding Laurie. It hasn't been an easy two weeks, and I've been in more meetings and part of more investigations than I care to think about.

Not only have I been working with Detectives Striker and Michaels on the arson and murder cases, but I've also been wrapping up the human trafficking case from Red Sunset. Convictions all around and life in prison for Crowley is like a sweet cherry on top. Bolo will be eligible for parole, but not until he's in his seventies.

Finally, Janice shows up, though I wasn't sure she'd come. But before she comes in the house, she beckons me outside. In front of the house, she pulls out her vape pen, taking long drags.

"I wanted to let you know, I just got off the phone with Detective Striker. Your aunt has pleaded not guilty to attempted murder of a federal agent. And she's determined not to take a deal. She wants her day in court."

I let out a long breath. "That's not a surprise."

"It's up in the air whether she'll get it or not. The evidence on the arson is circumstantial at best, though we do have her fingerprints on the pipe that nearly killed Agent Foley. The gun you mentioned hasn't been found yet."

Given how murky that water is, that also doesn't come as much of a shock. "What about Emily?"

"The coroner is ruling her death suspicious, and given your aunt's claims and the testimony from Dr. Archer, it will devolve into a she-said, she-said situation. Unfortunately, I don't know if you will ever get a resolution on it. If it does go to trial, all of the information about your mother will become public."

I nod. "I think my aunt is betting I won't have the strength to bring this to light, just like she did back then. Using the threat of coming out, of the embarrassment, to keep my mother quiet. I know my mom wasn't perfect, and I now know she had a dark past. But I'm not going to help her abuser keep that covered up. If she thinks I won't expose her, she's got another thing coming. We'll let a jury decide what the truth is."

Janice nods, taking another draw from the pen. "I'm glad you feel that way. But then there is the other matter."

I had hoped this could have waited until I got back to work next week, but I guess I shouldn't be surprised. When I invite my boss to a party after I've screwed up, I can't complain when she brings it up.

"Let me save you the trouble," I say. "I've been giving this a lot of thought, and I don't think I'm right to be SSA."

She stares at me. "And why not?"

"I don't like being in charge of my peers. I don't like feeling like they *have* to do what I say. And I'm having a really hard time resolving the fact I might have to ask them to risk their lives for me. That's causing me to fall back into some destructive patterns. And isn't something I want to do in the future."

"I see," she says.

"Before you offered me that promotion, I never even thought about what my future in the Bureau would look like, other than a nebulous idea that I would move up eventually. But now that I've really thought about it, now that I've been in that position, it's not what I want. I like being a field agent. I'm *good* at it. As much as I hate to say this, I'm not that great at giving orders."

"Nor at following them," she says. "You left your team to fend for themselves at a crucial point in an investigation."

"I know," I say. "And that's why I don't think I should keep the position."

"Good," she says. "That's the right answer. Because not only was I coming here today to tell you that you have been relieved of that position, but I was also considering putting you back on probation."

I drop my head. "Yeah. Can't say I didn't expect it."

"In fact, if you were any other agent, I probably would have fired you. You have made some amazing strides over the past year, Emily. I don't want to see you throw away your career because of forces outside your control. You should have left the investigation up to Michaels and Striker."

I nod.

"Still, your record since your return remains unblemished. You'll receive the credit for taking down Red Sunset, with a note on your record requesting a return to field work."

"No," I say. "Liam deserves the credit. He was at the center the entire time. And he brought down Crowley. If there is one last thing I can do, I would like to nominate him up for a commendation."

"So noted," she says, her face completely impassive. "I will, however, need to find a replacement SSA. Any recommendations?"

"Caruthers?" I offer. "He's professional, efficient, and dedicated to the job. And I hear budget meetings don't bother him."

She takes another puff, considering it. "Perhaps," she says. "I'll think about it. In the meantime, I still have a lot of paperwork to catch up on."

"Will you stay for a few minutes?" I ask. "Liam—well, Zara is grilling hamburgers."

"I'm a vegetarian."

"We have meatless options too."

Her eyes shoot back and forth until she finally makes a decision. "One burger." I smile as she heads inside.

As the afternoon goes on, Janice ends up staying, and the atmosphere relaxes. Even Elliott loosens up after the second round of mojitos, which is something I never thought I'd see. But it's the board games where he really shines, even going so far as to give Nadia a congratulatory hug when they win a round. The joy on her face is practically infectious. It's half past six when Timber goes to the front door again. Zara happens to notice and opens the door to find Theo standing there, preparing to knock.

"Well, hello love, got a bit of precognition, don't you?"

She smiles, wraps her arms around his neck, and kisses him as the rest of us try not to stare. "It was Timber. He always knows when someone is coming." Theo comes in, greeting everyone, including Janice, who he's never met before. She returns the greeting, but her gaze is cold and I'm not sure why. Though perhaps it's because none of us really know much about Theo, other than the fact at some point he might have been involved with MI6.

He shoots me a quick nod and a wink before placing a small black box on the counter.

"What's that?" I ask.

"Call it a housewarming present." He wiggles his eyebrows, and I have to admit I'm intrigued, but at that moment, Elliott knocks over a drink and we're all distracted helping him clean up. After a few moments, I've forgotten all about it.

Theo ends up reinvigorating the party and I can't help but step back and smile at what my life has become. These past few months have been pure hell, but somehow, we all made it through together.

"What's the smile for?" Liam asks, coming in the kitchen to get fresh glasses.

"You asked me if it feels like home?" I turn and look at all our friends, and coworkers, and Timber winding between them, searching for anyone who will give him something in exchange for puppy dog eyes. "Yeah," I say. "It finally does."

The End?

To be continued…

Want to read more about Emily?

Sun, sand and champagne. The perfect vacation. Except this is anything but. Local women are disappearing from the Caribbean island of St. Solomon and no one seems to know why. Even worse, the local authorities aren't doing anything about it.

Determined not to let these disappearances get any worse, Special Agent Emily Slate goes undercover for the first time since her life was turned upside down, hoping to find out who could be behind it all.

Except when she starts digging she'll get more than she bargained for. The tropical island holds a deadly secret, one that may drag Emily under with no chance to come up for air.

. . .

JOIN EMILY AS SHE DISCOVERS **BLOOD IN THE SAND**, *EMILY Slate Mystery Thriller book 15.*

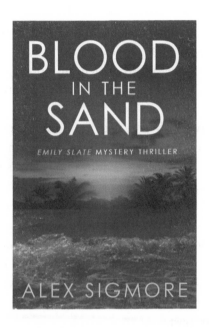

To get your copy of *Blood in the Sand*, CLICK HERE or scan the code below with your phone.

New Series Alert!
Dark Secrets Await…

I HOPE YOU ENJOYED *THE MISSING BONES*! WHILE YOU WAIT for the next installment in Emily's story, I hope you'll take a chance on my new series which introduces Detective Ivy Bishop. And as a loyal Emily Slate reader, I think you're going to love it!

Detective Ivy Bishop is celebrating her recent promotion with the Oakhurst, Oregon Police Department when she receives her first big case: a headless body that's washed up on a nearby beach.

Jumping into action with her new partner, Ivy is determined to show she has what it takes to make it as a detective. But she's harboring a dark secret, one that happened when she was young and continues to haunt her until this day.

Little does Ivy know this is no ordinary case, and will tear open old wounds, and lead her to question everything she ever knew about her past.

Interested in learning more about Ivy? CLICK HERE to snag your copy of HER DARK SECRET!

Now Available

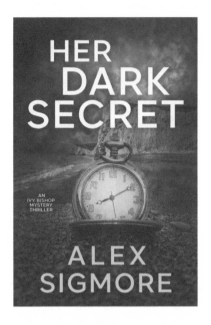

I'm so excited for you to meet Ivy and join along in her adventures!

CLICK HERE or scan the code below to get yours now!

The Emily Slate FBI Mystery Series

Free Prequel - Her Last Shot (Emily Slate Bonus Story)

His Perfect Crime - (Emily Slate Series Book One)

The Collection Girls - (Emily Slate Series Book Two)

Smoke and Ashes - (Emily Slate Series Book Three)

Her Final Words - (Emily Slate Series Book Four)

Can't Miss Her - (Emily Slate Series Book Five)

The Lost Daughter - (Emily Slate Series Book Six)

The Secret Seven - (Emily Slate Series Book Seven)

A Liar's Grave - (Emily Slate Series Book Eight)

Oh What Fun - (Emily Slate Holiday Special)

The Girl in the Wall - (Emily Slate Series Book Nine)

His Final Act - (Emily Slate Series Book Ten)

The Vanishing Eyes - (Emily Slate Series Book Eleven)

Edge of the Woods - (Emily Slate Series Book Twelve)

Ties That Bind - (Emily Slate Series Book Thirteen)

The Missing Bones - (Emily Slate Series Book Fourteen)

Coming soon!

Blood in the Sand - (Emily Slate Series Book Fifteen)

The Ivy Bishop Mystery Thriller Series

Free Prequel - Bishop's Edge (Ivy Bishop Bonus Story)

Her Dark Secret - (Ivy Bishop Series Book One)

The Girl Without A Clue - (Ivy Bishop Series Book Two)

Coming Soon!

The Buried Faces - (Ivy Bishop Series Book Three)

A Note from Alex

Hi there!

Congratulations, you have officially reached the end of "season 2"! If you've been with Emily since the beginning, you'll know that she doesn't get many breaks. And considering what happened at the end of season 1, I thought she deserved the rare happy ending.

Does this mean there won't be any more Emily Slate books? Absolutely not! Ever since the beginning I have loved writing these characters. In some ways, they have become a part of my family, and I hope yours as well. You can rest assured the adventures of Emily, Liam, Zara, Timber and all the rest will continue for as long as I can continue to think up new stories.

While you're waiting on the next Emily story, I hope you'll also explore my other series: the *Ivy Bishop Mystery* series, following a detective in western Oregon tracking down a number of harrowing cases, all of which seem to mysteriously point back to her own past.

And as always, if you haven't already, please take a moment to leave a review or recommend this series to a fellow book lover. It really helps me as a writer and is the best way to make sure there are plenty more *Emily Slate* books in the future.

As always, thank you for being a loyal reader,

Alex

Made in United States
Troutdale, OR
06/27/2024

20850830R00170